Henry Tuckahoe's War on Washington

Published by Commonwealth Books of Virginia
59 McFarland Point Dr. #12
Boothbay Harbor, ME 04538

ISBN (paperback): 978-0-9961368-6-0
ISBN (E-book/MobiPocket): 978-0-9961368-7-7
ISBN (E-book/EPUB): 978-0-9961368-8-4
ISBN (E-book/PDF): 978-0-9961368-9-1

Library of Congress Cataloging-in-Publication Data
CIP data applied for

Henry Tuckahoe's War on Washington

A novel by
Lawrence C. Melton

COMMONWEALTH
BOOKS
OF VIRGINIA
WHERE HISTORY, PHILOSOPHY, AND ART MEET

Boothbay Harbor, Maine

1

From a mile south of the National Capital Beltway, the lights of Washington and its suburbs sparkled and danced on the darkening Potomac like specks of green phosphorus on the scales of a sea-bound boa. On higher ground to the west, the last glow of a feeble sunset lingered momentarily over Potomac Great Falls as if waiting for a curtain call that never came and then disappeared into a twilight of reflected incandescence, leaving the Washington Monument as a pencil of reflected light thrusting itself spastically in the direction of a pale moon, struggling to consummate some desperate ecstasy before fading into the coal-dark river.

An unlighted canoe, weathered the silver of vintage teak, crisscrossed the flickering reflections of classical detail in graceful defiance of the strong ebb tide. A dusky figure, tall, heavy set and stooped, propelled the canoe by bouncing in the stern and shifting his weight for direction. The vessel was carved from a single trunk of the extinct bog oak. Its sides were embellished with carvings of eels and shellfish not seen in the Potomac for a hundred years, vanquished by the dark effusions of a growing population.

The man in the canoe sniffed at the breeze coming down river from the Capitol. His arms, outstretched for balance, held a thin wooden pole that had been hardened by fire and carved into a series of sharp barbs. From time to time his heavy, powerful legs turned the canoe sharply. He darted the spear into the passing shadows and then studied the fish struggling on the end of his barb carefully. Some, bass, chub or crappie, he stowed in a creel towed behind the canoe. Others, carp or eel, he brought wriggling to his mouth, bit into their flesh, and chewed them whole while singing a faint but simple tune that lowered the seventh degree of the scale half a step.

Finally, as if in boredom, the man crouched in the middle of the canoe and drifted downriver into quieter waters. As he moved, the moon played across a broad hairless chest, sloping, powerful shoulders and a full but muscular belly. His skin was the color of burnt umber and the texture of felt. His hair was shaggy and unkempt, cropped roughly at the top of his flat ears, and glued to his broad forehead with the thick sweat of the hunter at work and the river's condensing humidity. His heavy torso exhaled a bottom odor of organic decay as he garnered another carp from the depths and savored the crunching of bones and the emptying of soft body cavities into his mouth. It was an old urge, this hunger for the flesh of raw *Cyprinus carpio*, one he had not sensed for longer than he cared to express, but it was only one of many sensations, some new and some barely remembered, that he felt coming with the humid breeze from the Capitol.

He glided into the swamps above Mount Vernon and munched on the pulpy roots of a plant known as Golden Club to the fussier members of the Audubon society, and to week-end anglers as the common cattail. In between bites of the mud covered roots, while humming the oddly toneless melody, he watched for signs and symbols in the river's undulating reflections.

Changes were coming. He smelt them. He read them in the dead colors of the river's nocturnal surface. Some he recognized. His brother, he could tell, had died within the last half hour. That was expected. Schuler's death had long been imminent. A curse was a curse after all. But there was more. Something new in Washington had changed the scent of the evening air. He touched the surface of the water, scooped away the layer of pollen and dust on the top, rolled his eyes toward Mount Vernon rising on a bluff above the river and sniffed the residue on his fingertips. It was a rare smell considering that Congress had adjourned for the remainder of August, an odor of sandal and soot, rose and rendered fat, sweet cumin and caucasian boxwood, but stronger, deeper, more of the animal kingdom than the mineral, powerful, and yet as familiar as the ineffaceable memories of childhood. It was generically kin to the slime that formed on a freshly dead eel, he thought, as he belched up the one and compared it with the other. But it was more than a whiff of unsettled food. Things were happening. Not war or a change in the interest rates. He knew those odors without question. It was something else. It was deep, he thought, something beyond the ways of men and fish, something bound inextricably with flora, fauna and the cycles of fertility, something bigger than family and older than clan. There were odors of banking laws and accounting rules and odors he knew as peculiarly his own. Someone was going to lose a lot of money, and, to Henry Tuckahoe's way of thinking, that meant someone else was going to make it.

Henry groaned in ecstasy as his bouncing propelled the canoe back toward Alexandria. Twenty yards into the Cameron Run estuary he speared a fourteen inch channel carp caught in a web of rotting hydrilla and took the fat gaping head off with one bite. Waving the body and tail of the decapitated fish above his head, Henry bellowed an inarticulate syllable into the wind that sounded like the slow splitting of a frozen poplar. After stowing his canoe in a swamp of thorns and poison sumac, Henry packed his remaining catch in a styrofoam ice chest and tucked it in the trunk of a hand-rubbed, still immaculate Jaguar Mark XX. The engine wheezed to life and the car moved with the sound of willow boughs dragging against a strong current. Without turning on the lights, Henry drove toward the Alexandria waterfront and disappeared among the shadows.

Jason Potter, United States Senator for thirty-five years from a state so frequently confused with other flat, wheat producing states that he had come to call it South Kanaska as a joke, jogged complacently along the Rock Creek Park bicycle path. It was the one day of the year—an unpredictable day between April and October—when Washington weather approached the perfection he recalled as common from his unhurried youth. The atmospheric ceiling was high, the humidity was low, the temperature was warm, an imperceptible breeze turned a canopy of lush foliage from green to silver and back again in silent ripples. An errant jet stream pushed cirrus wisps across a sapphire heaven. A California day, the locals called it, but Jason knew better. It was a South Kanaska day. One never forgot the big skies and the high wispy clouds of the prairie, he reflected, recalling a boyhood of towering grain elevators against endless skies that could change in an instant from sublime to sinister and tended to humble a man by comparison, if not with the Creator exactly, then with the Creation. His youth, in fact, for all the signs of Sybaritic excess now carved in the surplus folds of his face, was closer to the ideal of Mid-America than he cared to admit, unless, of course, it was that relatively rare event, an election speech in the forgotten reaches of South Kanaska itself.

Jogging was a vital part of Jason's routine. Twice a week he broke from the monotony of legislative business for three hours, sometimes four, and lumbered from the Hill to Georgetown through Rock Creek Park and back. He had been filmed for the constituency passing the monuments, the White House, the historical sites and the swollen stream in the park where Teddy Roosevelt had exercised his horses. There were stills and videos that came out every six years, changed and updated to keep pace with the times and his barely perceptible aging. It was a wholesome scene, and his South Kanaskans were proud of the unathletic figure that would have embarrassed a more urban constituency.

Jason's route through Washington, as televised in South Kanaska, took some liberties with the local geography, understating the distances, triangulating the squares and Jason had at first objected. But the campaign professionals assured him that the same stunt was used without quibble in more than half the states, some, literally, within walking distance of the reorganized landscape. Jason acquiesced, certain that he would be exposed, but the professionals were right. Nobody cared whether Senators lied about Washington's geography. Nobody cared about Senators at all. One or two might be minor public figures. But most were not. They drove themselves home, did their own shopping and blended into the local scene, effaced by the real power of the President and the Pentagon. This invisibility irritated Jason at first. But, as the practical demands of simple pleasures superseded youthful ambition, he not only recognized but came to rely on the advantages of anonymity, so that after 36 years the assurance of obscurity in matching ends to means had become a necessity rather than a convenience. The thought of his constituents seeing more of his twice-weekly outings than he wanted now blurred his vision and shortened his breath. Besides, he reasoned, the burghers of Cornucopia City, the Capitol he had composed for South Kanaska, could hardly be expected to understand either the temptations of an unprincipled city or the obscurity so necessary to assure their prosperity. As Chairman of the low profile Senate Banks Committee he had mastered and used the filigreed laws of finance to amaze, encourage and enrich his heartland constituents in their annual need for easy money and low credit, a legislative process he considered a virtual raid on the banking palaces of Wall Street. And all without any danger of exposure.

A block away from the Russell Building Gymnasium, Senator Potter hailed a cab to a faded apartment complex opposite the Shoreham Tower Hotel, spent an hour, sometimes two, with a youngish woman of receptive disposition, and then afterwards jogged down the Rock Creek Park bicycle path to the Four Seasons Hotel where he took a cab off the rank back to Capitol Hill. The drivers rarely spoke English and never recognized him. It was a harmless vice as he saw it, one that hurt no one, least of all his wife of thirty years who had her own interests and rarely came to town. And besides, Esther Ann helped with his work. She had a perspective on finance that he lacked. Like this rule change at "Fizz Lick" as he liked to call the Federal Savings and Loan Insurance Corporation. He wondered why people cared about accounting rules. He didn't. The voters didn't. Words mattered. Numbers took care of themselves. It was one of his principles, one he shared with his ninety-nine colleagues. Not a math whiz in the bunch, he liked to mutter in homely fashion as the debates of substance were turned over to the staff at the end of a term. But, for a reason he couldn't identify, Jason didn't trust the bean counters anymore. Things were getting more complicated. Young people thought differently. Even Esther Ann—the only shining light in the mathematical gloom— had seen more to that Rule 502 thing than he had. The way she looked at it, even the *Post* might pick it up. And the *Post* could only mean bad publicity. He could handle it, of course, by moving the mess around. The Fizz Lick accounting scandal, if that's what it turned out to be, may have started in his committee, but he could see it wouldn't end there.

Jason Potter chuckled to himself between the rhythmic surges of his breathing. The Fizz Lick thing was merely a challenge in a career of challenges. He'd been in worse scrapes. And gotten out. There was something satisfying about all that experience, about having been there before, just as there was something soothing about the heaving of his own chest. A man his age, sedentary of habit and thick around the middle, could only take pleasure in such a steady sound.

Jason jogged on. The path was deserted and there was little traffic on the adjacent parkway. The clarity of light in the trees drew his gaze upward. It was a rare day he thought again and savored the sensation of air and light in perfect pitch with his body, his confident mood, his fresh memories of Esther Ann. It was a feeling of perfection he had known only a few times before, and it was, he recognized, as close to transcendental ecstasy as he was ever likely to come. Then, in the twinkling of an eye and the single contraction of an overworn heart, the strangely perfect light in the overarching oaks drew Jason Potter into the silver wisps beyond the dancing leaves and with a faint but sudden murmur, the Chairman of the Senate Banks Committee left the world of borrowers and lenders to a younger generation who knew the crunching of numbers and the taking of profit as transcendent experiences in their own right.

3

As Jason Potter's shade lingered uncertainly among the oaks of Rock Creek Park and gazed mournfully down at the fallen sack of earth which had once so fully consumed his attention, a young man named Aubrey Wythe, as pallid and thin himself as newly slipped coil, poured his last desperate dregs of cheap beer and lukewarm passion before an older, heavier woman of little beauty but great learning, named Lacy Swanda.

"Stage left overgrows . . . what was it? I'm sorry, I was looking for that waitress again, the one with the hair net," Professor Swanda said over the shouted conversations, jangled crockery and oldies jukebox racket of the Tune Inn, the only bar within a four mile radius of the White House that had not changed its name to flatter the slogans and provincial origins of a new administration.

"The fa-fa-fantasies of stage right," Aubrey shouted with determination through beer frothed lips, but she showed no sign of hearing him.

"The realities of stage left overwhelm the fantasies of stage right," Aubrey said again with the confidence that comes of authorship and pedagogical repetition. "The context is Latin Comedy, of course," Aubrey continued. "Every Latin stage was set with the city on the left and the port on the right, the quickest escape from a nagging wife being to hop a boat on the midnight tide."

"Right," Lacy said mechanically. Her broad back was turned to Aubrey. She glared intently at the stooped shoulders of an elderly waitress.

Aubrey pointed to the pitcher again with his left index finger, as if he were reading a paper to the Modern Language Association and said in a tone of stentorian splendor, "polis, responsibility, and civic duty." He then lifted the black and chrome napkin holder with his right hand, shook it for emphasis until a few thin slips of paper fell into a puddle of beer and said in a lilting tone he could have picked up from the overture to the *Mikado*, "escape, irony and personal gratification." He returned the soggy napkins to their place, knocked over a pepper shaker and stared with contempt at the dispensing contraption, as if some mystical connection between the spring loaded box and anti-social sensory excess were perfectly obvious.

Lacy, who had missed Aubrey's display in her continuing effort to obtain more beer, glared at him with incredulous frustration as the waitress fled again to the bar without taking her order.

"The dichotomy between stage left and stage right institutionalized the conflict between individual and society, you see."

"Virtue on the left," Lacy said to show she had been listening after all. "On the right vice." The final sibilant showed the orthodontically corrected front teeth Aubrey considered to be her strongest feature.

"If it sounds crude by our own standards, it could be because the line of legitimate social interest has been intentionally blurred by the rise of a liberal, individualist, bourgeoisie that exploits all sense of social obligation, pushing stage left off the proscenium altogether." To show what he meant, Aubrey pushed the pitcher off the table into Lacy's grip. She waved it in the direction of the withered serving lady passing their booth with platters of prawns and pitchers of beer for other revelers.

But Aubrey didn't notice the waitress or Lacy's cries of "Miss, Miss." Nor did he feel the lack of liquid refreshment as Lacy did. He had, ever so briefly, retreated from body, Tune Inn, and the Nation's Capitol altogether. He had launched himself into that brief paradise that comes with the encounter of a new idea, the ecstasy of scholarly delight, a revery for which he had once lived and which now came with dispiriting infrequency. The connection between the rise of an individualist bourgeoisie and the decline of civic virtue wasn't something Aubrey had considered in detail before it blurted out, almost of its own accord, but it sounded academically plausible, if not entirely cogent. And, all things considered, plausibility was as high a standard as even he sometimes had for his dissertation topic. He jotted the phrases on a napkin and drew arrows to show that as one ascended the other fell. Beneath the picture he wrote: "*Sic transit virtue civitas*, but he was uncertain of his Latin declensions and put it in his pocket before Lacy could find any mistakes.

Lacy, oblivious to Aubrey's fumbling with the napkin holder, cast her eyes around the Tune Inn for another waitress. It was a long, narrow restaurant with formica booths, mangy moosehead mountings and a doe's rump suspended over the women's toilet. The name had been attached in the turn on, tune in '60's, but the soul of the place was the hard-drinking, heavy-smoking 50's, when congressional drinking habits were out of bounds to *The Post* through professional courtesy. Low level pols and high level staffers swirled and cavorted with overdressed lobbyists and unattached coeds, up or down for the summer from quieter, simpler hometowns where Washington was confused with fading *Life* photos of the Kennedy inaugural address and JFK's "bear any burden, pay any price" was routinely confused with "climb every mountain, ford every stream."

Lacy, authoress, as she liked to put it, of the formidable tome *Diabolus In Musica: Structural Implications of the Crotchet In Anglican Plainsong*, and Aubrey Wythe, the Virginia scholar, were out of place, but the Tune Inn was the only Capitol Hill bar within the graduate student price range and an occasional smattering of scholars from the Library of Congress and the Folger Shakespeare Library mixed in drunken sympathy with the regulars.

"It's the only way a comedy of satiric ridicule can work," Aubrey said hoping to renew her interest, realizing that she wasn't following him at all, and, at the same time, that the relationship he was trying so desperately to cultivate required that he continue in the same vein. He searched for examples of comic literature that would strike a common reference point with a specialist in musical incunabula from the University of Indiana. It was a difficult gap to cross. His own knowledge was deep rather than broad, and the Tudor restoration of Latin drama severely limited meaningful dialogue to a pathetically small audience. *Adelphi* and *Eunuchus* came to mind, particularly the performances about 1545, but the secrets of Terrence and the arcane vagaries of the classical restoration were—as he realized—hopelessly remote to his listener, and desperately foreign to his purpose.

The sad truth was that even though Aubrey had thought of little but his dissertation for the last four years—"Ancient Texts in Search of Modern Experience" was the working title that had gradually become carved in marble—it was on this occasion the last thing he wanted to discuss. Every neuron in his fellowship-educated brain shouted for an abrupt change of topic, but, because his mind and his vocabulary had for so long been reduced to the substance and style of his dissertation, and in spite of the shrill warnings of a higher intelligence, "Ancient Texts In Search Of Modern Experience" plopped onto the small table in The Tune Inn amidst puddles of generic draft beer and became his lame hope of seducing Professor Lacy Swanda.

Aubrey's fellowship at the Folger Shakespeare Library, which included important residence privileges in the Folger Guest House, had finally expired beyond all hope of resuscitation after two extensions and fruitless petitions to the Board of Directors. He had no place to live, a dissertation at best eighty percent complete, a single suitcase packed with notes, and a firm conviction that if Lacy didn't agree to share her room at the Guest House with him he would join the ranks of the homeless wanderers who slept on the steam grates by the Supreme Court. Years ago, as an undergraduate in Charlottesville, Aubrey would have known better how to deal with the situation. Then, any instigation of sex required the use of love as a nominal if not actual prelude. It had, he thought, something to do with the technology of the times. Birth control pills were around, but single women didn't have them, or didn't take them, and, chivalry not being entirely dead, one was expected to marry a girl if she were impregnated by these 'I love you' rushes of undergraduate passion. It was a talisman of sorts to cover the obvious contingencies. But now, ten years later, love had become more a matter of conjecture than convention in academic circles. One could, he realized, speak to an academic woman of love, but the response was uncertain, and such a declaration was more commonly made after cohabitation of some years and prolonged examination of personal commitments and the compatibility of career objectives. It certainly wasn't made on the first date in an effort to entice someone into bed.

It might have helped, of course, if Aubrey had not virtually ignored Lacy for the year they had been neighbors on the third floor of the Guest House, sharing the pathetically small bathroom, bumping into each other daily, and hardly managing to meet. He had never even asked her out for a drink. And now he needed to move in with her. If it were possible to do this without sex, then Aubrey would certainly have proposed such an arrangement, but the rooms were tiny, with single beds, and in spite of his uncertainty about how to deal with academic women as women, he was positive that a proposal along Platonic lines would have been offensive.

"I'm . . . I'm really sorry I never got to know you better, Lacy," he finally stuttered, awkwardly groping for her hand under the table and finding hard gobs of chewing gum against the back of his fingers as he squeezed her palm tentatively. "I always felt that . . . well . . . you know . . . if my dissertation had been going more smoothly . . ."

But he couldn't finish the sentence. Her hand was fleshier than he had imagined and, for all his concentration on the immediacy of her presence, her name reminded him of an earlier generation. Her lilac scent, so reminiscent of his grandmother, brought to mind only dry skin, false teeth, fading chintz and clumsy enema bags hanging permanently by the toilet.

Not that there was anything really wrong with her looks, Aubrey thought, glancing up from the smears of crab cake and catsup on their plates. She had strong features, thick mottled brown hair pulled back in a short uneven ponytail and the kind of clean, but never smooth, and all too obviously flawed skin that seemed to have been passed out promiscuously at the world's centers of post-graduate education.

Flattery, Aubrey realized, was out of the question. One had to respect certain natural limits of credibility. Still, the matter had to be brought forward. He had to say something. But saying meant thinking. Thinking meant metaphor, which meant literature and in the case of a midwestern musicologist specializing in pre-1501 manuscripts one could never tell what she had read, if anything.

"You'll remember in the *Decameron*," he started, but the shadow across her eyes put him off, the stage left of the Textualist defeating the stage right of the Renaissance man.

"Like in *The Taming of the Shrew*," he started again, this time without looking at Lacy's eyes, and he launched into an account of the necessities of satire contrasted with free form comedy of delight.

"Like in Cardinal Wolsey's production of the *Menaechmi* in 1526," he said, returning involuntarily to his dissertation topic. "Tudor audiences wanted more than the ridicule of Aristotelian comedy. The medieval romance had taught them to demand spectacle, didactic message and love interest."

Aubrey looked up when he said 'love interest' to see if there were some response in Lacy's eyes, but she was still trying to get the waitress' attention. He cringed and blushed. He couldn't blame her impatience at the awkward literary metaphors of his erotic aims. But it was all he knew, the only trick up his sleeve, and as practiced in the quiet, but heady, groves of Charlottesville, a rhetorical style not without its own amorous potential. But, as Aubrey reluctantly realized in his increasingly frequent dark moments, the truths of Charlottesville translated to the vulgarity of Washington with an imperfection that bordered on the random.

"Ancient Texts In Search of Modern Experience." It was what he had become. It was the only love song he knew by heart. He lumbered into a description of *Miles Gloriosus* acted for Queen Elizabeth by the Westminster boys during the Twelfth Night revels of 1565, hoping that Lacy would notice that it was no longer a thing in its own right, but a means to an end.

"We'll get another drink quicker back in my room, you know," Lacy said, interrupting and withdrawing her hand. Aubrey realized that the perspiration he had attributed to her weight was really his own.

"Come on," she said, leading him past the stews at the bar and into the street.

Lacy knew what Aubrey wanted and what he didn't. But she also knew that the Post-Freudian age being what it was, men—even men like Aubrey Wythe—couldn't take space in a woman's bed without offering sex. It suited her. She had always found Aubrey awkward, coltish, too keen, too green, too concerned with things that didn't matter. But at thirty-six, Lacy didn't care too much about what gave her single bed such allure. Aubrey was available, and he was the kind who stayed around if one listened to him. Happy marriages had been built on less, she knew. And it was a bargain she could keep if he gave her the things she hadn't been able to get for herself, a marriage, a baby, and not necessarily in that order.

Almost certainly not in that order, she thought again as Aubrey rambled on about Tudor production costumes surviving in the attic of Queen's College, Cambridge to show how the comic structure of the original Latin had been reinvested with new meaning.

Poor little man, Lacy thought as Aubrey fumbled for her hand in the dark and then—when she decided it was time—found it.

4

As twilight faded into dusk, and Aubrey Wythe felt the ominous snap of the deadbolt on Lacy's door like a hammer blow on the sternum, bats twittered over Jason Potter's fallen head in mute competition for lightening bugs and mosquitoes. Furtive lovers coupled in oblivious ecstasy behind an adjacent laurel. A homeless grifter ambled by, probed the pockets of the Senator's jogging suit, removed a money clip, loose change, an emergency cigarette, and sauntered off as if a corpse in the park were nothing out of the ordinary. In impotent protest, hydrogen of bacterial decay eructed from the gaping mouth that had once held the final word on winter wheat subsidies and federally guaranteed bank deposits. Jason, hovering still in the trees, appalled that his remains could be ignored for so long, felt the embarrassment acutely. In death, as in life, it seemed, the gasping belches of this hulking form were an embarrassment to its owner, something he—if any form of gender still applied under the circumstances—would just as soon abandon if it were not the only familiar object in his new world, and so much more manageable than this new unthinkable form he had assumed.

Jason tried to slide a hand across his thigh to resolve the gender question once and for all, but what he had taken for a hand proved unresponsive and floated slowly toward the river as if with a mind of its own.

Jason wondered whether to abandon the ripening form of his former self to the spreading gloom and seek whatever fate lay beyond the glowing clouds that massed in the West beyond Georgetown and the Francis Scott Key bridge. Some force of radiant blue magnetism seemed to pull him in that direction, but with a force that was easily resisted, like a Spring breeze that one could sail into or behind as one chose. And there was no rush. The force seemed steady enough. It wasn't likely to die any time soon, he thought, and then felt a chill as the death word passed through his ectoplasmic mind and he looked disconsolately down at his undiscovered corpse. Some things one had to see through to the end. He decided to wait. Somebody had to notice the body eventually. He had been a United States Senator after all. It was bound to count for something.

806 Pretender's Street, named for the Bonnie Prince who sulked and drank himself to death in Parisian exile, was the most

formidable and least restored mansion in Alexandria. Since its erection in the 1780's, the four story structure—"federalist" one would say except the word lost favor in Alexandria after the debacle of the 1860 War—had been used as a tobacco warehouse, residence, counting house, slave market, union army hospital, workingman's bordello and meeting house for the United Daughters of the Confederacy. Its worn, somewhat tawdry, but still dignified and well-proportioned facade now housed the combined medical clinic and legal resource center of the Wombyn League, a title designed to avoid the verbal sub-jugation of the feminine gender to the masculine as the League itself was organized to eradicate the most inconvenient aspect of male domination. It was known more simply in Alexandria as The Abortion Clinic. And it was because of the medical pro-cedure referenced in the popular title that a plainly dressed, unfashionably sturdy and somewhat masculine woman stood resolutely outside ten feet of the short flight of deeply troughed red sandstone stairs that connected the building to the adja-cent sidewalk and displayed to the world at large a full color poster of uncertain but obviously biological content. The ten feet, rather than some other distance, was the boundary estab-lished by a local court between the privacy guaranteed to the medico-legal functions of the Wombyn League and the freedom of speech guaranteed to the Catholic Church for expression of its position that abortion and murder are one and the same.

As Sister Mary Scroggins of the Order of Mercy held her ground against principalities unseen, a shadow blue Chevy Camero stopped in front of 806, its engine idling at an artificial-ly high speed, and the roar of its open tailpipes rattling the win-dows of the surrounding buildings. A girl of unformed features pecked the driver's beardless cheek as he glanced furtively in the rear view mirror. She retrieved an overnight bag from the back seat. The front door creaked as she slammed it shut with a hollow, tinny clatter. The driver and the car were around the corner of Patrick Street before the girl alighted on the curb and paused to study the small brass plague beside the door.

The girl knew the address by heart even though she had never been there. "806" had passed from mouth to mouth in earnest pleas and fits of girlish laughter since she was twelve and barely cognizant of the connection between boys and the swelling of babies in bellies. Now that she was sixteen, the address, and a few hundred dollars, had saved the reputations of several girls she knew well and had become her only hope of avoiding a pre-mature marriage. She now couldn't imagine what had made her 'fool around' with the obviously immature driver of the Camero. His half-fledged moustache, carbuncular neck, and inarticulate concupiscence now revolted her. And besides, there was someone else now, someone she really didn't want to know anything about all this, someone at Virginia Tech who could invite her away to fraternity parties and whose approval meant more to her than the inconvenient state of her hormones.

As the girl hesitated, Sister Mary Scroggins lurched forward with her poster of the embryo in its various stages of legally abortable development. At six weeks, the embryo floated in a royal blue sack attached to a crimson umbilicus. The heart, like a poppy, swelled on its chest. Its short unjointed arms ended in four-pointed flippers. Its head was over-sized and laced with capillaries. A white spinal column ran from the crown of its head to its bottom, and dark brown eyes sat level with a small nasal swelling. All anatomical parts were labeled in bold, luminescent print to eliminate any confusion with tadpole or lungfish, and to show beyond doubt that these oddly formed, foreign-looking masses were, in fact, human organs. A yellow sack of yoke floated next to its feet. Its massive head—most of its body weight of half an ounce or so—was bent over in the posture of deep reflection, Rodin's "Thinker" with no arms.

The girl averted her eyes.

"How far along are you?" the older woman with the poster asked. "Six weeks? Eight weeks? Twelve weeks? The eyes, the mirrors of the soul, are fully formed at ten weeks. Don't let them kill your baby."

"I . . . Uh . . . Uh . . . ," the girl stammered in shock without giving an answer. Her left hand involuntarily covered her abdomen.

"At six weeks," the woman with the placard said, "your baby's heart beats about twice as fast as yours. That six week old baby loves you and wants to live." Through some trick of the airbrush, the background of the fetus' head had been lightened into a circle, to show without superfluous label, that the soul, which goes without reference in *Gray's Anatomy*, was here, of all parts, the most prominent if hardest to find.

As Sister Mary Scroggins' one sided colloquy with the frightened girl continued, a frail young woman of petulant, dark-eyed beauty emerged from the door of 806. A Wombyn League nametag that said Lindsay Hayden, Legal Advisor, was pinned to her silver and turquoise Thai silk blouse. She rested a clipboard on a well-turned hip and scanned the street impatiently until a police cruiser appeared slowly, even reluctantly, a block away at the Henry Street stoplight.

They could have used the siren and come on through the intersection, Lindsay thought, but she was used to the reluctance of police protection south of the Potomac. Without waiting further for the police, she descended the short flight of stairs to the street and tugged the young girl away from the picture of the floating fetus that appeared to have hypnotized her.

"It's all a lie," Lindsay screamed at the poster, taking a small can of spray paint and obliterating the fetal head, halo and all. "It's only a pregnancy, your pregnancy, and you can terminate it if you want to."

As flashing lights from the police cruiser bounced off the solid brick walls of Pretender's Street, and the officers opened their doors at a leisurely pace intended to allow any criminal at the end of their chase to escape before they arrived, Sister Mary Scroggins drew three feet of number ten chain and a Chubb bullet proof lock from her carry-all, chained herself to a parking meter and started to sing "Jesus Loves the little children, all the children of the world . . ."

"Arrest her," Lindsay shouted to the still dawdling police-men, her short dark curls swirling around her head like angry vipers. "The order says no closer than ten feet to the door, and she's about nine and a half feet now. I've got a tape measure here if you don't believe me." She offered a carpenter's self-winding tape to the air, as no one seemed concerned about exact distances.

The girl whose presence had initiated the confrontation shuffled toward the policemen as if she too needed protection.

"Don't let her intimidate you," Lindsay shouted. "You're not killing anybody. There's no such thing as a soul. It's your right."

"Is she really a nun?" the girl asked, not speaking to anyone in particular, and glancing furtively up and down the street.

" . . . red or yellow, black or white, they are precious in His sight," Sister Mary sang for the third time and then, without missing a beat, started in to "We shall over come."

"Couldn't you just move a couple more parking meters down the street Ma'am," one of the three policemen, pushed forward by the other two as their spokesman, said. He was in his early thirties, handsome and apparently fit, the model officer of a model city.   "Really, Sister, you can get up and walk away . . ."

"No. She's already in contempt. She goes to jail for this. It's in the court order. Look what she's done to this poor girl."
The girl in question shuffled even further away from the clinic.

"But, if she'll just move . . ."

"I've got your name and badge number. If you don't arrest her I'll call . . ."

"Well . . ."

"Ohoo . . . ohooo . . . deep in my heart, Ahhh . . . do believe . . ."

"You're probably a Catholic too. If you don't arrest her, Don-lon, I'm calling the Mayor right now."

Officer Barry Donlon looked back at his patrolmates. Duke Scribelli was a three-mass-a-week Catholic and Buster Earl was a Southern Baptist. Scribelli was the tenth of ten children. Bubba had a Downs Syndrome brother.

"You've got one more chance, Sister," Donlon, a lapsed Catholic with no strongly articulated views, said. "Move on."

"Do your duty, son, God will forgive you if you ask Him to, which is more than He will do for you Lindsay Hayden," the nun said turning from the policeman to the assistant legal advisor of the Wombyn League.

"Lindsay Hayden tells people to have abortions when she has no idea what she's talking about."

"Get the wire cutters, Scribelli."

"Does Lindsay Hayden know what it feels like to kill her own baby? Does Lindsay Hayden know what she is telling these young women to do to their lives?"

"They won't cut this, Barry, it's number ten chain."

"Don't go," Lindsay said, grabbing the young woman's arm. "Don't believe her. A fetus isn't really a baby yet. You have the right to terminate your pregnancy. It's your choice. Nobody has the right to judge."

"A torch?" Donlon asked. "You think so? Really?"

"No," the young girl said pulling herself away from Lindsay's desperate grip. "Really. I've changed my mind. I can still think it over for a few more weeks." The girl rubbed the deep red indentation from Lindsay's fingers on her forearm, and walked with increasing speed toward the bus stop on King Street.

Sister Mary prayed, getting down on her knees and repeating Hail Marys.

As the policemen dawdled and then retreated to the station for welding equipment, Lindsay's ire rose again, distorting her clear, regular features into a pinched mask of animal fury. She had tried, over the years, to treat Sister Mary Scroggins and her Catholic bigotry with the courtesy lawyers reserve for their professional adversaries. But, even though they knew each other on a first name basis, Sister Mary's personal jibes had gone too far this time.

Lindsay drew her right leg back and delivered a sharp kick to Sister Mary's hefty underside. Her pointed shoe sank into the soft flesh but seemed to cause its recipient little pain. Lindsay drew back and kicked again. Her stiletto heel caught in the worn paving bricks, pulled her aim high and into Sister Mary's ribs. There was a noticeable crack. Sister Mary winced and muttered a prayer written to be said in times of persecution. Lindsay drew back at the sound, but then, in a surge of hot-blooded fury, she hit the same broken spot over and over, forcing the pointed toe of her Georgio Armani shoe into the nun's chest cavity each time.

"Now you'll have to leave these poor, frightened girls alone, won't you Mary?" she asked sarcastically, and kicked again as the unspoken phrase "forgive them for they know not what they do" crossed the nun's lips.

"And I know perfectly well what I'm doing, " Lindsay said, scarcely noticing the echo from the nun's chest cavity. "You're the one who doesn't know what you're doing. Every time you scare a kid away from this clinic she'll get the same thing done illegally and be maimed, sterilized or killed. Is that what you want? You just like punishing kids in trouble? Is that it?"

"You have no children. You've never been pregnant. You've never had an abortion. Don't tell people to do what you've never done yourself."

"And you're a virgin, for christsake, how can you pretend to know anything about abortion?

"I am a virgin," Sister Mary said, "for Christ's sake."

Lindsay kicked blindly at the meaningless avoidance of the issue, and the numbing obstinacy of religious faith.

" . . . pray for us now and at the moment of our deaths . . ." Lindsay was not a Catholic and did not know one prayer from another, but the words reminded her again of Sister Mary's irrational justification for the misery she inflicted on unwilling mothers and unwanted children. She found a new spot on the nun's thinly padded side and kicked again.

" . . . and calm the wrath of our sister Lindsay . . ."

The return of the patrol car interrupted Lindsay's violence and brought her suddenly to the realization that she had committed an assault, possibly a maiming, and had pronounced, without consideration, thoughts which, in more rational moments, she would have considered impossible for one of her education and professed tolerance. She retreated to the doorway of 806 Pretender's Street as if she were watching the life of someone else.

"Are you alright, Sister?" Scribelli asked after he cut through the chain and helped Sister Mary to her feet. "You look a little unsteady."

"Oh," Sister Mary said stretching, "I'm fine. Sometimes sitting down too long makes me a little dizzy, that's all," and without further ado she started a new song: "My soul doth magnify the Lord . . ."

Jason Potter watched impassively from a thousand feet above Arlington Cemetery as the sun set for the fourth time since his death. The first few times, it had been exciting. The clarity of vision afforded his spectral form had turned the gaudy reds and purples of sunset into a fireworks exhibition that reminded him pleasantly of the Presidential inaugurations that, whether his party won or lost, had been the spiritual highpoints of his years in Washington. And the star-lit gloom that followed the colorful eruptions brought a sense of peace that felt as much like sleep as anything he had felt in his ghostly repertoire of new experiences, sleep without dreams, but with, it seemed, a continuing consciousness that surpassed both waking and forgetfulness.

The sense of being drawn toward the west by currents of soothing blue light had faded. The currents were still there. In fact, he saw them more clearly each day as his spectral eyes adjusted to new modalities of perception. The heavens swirled with vivid blue streams bearing souls westward into an abiding light beyond the horizon that he no longer associated with the sun. The two were distinctly different he could tell and wondered how he had ever confused them. The blue light was stationary, while the sun still moved like Apollos' chariot through its daily arc.

Jason lowered himself from the heights above the National Cemetery and flowed up the Rock Creek Parkway against traffic. He perched quietly above the brook, and watched the swirls of souls in the mainstream as they headed down to the Potomac and then westward. They looked happy enough if one could judge by their smiles and grins, their facial reflections of peace, and the words that formed on their singing lips. But, being a politician, Jason had long ago stopped accepting superficial expression as evidence of a larger truth. Even setting his natural doubts aside, the faces swirling so blithely westward blurred as they were swept away, and lost all resemblance to human beings long before they were over Harper's Ferry, which was about as far as Jason could see.

Yet, he had to admit to himself, even "see" wasn't the correct word really, for his sense of vision, his certainty of perception, did not rely on light and was not obscured by opaque objects. It was more a matter of mind than of perception, he realized, as was his sense of movement. He had first called it flight and twittered along the treetops, over Georgetown, down the river, across the Mall, doing loops around the Washington Monument, through the Capitol dome and across the river again to his house, an ante-bellum mansion on the Alexandria waterfront surrounded by topiary magnolias and covered with blooming wisteria.

It was fun the first time he did it. A prenatal dream of flying found expression in his airborne pirouettes. But, on the third pass, as he looked in vain for his shadow in the reflecting pool, Jason's post-mortem glee began to fade. He noticed for the first time that he was invisible to the world, invisible to himself and that even the other shades splashing through the blue river ignored him.

With sinking spirits Jason left Rock Creek Park and hovered over Alexandria. It was still rush hour. Cars streamed around the Beltway like rivers of fireflies, each entering and exiting as if preordained, as if the flecks of light knew where they were going and had some purpose. He pitied and envied the bustle of the world. It seemed impossible that he could miss the places and feels of the Senate so intensely, or that his absence could have left the world so unaffected. But it was so.

The vacancy in the Senate created by his death had already been filled. Jason tried to tell himself that he didn't care anymore. Most of what he had done during his living years seemed trivial from a thousand feet up and two miles across, he thought, realizing for the first time that he could expand his being horizontally as well as vertically. Yet even that realization made him sad, because neither "vertical" nor "horizontal" could describe what he was doing with his mind, as if mind itself made any sense. Language had become obsolete, inappropriate, the nexus of word to thing a mere bond of convenience that decayed quicker than flesh.

Jason, thoroughly depressed by now, sat, or rather compressed himself onto the roof of the old Alexandria Post Office. It was the federal courthouse now, a restoration in which he had once taken some pride. He looked down at the statue of the Confederate soldier in the intersection of Duke and King Streets. The young man, solemn and mustachioed, bowed his head toward Richmond in mourning for the Lost Cause. Jason, who in life had driven through the intersection at least twice a day and as quickly as possible, noticed the statue for the first time, and shed, within his incorporeal limitations, a tear of sorts for his own lost causes and squandered opportunities.

Jason's self-indulgent revery was interrupted at last by a crude, bumbling disturbance in the air, like the flutter of hummingbird wings. He looked up to find a being no larger than his thumb waving short gossamer arms in wild despair. The sun streamed through its crystal body refracting into rainbow hues that swirled into a spherical halo. Its eyes were closed, its mouth gaped in mute supplication, and Jason felt rather than heard a high-pitched cry beyond tears. He cupped the trembling spirit in his hands and floated with trepidation to the banks of a turquoise stream of infinite depth that flowed swiftly upward from the gates of Arlington Cemetery in dimensions he could not name. The tiny spirit's longing cry turned into mummering song as Jason placed it gently on the surface of the stream. The halo merged with the glimmering colors of the river and faded into ether. The tiny ghost went limp and, with peals of inexpressible joy, dissolved itself into chords of celestial harmony. Jason watched other spirits float past. They dissolved less quickly, but as their spectral resemblance to life faded he detected a rise in their general level of happiness, until, at the point of total dissolution from the world, their barely discernable expressions were bursting with unconcealed rapture. It was, he realized, the forgetfulness and dreams of Lethe's potion, the gulf where memory died and the world beyond death began. Seeing such joy on the face of those who floated past made Jason long to swell their number on the way to eternity. He was reaching for nonexistent clothes with non-existent hands to strip himself for the journey when a last memory of low chicanery rose to check his departure.

Jason cast his cerebral eyes down the Potomac. It was night again. A solitary canoe plied the waters of the Potomac south of the Beltway. He knew the face and the form of the lone helmsman. He had a body the ashen hue of old evil and a heart the texture of coral. And, Jason remembered, he had made a deal with the man that cursed any thoughts of entering the neverending stream. It hadn't seemed like much at the time. It was a small favor, a legislative mite so to speak, and, thoroughly deniable, like most of the bills he had sponsored or supported, something that could never be laid at his door except, of course, by his own conscience.

Jason knew it was wrong when he did it, but there were many ways on the Hill to give with the left hand and take away with the right without anyone being the wiser. And, if he had lived longer, there were ways of thwarting what was given without retracting it. If he had lived, he thought, concocting contingencies and possibilities that might have been. But the possibilities of his imagination evaporated as rapidly as he conceived them. The might-have-beens loomed across unfordable canyons. His heart sank into his ethereal shoes as he thought of what he had made possible but which he could no longer stop or control.

It was all the fault of that house on the waterfront, he thought. He had wanted it too much. He saw that now with the moral perspective of one with no physical needs. But he still remembered the desperate longing that had begun with simple admiration for a certain colonial style, blossomed into infatuation with the First Families of Virginia and a compulsion to rise above his plain mid-western origins. He began cruising past the house once a day, then walking through the neighborhood at night, picturing himself as the owner, the proprietor, the Lord of the manor. It was the most common fantasy about the South. After twenty years of pandering to votes on a common man theme, Jason needed to feel a sense of aristocratic detachment while he was on the job. After twenty years in the Senate, he deserved it. And then, while taking the evening stroll he had come to call his constitutional, a huge swarthy man of indeterminate age fell into step with his proprietary gait.

"Evening," the stranger said in the drawling confidence of old Alexandria that Jason admired.

"Evening," Jason said in angular, mid-western imitation of the same tone.

"It's a lovely property, wouldn't you say, sir?" the stranger asked pronouncing "sir" without the final "r" and indicating the property which had come to represent the "Massa Jason" of Jason Potter's imagination.

"Oh, yes," Jason said without trying to hide his enthusiasm.

"You know the history of the Mayberry-Lewis house, do you?"

"Well, a little, you know . . ."

The stranger launched into a history of the house from Alexandria's earliest beginnings to the present. There were sea captains, duels, wars, murders, elopements, maiden aunts, slave mistresses, mulatto bastards, a war of revolution and a wife seduced by Light Horse Harry Lee, cotillions attended by George Washington, financial panic, runs on banks, a War of Secession and Union occupation, years of decline and the sufferings of old blood in deep isolation.

Jason sighed when the stranger finished. He could too easily see himself telling the same story while having juleps served to his main contributors.

"Who lives there now?" Jason asked hesitantly.

"Why, the widow Sims, of course. As you may recall, Ambassador Lucius B. Sims was a China hand and emissary to Sun-Yat-Sen." The stranger spoke with a reassuring ease and total lack of gesture that rendered his strangeness familiar and made Jason trust him.

"Ahhh . . . ," Jason said in response, being somewhat vague on foreign affairs. "She must now be a lady well up in years," he guessed, finally placing Sun-Yat-Sen in his memory.

"Oh yes, the widow Sims has seen ninety summers come and go. You would call that 'well up', would you not, Senator Potter?" The stranger extended his hand. It was large and dry with callouses, more like the hands Jason shook back in South Kanaska than the soft, wet, even slippery ones he knew from the Senate.

"Yes," he replied wondering how the stranger knew his name, but feeling too flattered to ask. "And probably nearing the end of her summers, then, I would think."

"But bright as a button. Sharp as a tack. Good stock. Obadiah Sims came to Smithfield around 1690, you know, and he knew the value of land. It stays in the genes, that kind of thing does."

"You know her yourself?"

"Good Lord, yes. I sold the house to Ambassador Sims when he retired in 1948."

"You mean that your family lived here?" Jason didn't think that the stranger looked old enough to have done what he claimed.

"No. I was only the agent," the man said with a smile that showed teeth too white to be real, but too sharp to have been designed by a dentist. The man would have to have been at least twenty-five or so when the transaction occurred, Jason thought, and would be at least seventy now, yet he hardly looked it.

Jason shifted his position to see the man in a better light. His skin was creased, to be sure, but hardly wrinkled. His hair showed a speck of white above the ears, but it was almost as black as an oriental's and certainly as straight, falling with defiant resolution over a brow that was high without any hint of a receding hairline. His shoulders were curved somewhat, but powerful, the stoop of the weight lifter rather than the involuntary bowing of age.

Jason, a professional at sizing people up for what they could give and how much they would demand in return, resumed his evening stroll. He felt uncomfortable in the stranger's presence. He felt overmatched in some contest he hadn't planned to play, whose rules he couldn't fathom. The stranger moved easily with long strides he had to check to keep within Jason's limit. Jason noted the ease, silence, even grace, with which the man moved his considerable bulk as they walked side by side around the Mayberry-Lewis mansion.

"What do you think the house is worth now?" Jason asked, getting to the question that had been growing in his mind for over a year.

"Ah." The large man paused. "Price in today's market depends on many things. One would, of course, have to presume."

"But you must have some feel for the value of such a house."

"Oh. I do. More than a feel. I am the only realtor in the area who ever quotes firm prices without a written agency agreement from the owner. It is an old custom, largely abandoned I am sorry to say, but one to which I still adhere." The man's soft accent and choice of outmoded words again reminded Jason to scan his face for signs of superannuation. The effort was again in vain. Jason ascribed it to the night and the river humidity.

"Were I to give you a price, sir, on this property, I would commit myself to seeing that it was sold to you for that price or I would forfeit to you the ten percent commission I would otherwise receive."

"But realtors always represent the seller, not the buyer . . ."

"Henry Tuckahoe, sir, creates a market," the man said presenting Jason with a card that contained the name but no address or telephone number. "It is, as I said, an old, even ancient, custom, but one which I accept and which I am allowed to pursue under the grandfathering terms of my licensure with the Commonwealth."

Jason, who had bought and sold Washington area real estate for thirty years, starting in an Arlington Apartment and going through houses in Chevy Chase, Bethesda, and McLean prior to buying his present roost in the Rosemont area of Alexandria, had never heard of such an agent, but the arrangement implied certain exciting possibilities.

"If a gentleman of your stature, Senator Potter, were to approach a lady of Mrs Sims' intelligence, he would, I suspect, pay $840,000 for the property. It is, as you well know, unique, the only fully detached house in this part of Olde Town, and certainly the largest mansion of its type with a view of the river."

"Eight-hundred-forty-thousand," Jason repeated without expression. He discussed billions on a daily basis, but that was somebody else's money. When it came to what he could afford himself, $840,000 was a lot of money, more than twice what he had paid for his present house.

"But, on the other hand, if Mrs Sims were not advised as to the stature of her purchaser, the price could be lower," Henry Tuckahoe said, "considerably lower."

"You are talking about an agent for an undisclosed principal?" The relationship implied certain risks for the agent and was rarely used.

"Precisely."

"How low?"

"What price would you consider reasonable, Senator?"

"Oh . . . I'm not really in the market, of course, but, considering the house and all . . . and of course I've never been inside it . . . maybe as much as . . . uh . . . six."

Henry Tuckahoe absorbed the statement impassively. Offers for real estate were something he never got excited about. "It could go as low as that, if I were to waive my commission . . ."

"Well," Jason laughed nervously feeling an almost sexual excitement at the mention of such a proposition.

"If I get you the Mayberry-Lewis house for six or under, Senator, do we have a deal?"

"And your commission?"

"Something to be worked out later. I'm sure it won't be a problem."

Jason's excitement crossed the threshold into the sensual. It was a fantasy. It seemed so improbable. Whatever he promised couldn't matter. So he agreed. It was verbal. It was not legally binding. But in his heart he knew he had made a bargain he would have to keep.

But who could then have foreseen what the dusky giant would want, or what it would entail? Jason certainly had not guessed his demand or seen its significance at the time. A change in the accounting procedures of the FSLIC—the Fizz Lick of his jokes —seemed so remote, so arcane, so clearly within his power, and yet so picayunish as to be deniable in case of a backfire, that it could hardly hurt his career. It was a deal with the devil in a manner of speaking, but he had made them before. He felt, in fact, that dealing with the devil was his profession, a skill in which he had become expert.

Senator Potter had started to suspect that the change in the FSLIC accounting rules was more serious than expected even before he died, but now, with all the advantages of spacio-temporal disintegration, he could see the magnitude of what he had done.

Jason hesitated beside the stream he called Lethe for lack of a proper name and envied the loss of memory that would be his on stepping in and floating away. The time for him to go, however, had not yet come. He didn't know what his limbless mental power could yet accomplish if he stalked the face of the earth, but he intended to try. This deal with the devil had to be undone. If possible. It was a big "if." Jason sank back into the shadows of the Potomac. The river sprite, he had found, was the one form of all his astral possibilities most conducive to serious reflection.

"Knocking off early for a change, Granny?" The guard asked in a tone that was both apathetic and derogatory.

"Time to go out and celebrate," Frances Appleby said jauntily as she shrugged at the shoulder strap of an old, overstuffed briefcase and deposited it on the table for inspection. "A major breakthrough in my research, Louis," she said reading his name tag. She had prided herself once on knowing all the staff by name, particularly the fellow smokers like Louis O. Williams, who sometimes even let her into the union-sponsored smoking lounge in winter. But with the tumor off on its own malignant little course again, short term memory was getting to be a problem.

Francis knew that Louis, and the rest of the staff, had no interest in her research, and even considered books to be frivolous. She had, years ago, tried to bring them into the picture, to pique their interest in the painstakingly inscribed notes they inspected each day without question. But nothing roused their attention and she had, reluctantly, given up and accepted the limits of their vision. One had to make allowances for family members, and, since her retirement from the Fairfax County school system on medical grounds, the Library of Congress and its employees were the only home and family she had.

It had started as a place to go, a welcome respite from her small suburban apartment. But as the books came alive, the trip back home became too much trouble. The Library of Congress was the place she wanted to be, the place she longed for, the place she thought of as her destiny. And then, as the urgency of her research grew and the date approached on which the morbid but inoperable dilation of her brain would reach its natural course, Francis gave up her apartment and moved outright into the national library. It was the right thing to do with time running out. And, today, more than ever, she knew that the world's largest library, her home, would yield its secrets.

Deep in the third basement of the Jefferson Building, fifty feet below the genealogy room, two-hundred feet through a tunnel from the main dome, and at the beginning of a rarely used passageway into the Folger Shakespeare Library, on a shelf of unclassifiable materials labeled "Unpublished Virginiana," she had found the secret to the problem that had confounded her for the last thirty years, since, in fact, a stay in a Florence Crittenden Home for Unwed Mothers had interrupted her doctoral research at George Washington University and forced her to teach World History to High School sophomores as a career of necessity.

Frances' answer took the form of two handwritten tomes in an undecipherable language that looked to her like a previously unknown proto-semitic script. The paper in the earliest volumes was easily two-hundred years old, if not older. It had obviously been copied from something even more ancient, something that had been passed down from hand to hand, from generation to generation and treasured more than a pearl of great price. And it could be the proof she had been seeking for what she already knew with absolute certainly, that the Powhatan tribe of the Potomac Valley was one of the Ten Lost Tribes of Israel.

The key was that the Powhatan ate manna, just like the Children of Israel in the Wilderness. Of course, they didn't call it that. Linguistic shift being what it was, one wouldn't have expected it. But the early explorers recorded the Powhatan feeding on a manna-like substance that appeared at the base of the native river oak. The English settlers called it "indian bread," or "tuckahoe truffle." It was white. It was fluffy. It grew quickly, even overnight. It was proof enough for Frances. And this new manuscript promised to elevate her theory into fact.

But she would have to find someone who could read it first. There had to be somebody. There always was in Washington. Between the State Department, the CIA, the National Institute of Health, the Smithsonian and the Geologic Survey, somebody in Washington knew everything. But, usually one didn't even have to leave the Library of Congress. Everything was right there. So Frances rarely left the Library and knew how to avoid the guards and librarians when she wanted to, even to read through the night if necessary.

"Sleeping out tonight, Granny?" Louis O. Williams asked as he probed her carryall for contraband books, avoiding the soiled undergarments and the toothbrush worn to a stub and wrapped in toilet paper.

"Yes, indeed," Francis said, and walked briskly into the stagnant heat of the Washington night. The close air felt good after so many weeks in the artificially cooled and dried air of the Library.

Frances Appleby, "Granny Franny" to her familiars, old beyond her sixty years, marked by the poverty of one who rarely bathed and dressed with what came cheaply from the Salvation Army, strolled calmly across Independence Avenue, around the Eastern Market, where she helped herself to week old vegetables from a vendor's discards and then disappeared into an alley between 3d and 4th Streets. There was a grassy spot next to a garage in the middle of the block. The owner knew she used it on clear summer nights, but she never left a mess and nobody minded.

She needed a vacation. There were so many pressures on the researcher these days. So much to learn. So little time. It was nice to have a place to get away to. She called it a summer place, and hummed a tune from an old movie of the same name.

8

Clovis Tuckahoe, a heavy-set, thick-jowled woman in her late sixties with dyed black hair and deep layers of foundation make-up that gave her face the patina of antique *papiermache*, lingered in stunned silence by the still open grave of her husband, Schuler. The reality of his death had been slow to affect her. He had faded quickly. His passing was painless. And since then there had been a business to run that was itself so synonymous with Schuler that its details of cash balances, loan approvals, interest rates, and points at closing seemed to confirm his continued existence. Even the Burgh & Tuckahoe loan portfolio, so covered with Schuler's approving initials, seemed to prove the death certificate wrong.

Clovis didn't really miss Schuler until the casket was finally screwed shut. Then, for the first time, a deep sob shook the rubies on her ample bosom and rustled the black silk dress she had ordered by the yard from New York. It was a convulsion somewhere between a hearty sneeze and the terminal gasp of a consumptive poet and it came as a shock even to Clovis who, because of an early tendency toward fat, a generally disagreeable personality, and a socially insecure mother who tolerated neither, had been forced to master her basic urges and to meliorate the symptoms of raw emotion. It just didn't do to lose control like that, she thought, realizing all the while that nobody was watching and that she was performing only for herself. The thought brought on another heavy sob.

Birds twittered high in the trees above the Oak Hill Cemetery, the burial ground for old Alexandria families. *Magnolia grandiflora* shed petals onto the rows of headstones inscribed with pious verse, adorned with angels, laurel boughs, and masonic symbols. Long shadows of tall oaks spread across the hillside even at noon, the burying hour. Most of the guests—saddened more by death as a concept than by the end of a man they had known only professionally—had hurried back to their businesses muttering, "she wouldn't want to be bothered at a time like this," or, "we'll drop in later." A few, the long time Burgh & Tuckahoe employees, headed for the food and drink required by Southern custom.

Clovis glanced over the crepe myrtles beneath the oaks and maples, their deep purples and pinks banked in walls of color against the dark tree trunks and the verdant hues of rain-washed ivy. Schuler had loved crepe myrtle for its easy appeal and hardy growth. He always said that when he was a boy such vibrant colors were unknown, but Clovis had never taken him seriously on that or a lot of other subjects, and never bothered to ask him exactly how long ago that had been. And now it was too late for further questions. Another sob shook her breast and cracked the thick foundation across her face. Clovis hastened to repair the damage with compact, brush, and finally a liberal squirt of a perfume called Garden Bower.

A hummingbird, attracted by the synthetic ether of potable nectar, dove toward Clovis as if toward a bower of ripe wisteria, sensed his mistake too late, struggled to alter course in mid-air, tried impotently to regain altitude and then plummeted into Schuler's grave with a thump like the flick of a determined finger on a ripe watermelon. Clovis raised her head at the thin mewing from the grave and the faint drumming on the casket lid in time to see a minute chartreuse ball lift slowly on battered wing into the treetops. She blinked, gasped in wonder and disbelief. "Schuler's soul," she said, sobbed and waived a perfumed handkerchief at the retreating bird.

"Poor Schuler," Clovis said aloud but to no one in particular as a patient chauffeur seated her in the funeral home's black limousine.

"Poor Clovis" she said in the same tone of voice, as if there were no difference. They had been so much alike, after all, so devoted to each other, and yet there was so much that she did not know about him. Clovis had been almost forty when they met and married. Schuler was much older, though she never knew his exact age. He seemed almost timeless, and his constitution would have done credit to a man in his twenties.

After their only daughter, Daphne, and her Wall Street law-yer of a husband produced the baby Tabitha, Schuler faded quickly, as if he had lost all interest in living. He seemed to accept it, refused to see a doctor, and Clovis resigned herself to the state of confused acceptance that had generally prevailed when it came to Schuler and his personal affairs. Now, Daphne and the baby had already gone back to the family home on King Street next to the Burgh & Tuckahoe Savings & Loan. They were all she had left, but there was little room in their lives for the overweight, over-indulged, easily-miffed, quick-to-pout Clovis. She knew herself for what she was, knew that her fate was to be loved by one man only, and he now gone before. Clo-vis sobbed again and rustled through her purse for the compact and perfume as if she had not used them only a few seconds earlier.

As she shoveled talc and camphor into the natural lines of ageing, Clovis suddenly thought resentfully of Schuler flitting off blithely into the afterlife, abandoning his responsibilities, not even stopping to dip a wing or circle round her head. The painful mews she had heard turned in her memory into happy chirps. It wasn't fair. Everything was gone now, she moaned, everything. Unless, that is, one counted Schuler's younger brother Henry. She sobbed again at the thought and patched the broken veneer on her face.

Henry huddled in a corner of the limousine as far away from Clovis as possible. Clovis looked intently away from her broth-er-in-law, but there was no comfort for her in the familiar scen-ery outside the window, Schuler's world carrying on, blooming and bustling, but without him.

Clovis knew Henry had never really approved of her. He had envied the influence she had over Schuler, and now he seemed to blame her for Schuler's death. Not that there was any basis for that, of course. She had doted on Schuler. Wife had never loved husband more.

Clovis wept into a Garden Bower scented lace handker-chief, realizing for the first time that she was left alone with a

Savings & Loan that had been losing money for several years, and an unsympathetic brother-in-law who had finally inherited enough stock to sit on the Board of Directors.

Clovis felt tired and defeated as she turned her thoughts to the crowd of unwelcome mourners who would be waiting for something to eat at the reception. It all seemed to Clovis like more than she could endure and she recalled with envy the yellow-green puff of immortality disappearing into the heavens.

The call of the loon, plaintive and strange in the first light of dawn, spread on expanding ripples across the cold blue surface of Lake Chemquasabamticook to a rustic cabin isolated deep in the Maine woods where the solitary figure of the Honorable Jenkin Carroway, Judge of the United States Court of Appeals for the First Circuit, sat in a worn, bumpy Adirondack chair and labored intently over the written word. A knob from the chair's rough back dug into Jenkin's shoulder and he shifted position. He had lived with the pain since inheriting the chair from his grandfather and installing it more than twenty years ago in his sparsely furnished room overlooking the Harvard yard. He knew the pain from the well-worn knob and loved it in the way that one loves even the inconvenient quirks of one's own personality. It was a constant reminder of a life which, while it was hardly an ideal he might have composed for himself, was at least his by right of birth and force of achievement. Besides, as his father's fathers back to the Mayflower and beyond had said before him, getting too comfortable was bad for the circulation.

Jenkin hunkered over a steaming mug of instant Maxwell House, the bachelor's brew. It was easy to make and tasted so unlike freshly perked coffee that it could never offend even the most refined taste, something Jenkin's Yankee heritage found alien and even somewhat dangerous. Yet, he thought, one never knew who might drive up the two-hundred miles of deeply rutted dirt roads for a visit this time of year. There was, in a sense, no escaping such people, and he recalled with undiminished horror the time, almost twelve years ago now, when Aunt Anthea Brewster Carroway, Great Uncle Robert's widow, had come up for the day, just to see the old place, just because she remembered Uncle Robert talking about it so much back in '42 when he still used to fish, and just because she was sure, as she had been for the last forty years, that her days on the earth were few. But her comments about his coffee were inexcusable, he reminded himself, the exception to the rule of stony politeness kept by the Carroways, and something, in all Christian charity, he should have forgotten years ago. Aunt Anthea's being a Brewster of the Salem Brewster's explained it, of course. Massachusetts was too far south to be taken seriously, too corrupted with Congregationalists, Quakers, even Antinomians for all he knew. It was a case of *non-noblesse non-oblige* and, even as a young man of twenty-two Jenkin had wondered, even making the necessary adjustments for the ravages of age, what Uncle Robert could have seen in Aunt Anthia. Any one who would carry on so uncharitably about his coffee—perfectly good Ann Page grounds dried out and reused—seemed incapable of the self-sacrifice he associated more than any other virtue with marriage.

Jenkin warmed his hands with the mug and inhaled the steam. It was cold until the sun rose above the jagged line of the virgin spruce forest. By ten-thirty the temperature would climb up into the fifties and hover no higher than sixty-two before heading back down around 4:30. He liked it like that. The cool air kept a man vigorous, and, turning back to the thick pile of typed papers, he realized that he had brought more work than he realized. Still, it made for a challenge, and that, perhaps more than anything else was what he lived for.

Gaging the morning light against the whiteness of the page he was correcting, Jenkin lifted the globe of a kerosine lantern and extinguished the flame with snuffers that had belonged to his great-great-grandmother Winthrop. The natural light made a difference to the choice of words on the page and he was soon busy with his pencil, striking out whole lines with energetic vision and interlineating new paragraphs.

Hours passed. Jenkin hardly moved except for the periodic shifts from side to side in the Adirondack chair and the regular marking of the manuscript. At 11:30, a trickle of perspiration formed under the wool collar of his frayed Pendleton shirt and reminded him of a call of nature that he had suppressed for the last several hours. He stood, stretched and walked to the squat bark-covered outhouse behind the cabin.

A window in the shape of a five-pointed star allowed a column of light into the natural gloom of the privy. Jenkin picked up a *Bangor Herald* from a stack on the floor that served his simple requirements. It was only a week old.

His picture was on the front page. He wasn't surprised. He was not, as a rule, surprised by anything, and federal appeals court judges by way of regrettable necessity it had always seemed to Jenkin—were used to a certain amount of publicity. The headline under the picture did, however, cause him to read twice. He had, according to the article, been nominated for the United States Supreme Court. Again, not a surprise. A seat on the Supreme Court was the natural ambition of every judge, and he certainly had the academic qualifications and the temperament. But this was something he would not have considered plausible for another twenty years. He was only forty-three, after all.

Jenkin read on. His chief qualification, according to the article, was that he had never decided an abortion case, written, or spoken on the subject. It was true, he thought. He had hardly ever thought about the matter. Pregnancy, abortion, things like that, were, he thought, like the connoisseurship of fine coffee, things with which serious intelligent bachelors were not concerned. He knew the Supreme Court dogma on the topic, of course, as he knew the Supreme Court dogma on every topic, but he had never thought the abortion issue through for himself. Pure of mind and chaste of body—*meno sana in corpore sano*—the issue had simply not presented itself.

It was the wrong reason to be appointed to the High Court, Jenkin reflected as he put the paper to more practical uses, but he had never put his faith in princes and he fully expected that when his moment came it would be for someone else's reasons and not his own. There was this irrational element to life, Jenkin reflected, and Aunt Anthia came to mind again. Besides, most of his life experiences had been oddly thrust upon him, matters of duty rather than desire.

Still, he thought, casting the *Herald* into the nethergloom, there was no rush in verifying the paper. The story said he was unavailable for comment. That wasn't true. His mother knew where he was. But, true to the code of the Carroways, she was having nothing to do with the Fourth Estate. And there was no point in running down to Boston to see what was going on. If it was true it would still be true in another two weeks when his time at the Lake was over.

Having dismissed the matter from his mind, Jenkin returned to the pile of typewritten pages in front of his Adirondak chair and resumed the task, as he explained it if ever interrupted late at night in his judicial chamber, of proofreading for a lady novelist friend.

——· 10 ·——

Henry Tuckahoe prodded the crumbling masonry vault with a bent coat hanger and covered his head as plaster and mildew were followed by a damp chunk of decayed brickwork. He turned off his small flashlight. A faint light shown from the river side of the tunnel. The stench of sewage, diluted by summer rains but never offensive to Henry in even the driest seasons, was relatively friendly. Only the oldest buildings were still allowed to discharge their pourings and droppings directly into the Potomac. The rest of the City, everything built since 1952, channelled its ordure into smooth concrete sanitary sewers that led directly to the devices of Alexandria's treatment plant on Cameron Run. The ordinance preserving the old sewers was one of Henry's dearest achievements, and he prided himself on his intricate knowledge of their layout and structure. Besides, he never really trusted the modern sewers. He didn't trust any concrete structures for that matter, piles of mortar with no stone or brick.

Henry prodded the masonry, stood in the darkness and listened to the echoes and reverberations in the long tunnel. He was looking for the biggest building on the block. There would be a distinctive sound. He waded into a rivulet bobbing with fresh feces, tapping the vault as he went and listening for a change in the returning echoes. There should be a different odor about the place too, he thought, something fleshy, even a little bloody, if what the papers said about centrifuges was true.

He stopped after a few more yards of thumping and sniffing. This had to be it, he thought. 806 Pretenders Street. Henry knew the building well. He had sold it often—the transition from tobacco barn to gentlemen's knocking shop had been his idea—and he still admired the building for both personal and financial reasons. There was a tremendous demand for large, historical, but as yet unrenovated properties, and the Wombyn League had not done much with 806 from the architectural point of view. They kept it painted and scrubbed, but the windows were original, the tin roof hadn't been replaced since 1921, and Henry could tell by listening with his ear against the external walls that the central circular staircase was sagging, its supporting cross-beams gradually pulling away from their wall sockets. Whoever sold it now would get a commission in the six-figure range, even if it were in very poor condition. With appropriate zoning changes, the commission itself could be a million. The building had sixteen rooms, two of them large enough for conferences. The halls were fourteen feet wide and the ceilings were ten to twelve feet high. Law firms paid fortunes for these buildings when they came on the market. And that was the problem. The Wombyn League didn't want to sell.

Henry had dropped in repeatedly on its President for the last year. There was, he noted in the polite tone he expected old Alexandria to revere, every reason in the world to sell. Henry had drawn curves showing the rising costs of maintaining the building against its maximization of value. The cross-over point was now, he kept saying. Besides, it was a poor choice for a clinic. The Health Department kept demanding an elevator for the third floor patients, and elevators were expensive. The head of the League had finally sold him an option, but it was really a right of first refusal and it meant nothing unless she decided to sell. Still, Henry was confident. Time was his ally. And the decision to sell could be assisted.

Henry found the cast iron control to the master valve for the building, put his full weight against it and felt the rusted threads of the old machinery start to give. A ribbon of red water, lumpy with small bits of meat like a hobo stew, thinned to a trickle and then stopped entirely. Henry relaxed. It was a good valve. Built around 1873, he guessed, and taking a can of 3-IN-1 out of his coat pocket, oiled it to be in better working order next time.

They won't like that upstairs, he thought. And the Health Department wouldn't like a clinic, even an abortion clinic, with no working toilets. It was bad enough to pee in a jar, but what were they going to do now with the things they aborted, he wondered, and laughed at the simplicity of frustrating the most basic needs of over-civilized people. A turn of the right wheel would send them into a panic. A call on the 'phone and the Health Department would shut them down. Plumbers would look at everything before they thought of the master valve in the sewer, and then a week or so might have passed. The value of the building, as he said, had passed. It was time to sell.

Henry walked confidently toward the river exit, hurrying to beat the high tide. If only his other problems were so simple, he thought, and his mind turned to the venerable Burgh & Tuckahoe Savings & Loan. Now that he was on the Board, he couldn't ignore its problems the way Schuler had for the last several years. Not that it was Schuler's fault. Saving banks all across the country were in trouble. Thanks to a lot of congressional interference, banks and stock brokers had been allowed to offer higher interest rates. Money that should have been deposited in the Savings & Loans was being deposited in other places. The Savings & Loans were running out of money to lend. It was called "disintermediation" by the economists, but naming it didn't help. Still, there was a way to make the Burgh & Tuckahoe competitive again. Henry had seen to that. Money didn't mean much until it was accounted for over time, and the new changes in the accounting rules, changes Henry had first conceived in this same sewer when he was helping the late Mrs. Sims in that difficult decision to bring a property on the market, would make the Savings and Loans not only competitive, but phenomenally lucrative. If, that is, one had the visceral wherewithal to use the new rules. Schuler had not. But he was gone. And Henry did. That is if he could convince Clovis to go along. And now that he had a seat on the Board, there was no reason why he couldn't.

——·11·——

"Lindsay, I saw it. I can see the whole street from my window," Karen Moelders, the President and General Counsel of the Wombyn League said chidingly. "You deliberately kicked that nun in the ribs. Several times. Hard. It's bound to have left some kind of bruise. If she sues, it'll cost us a fortune. And the publicity will stink. It's bad enough they accuse us of killing babies."

Karen Moelders was a heavy set woman—square-rigged a sailor might say—in her early forties, with prematurely grey hair cut short and straight. Thick padding in the shoulders of her coat and a full skirt accented her size. Perfectly round grey steel glasses washed the color from her complexion and heightened the natural irregularity of her otherwise pleasant features.

High, thick heels added four inches to her natural height of five foot six and she chain-smoked unfiltered camels. Karen's was a striking figure made more imposing through a genius of design that she not only denied but which she publicly disparaged, explaining in the clearest terms that she pitied those who noticed, much less mentioned, such superficialities.

Karen paced back and forth against the Palladian windows that faced Pretender's Street as she lectured a contrite Lindsay Hayden. Ashtrays were conveniently located along her route, on the credenza, desk, window sill, coffee table, revolving book case with the Lawyer's Edition of the United States Supreme Court Reports, and on a plant stand for a nearly asphyxiated stalk of false aralia near the door. Each ashtray was full and the office reeked of week-old, month-old, even year-old tobacco.

As she paced, Karen dodged the poster of embryological development that had been forcibly confiscated from Sister Mary Scroggins. An embryo at five weeks, big-headed, hump-backed, long-tailed and reptilian stared at her with the sketchy eyes of a pencilled outline. By another week, definite arms and legs had developed, the eye was filled with dark pigment and a distinct nose had emerged.

Karen hated the poster. It was unfair. Girls didn't know they were pregnant at six weeks. The whole process crept up on them before they were aware of it. It was cruel to show them the posters. They could think more clearly, exercise their freedom of choice more confidently, without knowing what the thing inside them looked like.

Lindsay hung her head. Karen was right, of course. She knew attacking Sister Mary was counterproductive. She kicked at the poster and wished Karen would get rid of it. She hated the pictures. They made her feel queasy. If Karen hadn't been around, or if Lindsay had been on a stronger moral footing, she would have at least turned the thing over. It just wasn't a good thing to look at.

"I just lost control, Karen, I'm sorry."

"It's alright," Karen said, stroking Lindsay's neck. "You lose control and lash out sometimes. I know. It comes from letting yourself get fucked," which was the only expression Karen ever used to describe intercourse between the sexes. "Letting yourself get fucked and being owned are inseparable. Men fuck to own and dominate. Fucking and getting fucked breeds self-hatred. Self-hatred needs an outlet. You can't hold it back. It makes men violent. It makes women violent. It's not your fault."

Lindsay knew Karen's views on men and she knew to keep any criticism to herself.

"Deep down inside you think it's a human being, don't you?" Karen asked accusingly, holding the confiscated poster up in Lindsay's face.

"Well . . . it does look sort of like a baby . . . in an abstract . . ."

"Of course it does. But you've got to learn to live with that don't you?"

"Yeah."

"And it disgusts you to kill a thing like this, doesn't it?"

"Well. . . ."

"Then you've got to remember that this is something forced on a woman by a man. This," she said pointing directly to the macrocephalic head of the seven week old embryo, "is the natural product of a rape."

Lindsay nodded in response. She had never felt raped. There had been times—many times in fact—when she was less enthusiastic than her partner, but even then she never felt raped afterwards. And she had thought from time to time—in high school and college mostly before she went on the pill—that she might be pregnant, but even then, even thinking about the possible consequences, she hadn't felt raped.

Sister Mary had been right in a way, Lindsay admitted to herself. She didn't know what she was talking about when she told girls it was alright to get an abortion. Her immediate reaction in those few and fleeting moments in high school when she thought she might be pregnant by Jonathan Wildermute, the back-up quarterback and debate team captain, was to get

married and have the baby, work, put Jonathan through law
school, or medical school, or whatever he wanted. But those
had been simpler times, back in the 'sixties, before the Beltway linked the whole National Capitol Area together, before
sexual liberation and reproductive autonomy were even talked
about. Those old responses, she knew, were outmoded, arcane.
Now she didn't know how she would react to the knowledge of
an unwanted pregnancy, and considering the age and inclina-
tion of her present companion, there was little chance she ever
would. Sister Mary was right. It galled Lindsay to admit it even
to herself.

"It's not whether the fetus is human or simian or reptilian
or even a spark of the godhead, Lindsay, it's a question of who
gets to choose what to do with it. It's not a matter of right or
wrong, but of who gets to decide. Somebody has to decide. It's
existential realism. Not deciding is a decision. Not deciding lets
the state decide, and that may be Nazi Amerika, but its got to
change."

Lindsay winced at Karen's forced germanic pronunciation of
America, but, knowing the convoluted lecture that would follow any protest, she let the remark pass.

"Karen," Lindsay started, "Sister Mary . . ."

"Don't call her 'sister.' I'm more your sister than she is. She
has no sisters. None dare call her sister." Karen ignored her
own inadvertent pun. Puns were frivolous.

"She said I didn't know enough to tell people it's alright to
have an abortion. I mean I've never had an abortion, or a baby
. . ."

But Lindsay couldn't finish the thought. A dark stream of
polluted water trickled from behind the door of Karen's private
toilet and penetrated the heavy tobacco odor with something
stronger and more repulsive.

"My God," Karen shouted, dancing a Highland jig of sorts
and looking desperately at the bottom of her right foot. "Get
the janitor. Call a plumber. Christ, it smells like shit in here."

"It's coming out of your toilet . . ."

"It's not mine. Don't think I did all that. Other people come in here and shit when I'm not around. It could be the patient's . . .

"But look at the color. It could be . . . You don't think it could be . . . ?

" . . . fetal juice? Christ, it could be. You know what goes on downstairs . . ."

Lindsay put her head in Karen's trash can and waited for her stomach to convulse. She didn't have to wait long, and as the remains of Monterey Jack with bean sprouts on pumpernickel re-issued in altered state, her mind cleared and her prime concern became the cleaning bill for Thai silk.

"Look at that goddamn crapper," Karen said emerging from her small lavatory with a failed plumber's friend held at arm's length in frustration. "The whole system's backed up. This doesn't happen in any other building in the city. This goddamn building's too old, Lindsay. Get the thing fixed. Or, I'll call that Henryfuckingtuckahoe and sell out yet."

——·12·——

Later that afternoon, after the regurgitating toilets had been put right at 806 and after Karen had reluctantly approved a half day of sick leave, Lindsay Hayden lay on a ball and claw chaise beneath the wrought iron wisteria bower of a Georgetown mansion entwined in slow copulation with Max Aceldama. She rested on her side against pillows of Egyptian cotton, hand-printed in Mysore to an Aubrey Beardsley pattern, and fondled red Chilean grapes, sliding one slowly into her mouth as the periodic and varying rhythm of intercourse allowed. Max, a carefully exercised fifty, flat of tummy, firm of flesh and grey of stylishly elevated mane, lay behind, around and over Lindsay as the changing positions of "Mandarin Ducks," one of the thirty heaven and earth postures, dictated. He guided his jade stem, one of several Chinese or Indian terms he used for the external genitalia, into the coral gate between Lindsay's long, delicate legs. It was a posture intended to stimulate sublimity of mind while gratifying the subtlety related needs of the body.

Max, ever sensitive to Lindsay's moods, had perceived her need as soon as she came home. He had been in his study working on a sequel to his best selling *Food As Foreplay*, a treatise on oral sex as an extension of *nouvelle cuisine* that analyzed the chemistry and tastes of sexual secretions and the flavors which best prepared the palate for their enjoyment. The *Post* had coyly reported a "seven figure advance," but the royalties, and even the film rights, made the small fortune somewhat grander. Still, for all his success as a writer, Max had not considered resigning his endowed chair at Georgetown Law School.

"Of course, Lindsay, if you feel this abortion is something you must have to participate fully in life then you should have it," Max said as he plucked a cluster of wisteria flowers, blew the petals across her breasts and proceeded to catch them up on his tongue and transfer them to Lindsay's mouth in what he liked to call the columbine kiss.

"It's not something I necessarily *want* to do just for the sake of doing it," Lindsay answered apologetically and without noting in her tone the cadence of Max's continued thrusting toward the heart of her womb. "It's just something all the leading feminists have been through. Gloria Steinem, Germaine Greer, Sarah Weddington, they've all *had* abortions. They *know*. It gives them authority. But they didn't do it on purpose. It just happened to them . . ."

"You assume that."

"Well I can't imagine . . ."

"But you don't know."

"Well, no. I couldn't *know* it, but women . . ."

"Ah, Lindsay, sweet *naif*," Max said savoring the combined flavors of her salty left nipple, a fully sugared grape, and a particularly succulent wisteria petal as a gentle puff of summer air caressed silver Tibetan prayer bells hanging in the top boughs of a five-fingered crimson *Aser horizontalis*, an endangered species from the snow-lined rim of the Honshu littoral, "you underestimate the low native cunning of both sexes. My own first divorce—from the over-spending Julia you will recall—was, I am now quite sure, caused in part by the depth such an experience added to my own maturity and the credibility it lent my purely academic approach to the law. Not that this yearning for experience made poor Julia the financial profligate she was, but some knowledge of my own advantage, and perhaps a modest dose of curiosity, certainly inclined me to that solution. It wasn't easy. I was still a member of the One True Church at the time, laboring as a poorly salaried associate of a large cold-hearted firm and an unpublished adjunct professor of law."

While speaking, Max rotated Lindsay through a series of positions known as the "pair of swooping eagles" in which they rolled over and under each other from side to side of the chaise. They finished with Max on top, using the "seven shallow six deep" series of thrusts designed to increase friction on her "G spot."

Gradually, as his speed increased, Lindsay uttered a series of low guttural moans from deep within her body and Max transferred his gaze to a Japanese rock and sand garden—pure geometry contrasted against naturally and symbolically irregular stone—intended to be an object of contemplation during the final moments of sexual ecstasy, a method of transferring physical into spiritual delight. When Lindsay's moans subsided, Max rolled to his left and assumed the lotus position on a bed of blue Siberian moss surrounded by pale lavender canna lilies in full bloom.

As Max withdrew, Lindsay made a sprightly retreat into a lavatory under ivy covered stairs that led from the courtyard into the beaux art mansion. She had long ago lost any modesty about scampering nude from the wisteria bower to the lavatory. There were neighbors, of course. Being in Georgetown meant having neighbors a few feet away on either side no matter how much one paid. And even Max's twelve foot walls of slave-made bricks from the remains of a moldering plantation near Tangier Island could not keep out all prying eyes. But the MacCrackens on the left were in their eighties, rarely went out and would be too polite to mention anything they saw. And the house on the right belonged to Bruce Sobel, who even though he was in his forties, and living with which ever wife he was on at the moment, also had houses in Boston, the Virgin Islands, the Virginia Hunt Country, and was rarely in Georgetown. When Bruce's blue sable Jag was in the circular driveway, Max was simply a little more discrete in where he asked Lindsay to oblige him. The wisteria bower was, after all, hardly his only "sacred place" for love making.

Lindsay closed the lavatory door. It was against Max's preference for her to urinate right after intercourse. It broke his mood of intimacy, he said, even made him feel she hadn't been enjoying it. She denied it, of course, but his accusations were true in a way that Max, for all his intelligence, could not understand. She had long ago admitted to herself that Max's progressively more sophisticated, even spiritual, approach to sex had left her behind. She had been his student at Georgetown Law School when they met. He was twenty-one years older, vastly more experienced and learned. His lectures on Constitutional freedoms were a revelation. She became his disciple, his research assistant, his willing bed companion, and his live-in lover. Max had introduced her to Karen, gotten her the job at the Wombyn League. Max was a visionary, a television personality, a Moses of Constitutional law. All in all his quirkiness about vaginal orgasm was not much to put up with, she thought, as her stream of hot urine gurgled into the toilet and her hand slipped between her thighs to relieve the nervous tension Max had aroused.

Lindsay had tried to bring on the elusive and much ballyhooed vaginal organism. She had read the books. She had squatted over a mirror and studied her private parts, analyzed her feelings, exorcised the sex taboos learned from her mother, a demure and saintly soul who shrunk even from the idea of french kissing, and gone on with Max to read the basic primers of Taoist sex, then the *Kama Sutra of Vatsyayana* and its modern adaptations. But it had not increased her High Sex potential or awakened her Inner Lover. She had gone to the Skydancing Institute in Zurich, heard the lectures and studied the diagrams of energy centers connected by the Hindu serpent-god Kunilindi. She had listened to the *Dervish Symphony*, the *Missa Gaia*, the Leonard Cohen poems and the Lady Smith Black Mozambo songs, practiced sexual breathing, visualized the air entering her vagina like a rushing wind, and meditated on the painting of inner light that Max kept in his study, a woman seated on her lover, kissing, and hugging while fountains of psychic energy gushed from a lotus blossom in the space where their two heads met and enshrouded their bodies in streams of glorious burning, embracing light.

Lindsay brought on her orgasm efficiently and without the groaning flourishes with which she had announced the artificial version. She flushed the toilet, half covered herself with an antique silk kimono Max had brought her from the Forbidden City and walked slowly, as befits one whose spiritual needs have been fully met, back to the pleasure dome. Her breasts, not overly large but well shaped, jiggled between the teal blue pheasants of the kimono.

It was the right place for love even if she couldn't appreciate it properly, she thought, admiring the delicately textured tiles from a defunct Yucatan monastery, the Tanagra figurines, the finely wrought bonsai garden and the golden carp swimming lazily in a pool of opalescent verdigris.

As Lindsay peered through the cascading wisteria, Max was still in the lotus position. His eyes were rolled upward and his penis was fully erect. He was trying again, she saw, for the inner orgasm. He had explained it all to her several times, but it seemed to Lindsay like more pleasure than one was entitled to on earth, like hearing voices and seeing signs. Things so good simply didn't happen to people one actually knew.

"Let me help bring you off, Max," she whispered in his ear while massaging the base of his penis and starting to straddle him.

"No," he said almost bruskly, pushing her aside. "I feel it coming this time. I know I can do it."

She kissed his ear and curled up to watch. It was what he wanted, what the books all recommended. Nothing was to be kept from your partner. Her own furtive bathroom pleasures violated every canon of sexual ecstasy, even as ten years ago they had offended the moral law. It was, she realized in the rare moments when she bothered to think about it, merely trading one kind of guilt for another. But those thoughts were far from her mind now as she watched Max with half an eye and ruminated on her more pressing problems.

The idea of getting pregnant to have an abortion was strangely exciting and repulsive at the same time. Knowing the reality of what she had, for so long, been advocating for others had a deep attraction. If she just happened to get pregnant and just happened to need an abortion, that would be different. She had no qualms about that. And, it could just happen, of course. Max did still ejaculate occasionally. And, if she got pregnant from Max she knew he would want her to get an abortion. He made no apologies for not wanting children at his age. Neither of his two wives had children with Max, although both did in later marriages. What, as he put it, did a life so full need with children? It was a hard question to answer without implying some criticism of his obvious accomplishments.

Max shuddered and fell back on the chaise. "Oh, God. I did it." The salt and pepper hair on his chest dipped and waved as if a field of static electricity had passed over.

Lindsay looked dubious. Max took the higher sex manuals too seriously. It was, she thought, a problem that came from being an author himself, authors tending to take the written word too seriously. She looked at his penis as it shrank quickly back into its normal state of detumescence, waiting for some drop of liquid to appear. Max's ejaculations never were very copious. Max's new theory—based on Taoism or Hinduism or a syncretistic version of both—was that ejaculation was bad for male health, taking protein out of the body, and causing lower back pain. Ejaculation had become something to avoid.

It all sounded odd to Lindsay who had carried handkerchiefs on dates long before giving up her virginity to wipe up the natural results of the manual arts she had mastered along with most of her high school girlfriends. Ejaculation had been presented as a physical need then. It was considered unfair to keep a boy in a state of prolonged excitement without offering some form of relief. Lindsay and her friends met on Sunday nights at the local Shoney's to compare semen stained handkerchiefs and debate the pressing question of whether virginity had anything to do with purity of heart or was merely ignorance to be lost as soon as practicable.

Max closed his eyes and fell asleep. Lindsay covered him with a thin muslin sheet, drew a mosquito net around the chaise and went in to change for dinner. Above the back door, carved in stone made to look medieval in texture and impregnated with a dark shade of moss green, was Max's favorite passage from Flaubert: "I seek new perfumes, larger blossoms, pleasures still untasted." Lindsay had known for a long time what it meant to Max, the unapologetic hedonist, but on this afternoon it struck her with a new significance, as her own taste for the unknown, albeit one without obvious pleasures, struggled with another, older verse: "In the day that you eat thereof, then your eyes shall be opened, and you shall be as gods, knowing good and evil." She wondered.

—— 13 ——

"Vernon? Vernon Fargoes?"

"Uhhhh . . . yeah . . ?"

"Henry Tuckahoe here. You remember . . ."

"Henry Tuckahoe . . . not from . . ."

"From the NSLA . . ."

"Well goddamn," Vernon Fargoes said as fuzzy memories emerged of a National Savings and Loan Association convention at the Mayflower Hotel in Washington and a long alcoholic night spent in the company of a heavy-set, dark-skinned man with a formal way of speaking who seemed to know everything about the thrift industry and finally helped him negotiate a blow job in the parking lot of the U.S. Treasury Department for thirty dollars even though he had been too drunk to get his rocks off.

"Well Jesus H. Christ."

"You remember?."

"Sure. It's Henry. Henry from the little Savings & Loan in . . . now where was it now . . ?"

"Alexandria. Alexandria, Virginia. Just across the Potomac from Washington." Henry looked through the dust caked window of a telephone booth on U.S. Route 1. A cloud of yellow leaves, crisply dried in the September sun, was sucked into the trail of an accelerating tractor trailer.

"Well, long time no hear from, Henry. How the hell are ya?" A note of doubt crept into Vernon's voice. His recollection of what happened after the blow job was vague, and he had learned from experience that what happened under such dense clouds of forgetfulness seldom did him any credit.

"Well, Vernon, I could be better. The Burgh and Tuckahoe could be making money instead of losing it. It would not be happening if Congress had prevented this disintermediation situation. I suppose you have that down in Texas too?"

"Hell, yes, man. I'm losing my goddamn ass with dis-fucking-intermediation." Vernon relished using the F word. Few people knew what disintermediation was, and even fewer cared. It was ruining his life and he couldn't even talk to his wife about it. Placing the intensifying tetragrammaton after the first syllable was uninspired, he realized, but extensive experimentation had shown no more euphonious location. The little word, like the phenomenon it described, always managed to get the better of Vernon.

"Red ink on the books like cow shit," Vernon continued, but a convoy of six heavy trucks drowned out the rest of what he said and threw a heavy rock against the already broken door of the telephone booth.

"What the fuck was that noise, Henry?"

"Trucks going by. Sorry. I'm calling from a pay telephone, Vernon."

"A pay 'phone? What for? I mean this is not something . . ."

"Yes, it is something . . ."

" Oh . . . I get it . . . a *pay* 'phone, a *'phone* booth. Say no more Henry. Gotcha. Right on. Give me your number. I'll call you right back in ten minutes, maybe twenty."

———— · **14** · ————

Sister Mary Scroggins let the metallic fire door slam noisily behind her. It was thick enough to stop any fire, but it was crude, heavy, and awkward, making her feel unwelcome when she pushed it open and unloved when it slammed behind her. It was not the kind of thing she was used to. Her career as a Catholic nurse had been relatively comfortable. She had always worked in good hospitals, lived in comfortable residences maintained by private endowments and furnished with the provident bequests of significant estates. She had never envied the rich, but, at the same time, her father had a seat on the Chicago Grain Exchange, she was educated at the best Catholic schools, and she had never felt a call to poverty as such. Still, she thought, squaring her shoulders and squinting into the early dusk of the shortening September evening, one went where one was needed, and Mother Superior had made it very clear that God wanted Sister Mary to serve her six month period of community serve at the Carpenter's Shelter. It was an interfaith mission to the homeless next to the Alexandria railroad yard, the poorest, roughest quadrant of the city that had become a haven for dealers in crack cocaine and a battleground between rival drug distributors.

There were, on average, four murders a night. Most of the victims were in their teens. Most were gunned down by automatic weapons that rivaled the firepower of a marine corps platoon. A third of the housing was derelict and legions of homeless people, men, women and even families, wandered the streets, begging, stealing, living on the street-corner handouts of the City's churches. Most avoided the Carpenter's Shelter. It was too strict. But when they were sick, starving, or freezing, they came in with their few pitiful possessions and stayed until they were fit enough to head back onto the streets. Many were mentally ill, paranoid, schizophrenic, or deranged. Some, she thought, were simply sociopathic, even anti-human, holding themselves and others in equal contempt, scarcely house broken. God's creatures, she thought without the sense of elevation she found when applying the phrase to the unborn. "Lord I believe," she prayed, "forgive my unbelief."

To add insult to injury, Sister Mary had been ordered not even to mention abortion during her six months of probation. It was a hard order to live with. The issue was, she thought, the fullest expression of her faith, her best opportunity to give witness. And it was hard not to be able to respond to her critics. Even as the door slammed, she was smarting from the self-righteous jibes of a Methodist layperson who preached abortion as a Christian duty, part of preserving the environment and eliminating human suffering. Mary had treated her with stony indifference. She didn't know anything about the Reformation, much less Methodism. Method-ism. What was the "method" in their "ism" anyway? It didn't even make much sense as a word, method not really being one of the "isms." Mary wondered sometimes why the protestants even bothered to call themselves Christians.

As Sister Mary gave silent thanks for her staunch Catholic upbringing, a clatter of tumbling garbage cans drew her attention into a long dark alley between two empty warehouses. She quickened her pace and, against all advice to volunteer workers at the shelter, approached whatever mayhem was hiding in the dark shadow of a decrepit Dempsey Dumpster. She heard the scream of a female voice. Someone, the voice of a mere boy, she thought, mentioned a knife. There was excited talk of seconds and thirds.

As her eyes focused on the scene, Sister Mary saw four young men, youths she would usually have called them, straddling a girl's arms and legs while a fifth, a boy who looked no more than sixteen or so and had his pants around his feet, held a knife to the girl's throat and raped her. Her slender athletic legs, pinned against the concrete alley at unnatural angles, belonged in a hockey skirt or a tank suit and protested by their youth the use to which they were being put. She was hardly fourteen. Her face was contorted with terror and she screamed as her assailant's naked buttocks lunged back and forth, his pounding threatening to crush her ribcage, and his knife drawing blood from her throat in long scratches. The boy laughed self-consciously as his desperate pushing signaled an approaching orgasm. In an apparent effort to sound experienced, he described the victim to his waiting friends in a voice congested with sanguinary excess as "good ass" and "sweet pussy," phrases that Sister Mary had never heard, but which she did not need to understand.

The girl shrieked again and Sister Mary, swinging a sturdy umbrella, charged down the alley singing at the top of her husky voice "The Son of God Goes Forth To War" to the tune of "The Minstrel Boy." She took the boys by surprise, laid into them with her umbrella, struck a fierce blow where it counted to the boy with no pants on, and saw the rape victim escape up the alley. But, raw numbers quickly overcoming righteous zeal, the gang rallied, tackled Sister Mary at the knees and, their hormones having already been raised to fever pitch, substituted Sister Mary for their younger victim.

They took turns. One raped Mary while four held her down and then they rotated positions as if they were on a volleyball team. She squirmed, fought and screamed, but to no avail. The girl who escaped did not, as Sister Mary hoped, call the police. Nor, when each had raped her, did the ordeal cease. There was a stigma attached to having a one shot dick, and certain lies about sexual potency needed to be proved. After going in order twice around the victim, however, erotic fatigue set in, and one, bored with watching what he had already seen, and blaming his apparent lack of virility on six noontime encounters with an insatiable girlfriend, picked up Sister Mary's purse to look for money. He pocketed the few dollars she carried and sifted through her assorted cards for something worth stealing. A driver's license fell out. He picked it up and studied.

"Hey. You. Ramone. You fucking a nun, you know that? You fucking a nun, man. Ain't that right Sister Mary? You a nun, right? Ramone fucked himself a nun." The boy speaking stood up, releasing Sister Mary's arm. The others rose. Some were in shock. Others were laughing.

"Ramone, you going to hell man . . ."

"Me?" the boy called Ramone asked withdrawing from his victim's body and standing up. "Shit. I didn't know she was no nun. You fucked her first, Leon. Don't you accuse me of fucking no nun, man." His still erect and somewhat bloody penis stuck out incongruously as he spoke, and he struggled with his pants as the boys broke and ran back toward the city lights.

"It ain't my fault. She got a cunt like anybody else. Fuck-a-shit-piss, man. She didn't have no habit on. How're you supposed to know? Cunt's cunt, man."

"Ramone thought nuns didn't have no pussies."

"Ramone ain't never fucked a virgin before."

"Ramone ain't never fucked nothing but his hand before."

"You fuck her twice too Leon. You fuck a nun twice."

"I fuck her but I didn't know she was a nun see. But Ramone he knew. He moving his dick around after I said she a nun, ain't that right, Jerome? "

"Your dick gonna fall off, Ramone."

"Ramone going to hell."

"You just pissed off 'cause I fuck her four times."

"Four times! Shit!"

"Bullshit. Four times? That's bull-fucking-shit, man."

The voices became more lighthearted as they faded into the distance, converting the first shock of sin perceived into a ripple of insignificant boyish naughtiness and making Mary realize that she had overestimated their ages by four to six years.

When she was alone, and the alley was perfectly quiet, Mary Scroggins rolled onto her side and drew her knees up to her chin. Streams of tears poured through the pungent alley dust caked on her face. Soft sobs of grief, shame, disappointment and pain convulsed her frame. She lay on the ground for a long time without moving, but as a steady rain began to fall, she rose slowly to her feet, straightened her clothes and walked unnaturally toward a bus stop that now seemed miles, even worlds, away.

─── **15** ───

"You were saying, Vernon, about your Rock Of Ages Savings and Loan losing money . . ?"

"Red ink like cow shit in a spring pasture, Henry, you know when they're eating all that green grass and running like faucets. Red inky shit all over the Rock's books, Henry. All over."

"Losing money, then," Henry said as the significance of Vernon's Texas imagery hit him. A soft September drizzle, so different from the violent storms of the summer, had turned into a steady downpour and the trucks were splashing oily water through the holes in the glass walls of the telephone booth. Henry retreated into the booth's far corner to keep his shoes dry.

"That little sleepy fucker's going belly up some day if I don't do something. Why don't you buy it from me Henry? Six million. You get all my stock. Control. Loan portfolio. Everything. Six million. Hell, I'd even throw in my wife and golf clubs at that price. I could put a few mil in a little Brazilian gold mine I've been looking at, shack up with about eight Rio Negro whores, and make real money." Trucks roared in the background and Henry imagined Vernon huddled in a booth on the Fort Worth Bypass, one of the few places in Dallas that Vernon had mentioned during their long night together in the Pilgrim Lounge of the Mayflower Hotel and on the town looking for a prostitute to service Vernon at Dallas rates. He tried to picture the strip of bars and massage parlors Vernon had described. His mind regurgitated the image as too hot, too dry, too foreign, and the details would not come into focus. Henry saw Dallas, all Texas for that matter, as a series of parched Fort Worth Bypasses, straight roads, cadillacs doing ninety and dead armadillos heaped along the shoulders.

"What do you say, Henry? Don't keep me waiting. This booth's not air conditioned, you know, and it's still hotter'n a three peckered billy goat down here."

"Forget the millions, Vernon. Rock Of Ages can be worth Billions." Henry paused for effect. The word was magic. "Billions, Vernon. With a 'B'."

"I heard you, Henry, but—excuse my French—you've gone fucking loco. We do home loans, Henry, same as you. Home loans. It's Mom and Pop, Henry. We still manage by Daddy's three-six-three theory, you know, take in deposits at 3 percent, lend them out at 6 percent, and tee up at the country club at 3:00 p.m."

"Except, if you're as typical as you say, you are borrowing at 12 percent and investing at 9 percent."

"Right."

"You can't do that unless you are prepared to let your company go down the drain."

"No shit, Sherlock. But what do I do? What about this billion?"

"Billions. I said billions, Vernon, with an 's' on the end. As many 'ss' as you want. The sky is the limit. It's gold rush time and you don't have to go to Brazil." Henry, always one to use language carefully, spoke the word "billions" deliberately, but without any definite point of reference, much as a romance novelist might use Estramadura, Rajputana or the Barbary Coast as a setting for exotic action, aids to the imagination, words of sensation rather than reference. Henry's limited but intense experience with Vernon—there is surely no other way to describe the scene in the Treasury Department parking lot with Vernon's heart covered drawers caught in his eel skin boots—suggested that such large figures discussed in a telephone booth would have a dramatic effect on the man's imagination. Stuck in an inherited Savings & Loan for twenty years without making any serious money, Vernon chafed at the community pillar model of the small town Savings & Loan president portrayed by Jimmy Stewart in the film *It's a Wonderful Life*. There was, he knew, something about the Savings & Loan business that was incompatible with his Texas heritage. There was something wrong, Vernon liked to say, with the federal government guaranteeing deposits and limiting the risks a Savings & Loan could take. America wasn't settled with any guaran-damn-tees. It was settled by risk takers, and taking risks was the only way anybody ever made money. But how to do it was the question. And there were so many reasons not to take risks, so many attractions to the 3-6-3 style of life, so few demands on one's imagination. Still, over the bar of the Pilgrim Lounge, Vernon had left Henry with no doubt about where his ambitions lay and what would tempt him to change the uninspired investment practices of his modest institution. "It's other people's money, Vernon," Henry kept saying as one bourbon with gingerale became a third scotch on the rocks and then a sixth Glenlivet neat. But Vernon needed an excuse, some windfall of ready funds that would keep his auditors happy, some nudge into more exciting investments.

"Vernon, we've already talked too long on these telephone numbers. One cannot be too safe in matters like this. Call me in two days at 683-3441. Same time."

"Right, Henry. Two weeks." Henry listened to the receiver click. It was all very serious, but if he told Vernon all at once it might not sink in. Vernon was smart enough, but greed blocked his brain. Henry closed the phone booth door, surveyed the pattern of rain falling across the surface of the dark Potomac and headed for his canoe.

——·16·——

Esther Ann Hendricks sat despondently on the balcony of her twelfth floor apartment overlooking Rock Creek Park and the

Calvert Street Bridge. The fall rains had come, as usual, right after Labor Day to break the heat and make the little concrete balcony, for which Jason had paid so much, comfortable for a few weeks, until it got too cold. Esther Ann liked the view of wooded hills in the middle of the city not because, as Jason had thought, it reminded her of West Virginia, but because it was so different, surrounded as it was by towers of brick and cubes of glass, intersected by parkways and paved footpaths, so entirely removed, in fact, from the scarred, poisoned, wild and vengeful mountain forests that rose above her native river valley and the home town she could, even after so many years, describe only as a low, mean, sorry place of low, mean, sorry people.

New Alloy, West Virginia, abandoned even before Esther Ann's time by the steel mill for which it was named, serviced a barge cleaning station and a coal mine that laid off more people every year as new machinery came in. Yet, New Alloy, with its treeless, unpaved streets, rotting shanties, state liquor store, welfare office, and four clapboard churches, different in denomination but similar in temple-form style and hard shell theology, seemed like an oasis of life compared to the polluted river and dense forested mountains that surrounded it. Except for the occasional bunch of ginseng she sold in Charleston for a dollar a pound, the woods brought little pleasure and frequent bad news in the form of snake bite, poisoned moonshine, hunting accidents, rabid foxes, and girls who went there at night to find babies and boyfriends who would rather join the navy than get married. After seeing a sister emerge from the forest in the former state and a brother go off to see the world in the later, Esther Ann, with three younger siblings still to find their way in life and no prospects for a job or an education, took to heart her mother's sobbing voice when she learned, at forty-five, that an eighth little baby was on the way: "At least make'em pay for it, Esther Ann."

The precocious twelve-year old, who could not help but overhear her father's desperate attempts to affirm his declining manhood and his refusal to use rubbers with his wife—"What'da you think I married you for Janey?"—knew the act of which her mother spoke. Two years later, after her mother's ninth pregnancy ended in death at the hands of a Powten Hollow abortionist, and fearful of her father's furtive glances, Esther Ann sold her virginity in the back of a hearse to the undertaker of a neighboring town, bought a ticket on the C & O Railroad and rode over the mountains to Washington.

She remembered still the descent from Covington to Charlottesville in the early morning, a thousand feet down in two hours as the sun came up across the foothills of the Blue Ridge, piercing the mist and laying out before her the unlimited possibilities of new life in a world that knew nothing of what she had endured in the back of the hearse, or the small comfort that it was the only Cadillac in town. She stood in the day sleeper as morning broke over the still rivers, fat cattle, and picket fences of gentleman farmers. It had been early autumn then too. The maples were starting to turn red. Esther Ann should have been leading cheers for a football team that, with few exceptions, owed its street shoes as well as its cleats to the booster club. But the pain in her middle and the money in her purse left by the undertaker's passion eclipsed the thought of boys and mums and pompoms forever. She thought only of new worlds and new experiences as the odor of ripe apples rose strong and clean from the land to purge from her lungs the black soot her father wore every night when he was lucky enough to find work at the mine and that washed across the surface of the river for days at a time after the barges were scoured. The odor of apples revealed a more benevolent universe than the one she knew, a world she had known only through the yellowed pages of *Redbook* stories handed down from an aunt in Charleston. Toward Culpeper and Warrenton she saw horse farms and the first trappings of a fox hunting life that even the back pages of *Redbook* associated with other times and foreign countries. New Alloy, the town trapped by the dirty river and the dark woods, retreated like a bat at dawn.

Esther Ann had emerged from Union Station in an ebullient mood. She saw the Capitol dome rising on a far hill where she expected it from having watched "Mr. Smith Goes To Washington" five times, and she spent the day walking in a daze to the Washington Monument and back again. Geography had been her best subject. She knew about the monuments and the Smithsonian Castle. And there was so much more than she had imagined, so many more people than she had expected. She looked at the faces in the crowds hopefully, feeling for no reason that someone would recognize her or offer to help her. But, in a city with little use for hillbilly waifs, her early optimism was quickly supplanted by a sense of permanent loss and the dread of having no where to stay.

She slept on benches back at Union Station until the undertaker's last dollar was spent on a sour and greasy Crystal hamburger and the necessities of life forced her to turn to the only trade she knew. Fortunately, after selling a quick trick or two without knowing what to call it or what to charge, she was arrested trying to solicit outside the Hay Adams Hotel and sent to the more refined procuring ground of the Juvenile Detention Center. There, her exceptional youth and energy were quickly noted by a desk matron who recruited raw talent for the bordellos of Capitol Hill and from which, having quickly mastered the arts of Eve, she was shortly elevated to the position of kept woman by the Senator from the state she had now come to call, with affected familiarity, South Kanaska.

Jason Potter, old, flabby, not too demanding, and more talkative than any man she had ever known, except the undertaker who had grown strangely sullen once he paid for and got what he wanted, had been her life. He had paid for everything, the apartment, her allowance, her trips to Maine in the summer and Bermuda in the winter, her T-Bird, her subscription to *Redbook*, and her case of Silhouette Romances eight feet high and twelve feet across. He was a generous old bird, not jealous of younger men hanging around and willing to share with her the concerns of a life he found increasingly complex and beyond his control.

Jason's fatal heart attack had not surprised her. There had been some tension, fear, or, she sometimes suspected, guilt, that sex couldn't relieve, some constriction of the soul that her art couldn't reach. She had asked Jason to tell her about it, but he always wandered off into discussions of the Regulatory Accounting Principles, how they differed from the Generally Accepted Accounting Principles of real accountants and who was profiting from the changes. Jason didn't mind people profiting from the government—a nibble at "Uncle Sugar" he called it—but he drew the line at piracy. Except this time he couldn't tell who the pirates were. The accounting rules crossed him up. They had gotten too complicated. His staff understood them, but he was too deaf to hear what was said in the meetings and too embarrassed to wear his hearing aid in public.

Esther Ann had tried to explain it to him as best she could. Some things were pretty obvious. Rule 502 removed the cap on the interest rates Savings & Loans were allowed to pay their customers, lowered the required ratio of net worth to deposits from four percent to three percent, and in what seemed to Esther Ann, to whom losing even five dollars meant an immediate pinch, the oddest thing of all, let the so-called "thrifts" sell their loan portfolios at a loss and then spread the loss out over twenty years, as if they hadn't really lost anything.

"You can't do that with cash," she told Jason as she tried to rub his reluctant flesh into a state of workable excitement.

"Once you write the numbers down on paper, though, it isn't cash anymore, honey," he said.

"If I read it right, Jason, this section 502(b)(5) means a bank can sell its loan portfolio at a loss and still show a big profit on the books. She opened her hand to make sure she hadn't worn a hole in his thin, old penis skin. It looked okay and she started again. Sometimes this got him going and sometimes it didn't, but it was worth trying.

"Yeah?" Jason asked kicking the sheet off the bed to make Esther Ann's work easier and exposing his protruding belly in the process, "it probably has something to do with it being a twenty-year loan. The interest would come in over a twenty year period, so the loss should be shown over the same period."

"Oh," she said placidly and rubbed on, feeling no response in either his passion or in her understanding. Sometimes it took a while.

"You need to be an accountant to understand these things," Jason said. "It's what we call esoteric." He nuzzled his prickly old face against her chest and took her left nipple into his mouth.

"Oh." She adjusted her breast to keep his teeth from hurting. It was a pleasant sensation that made her feel maternal even if he was an old man paying for sex.

"Boring as hell, isn't it?"

"Well . . ."

"It's why I went to law school," he said and laughed. It was a remark at which he always laughed. But he increasingly laughed without conviction.

"It sounds to me like having your cake and eating it too, Jason. I mean if you sell the $50,000 note for $40,000, couldn't you put the $40,000 in cash on the books right away?" He moved her hand back to his flabby penis. It was hard to tell when he was ready to give up.

"I suppose. But, like I say, you know, it's an esoteric thing. Hard to understand unless you understand it. That's what I mean by es-o-teric." Jason reveled in big words. They formed a large part of his South Kanaska campaigns. People liked thinking their Senator knew more than they did. He cupped her breast in his hand and sucked steadily. As years and cholesterol had clogged his plumbing, this taste for the breast had become his greatest need.

"And your loss of $10,000 gets spread out over the next twenty years, so only $500 of the loss would show up the first year," she said. Some sap was rising in the nether limb, she noted, not spring exactly, but maybe the end of winter.

"Yeah? Well?" Jason slurped and gurgled, reluctant to let the nipple out of his mouth.

"Well it makes you look richer than you are. It turns a $10,000 loss into a $45,000 profit."

"Only in the short term, honey," Jason said with popping sounds between words as he tried to suck on Esther Ann's turgid nipples as he spoke. "When you look at the balance sheet you have to read the long term liabilities and amortization of losses along with the cash accruals. It's the way the accountants think. Esoteric. Like I said." He borrowed back into her chest, put her hand on his quickening stem and encouraged her to pick up the tempo.

Esther Ann did not understand amortization and cash accruals. She started to ask Jason how the semi-educated people like her were supposed to understand a financial statement, but she decided not to. She knew she was young and poorly educated. Thanks to Jason, she had a community college diploma and a real estate agents' license. He wanted her to do something else when he was gone. In fact, he had been really sweet about it.

"I won't be here forever," he said. "And you can't sell pussy all your life." But getting her realtor's license hadn't taught her much she didn't already know, and as long as Jason was paying the bills she was content to postpone learning all the things the instructors said you just had to pick up through experience.

"Well who could get hurt by this, Jason? Look at it that way." Something had to be wrong with Rule 502(b)(5) or it would not have made him so uncomfortable for so long. He lay on his back and admired his erection, a half hearted affair at best, and she straddled his girth and started working her pelvis back and forth, thinking more of the activity as exercise than as sex.

"Nobody ever gets hurt by these things, Esther Ann. Nobody. Uncle Sam guarantees all savings and loan deposits. If the institutions fail then the Fizz Lick pays off the depositors. Trust me," he said, "I was there in the beginning." And Jason, who liked to talk legislative shop during intercourse—connecting the two in his mind in a way he could never quite express—explained patiently to Esther Ann for what must have been the fiftieth time how Roosevelt had opposed federally guaranteed bank deposits on the advice of the big Eastern banking interests, until, thanks to a young populist from South Kanaska whose works the history books mistakenly attributed to Henry Steagall of Alabama, Congress passed a bill guaranteeing deposits up to the then-astronomical sum of $2,500. It proved popular and Roosevelt took the credit. "That's what presidents are for," Jason added. "They take the blame, so they get the credit." He laughed and felt a surge of blood into his penis.

"Federally guaranteed bank deposits! It's a crazy idea if you think about it," Jason said, starting to move his pelvis a little. Esther Ann felt his heart begin a final sprint. She knew what he was about to say and stopped his mouth with her tongue. She'd heard his speech often enough.

In 1930, almost two-hundred Savings & Loans failed. The depositor's lost millions. The crises got worse in 1931. By 1933 the country had lost about $44 million. The weak S & L's were pulling down the strong ones. It was only a matter of time until everybody's savings were wiped out. Jason could tell the story in his sleep.

He was rocking back and forth now, putting his whole body into the effort, pushing for all he was worth. Esther Ann held her pelvic muscles tight to increase the friction, knowing that he couldn't keep this up for long.

"Somebody had to do something," he blurted out. "The thrift industry was dying. Depositors lost their savings, their houses, their farms, hit the road, landed on the streets, became destitute and stayed that way. People were waiting in bread lines, queued up for soup kitchens, sleeping in parks. Somebody had to do something. Money was going from the banks to the bag under the bed and the economy was moribund. Barter replaced cash. A hotel in Oklahoma City accepted pigs and chickens. A newspaper in Maine quoted prices in bushels of corn." He was on the verge of an orgasm. His round, old face was red and mottled like a wasp-stung mackintosh. Esther Ann ground her hips into his crotch, bent over and thrust her tongue into his ear.

"And so we guaranteed the nation's savings and created Fizz Lick to keep the Savings & Loans from going wild with other people's money. The people were safe. Only the Government could lose." The last phrase brought on the spasm he had been working for. His old joints quivered and he moaned like an alley cat. Esther Ann smiled in obvious satisfaction. She knew "putting out"—the high school euphemism she still commonly used for sex—wasn't a respectable way to make a living, but there were some rewards.

Still, she thought, handing him one of the little pills he took after orgasm, Jason's history of the savings and loan industry hadn't enlightened her much about Rule 502(b)(5). Esther Ann had heard it all before and found it a little tedious. But it had the right effect on Jason. Repeating what he knew of the past seemed to resolve his doubts about the present at least enough to let his body experience basic pleasures.

He rolled over on his stomach and she rubbed his back until he fell asleep. He would sleep for twenty minutes now, and then "jog," as he called his manner of strolling along with his arms held up in a semi-running position, back to work. What she did, as simple as it was, seemed to help him.

But, in hindsight, she admitted that she'd never calmed his anxiety about Rule 502. He seemed to feel responsible for it to a degree that was quite unlike any other legislation. He never relaxed again like he did in the old days. And now he was gone.

Jason had not left her any money, of course. It would have caused too much scandal. He had explained everything carefully. And she had agreed. For all its closeness theirs had been a business relationship. And she was only twenty-six. Still, after ten years with a man, ten years during which she was closer to him than his wife was, she had come to expect something even while telling herself not to get her hopes up. With Jason gone almost two months now, a new Senator appointed from

South Kanaska, and his wife already re-married—evidently
something had been going on there that Jason had never mentioned—all hope of an envelope appearing out of the blue, or
a call coming from some unknown attorney, had passed. Esther Ann's little stipend was gone. Her savings were running
out. She would have to find some other method of support.
She could have other Senators, of course. Younger ones. More
important ones. Wealthier ones. Several had made offers even
before Jason died. Others had come forward since then. Senators who would never have acknowledged her existence while
Jason was alive dropped by to offer condolences, and stayed to
inquire about the amount of her rent. But she didn't like the
new propositions, because that's all they were. And going to
bed with a man just for money didn't feel right anymore. Jason
had never made her feel like a common prostitute. And with
the realtors license he had helped her plan for this unhappy
certainty. It was his only legacy.

A modest cyclone, not unseasonable for early October, twisted through the bed of Rock Creek, lifting urban debris up to
Esther Ann's balcony. A two week old *Washington Post* opened
to the Saturday Real Estate section. Houses were for sale everywhere. The market was booming. Interest rates were down.
Prices were up 17% over the last year, and going up at more
than 1 1\2% a month. People were moving. People were buying.
People who bought three years ago at 18% were re-financing at
9 7\8%, paying 4 1\2 points and glad to do it. There were not
enough appraisers or enough agents.

Esther Ann looked the old paper over carefully. It was a sign.
Jason had done it. The odds of this paper on this day open to
this page for this person were insurmountable. Esther Ann did
not believe in chance.

She looked at the paper again, more carefully this time. Old
Town Alexandria was the place to go. Jason had loved his old
mansion on the waterfront. She even visited him there when
Mrs Potter was doing whatever it was she did back in the
home state. Old Towne had pleasant associations. "Esther Ann

Hendricks Realty and Appraisals." It had a nice business-like ring to it.

It's what Jason wants, she thought. A dust devil twirled above the Potomac, hovered where Rock Creek flowed into the river, and then disappeared downstream. It was another sign. Esther Ann knew she was doing the right thing. For the first time since she wriggled out of her panties and spread her legs in the back of the 1954 Cadillac hearse—it was the same one that had carried her mother to the cemetery even though she made the undertaker promise that it wasn't—she had a strange sense of new worlds being born.

——·17·——

"Go whole hog, Henry? Sell the whole portfolio? I'm hav'in trouble hearing you. Speak up."

"The whole portfolio, Vernon. Sell every home mortgage you own."

"The Rock has been building that pile of investments up for fifty years, Henry. It's half of the houses in the Big D. You know what my board of directors will say? I mean have you got any idea?"

"They'll say what Clovis said. But they'll go along. There's no other way unless you want the Rock to fail."

"Christ, Henry, I don't know . . . selling out at a loss just doesn't sound smart," Vernon said, his Texas twang fading into the sounds of "Dallas Does Debbie," a rodeo singles bar. It was Wednesday, which meant that women over six feet tall were given free drinks until midnight, and men who attended had to sign a form acknowledging that it was legally impossible for a woman to rape a man in Texas. A mechanical steer of the type made popular by the film "Urban Cowboy" had been transformed into a ten foot cowgirl clad only in chaps waiting in the classic posture of erotic welcome for those cowboys who thought they could ride her down. Many were called. Few were chosen. But the thrill of watching oil field roustabouts climb on the plastic statue and ride for their lives, drew cheering and hooting throngs, sold Lone Star beer by the thousands of tall bottles and made the bar's telephones notoriously hard to bug on Wednesday nights. Vernon had waited for a variety of South American marijuana traders to complete their calls before calling Henry on what he felt was equally discrete business.

"Are you listening carefully, Vernon?"

"Yeah. Christ almighty, Henry, you wouldn't believe . . . there's this plastic woman with the biggest . . ."

"You could sell the Rock's portfolio for $36 Million, Vernon. It's a loss of over $6 Million, but in the first year your booked net worth would jump twenty fold. The Rock's financial statement will look golden. You'll have money to lend. You can pay dividends. You'll attract investors. The losses, of course, won't show up for years."

"Couldn't you hurry up Henry? Christ. You wouldn't believe it. They have this thing called a 'ride me cowboy' contest, see. All the women put money in a jar and the guy who humps this plastic woman the longest gets it all. I've heard about this, but I've never seen it. Oh shit. They've got a thou' in the kitty. You wouldn't believe it."

"You take the cash surplus in the first year and use it to pay interest of around 12% to 14% on the overnight market. The big Wall Street Brokerages have billions to keep in their management accounts. They can wire it anywhere. Dallas and Alexandria are as good as L.A. or New York. You go from an additional $30 Million in cash deposits to Billions. All in a few days."

"Hell, Henry, I'm better'n those guys. You know. You saw my tackle when I gave it the breeze behind the Treasury Department. You remember why that whore wanted double . . ."

"You then go public with your stock. The whole thing can be done in a few weeks. You've got this huge amount of cash on hand and a few long term debts that look quite small in comparison. The underwriters and investors will love it, snap up your offering, and then you have equity to pay the high interest rates that have attracted the overnight deposits and more and more deposits to attract equity and . . ."

"Aren't there limits on how much of those overnight parked accounts you can handle?" Vernon asked as he watched a stockbroker dressed in nothing but his horn rims get thrown off the bucking cowgirl.

"There used to be Vernon. But the new legislation did away with it. It's free competition now, Vernon. It's the range war you've always wanted."

"But somehow you've got to invest all this cash you've roped in, Henry. You've got to invest it to make a lot of money, a hell of a lot of money fast if you're paying out 14% interest on all those billions."

"That's the best part, Vernon . . ."

"God damn it! I'm going to enter this contest and win the whole pot. I can't stand it. I'll call you in a few days from out on the Fort Worth By-pass . . ."

The telephone went dead.

Henry closed the door of the booth placidly and looked at his watch. He had exceeded Vernon's four minute attention span. One had to move cautiously. He studied the moon. Too late for the river, he thought. Henry Tuckahoe retired to his Jaguar and drove into the deep miasm that formed on autumn nights under the Woodrow Wilson Bridge.

——·18·——

Aubrey listened intently to Lacy's breathing. There was a low-toned roll of the diaphragm that distinguished the long sighs of erotic glut from the deep trance of true sleep, the state, he liked to think, beyond the point of recall. He had certainly come to know her breathing patterns well during the last two months. Such intimacy was unavoidable in a small room with a single bed. There was nowhere else to go. No place was out of sight. The bed was cramped, and any flopping around brought him in contact with her face, her lips, her breasts, and then she drew him in until they were both exhausted.

It was his first experience in actually living with a woman, and, to his surprise, he found the loss of privacy intolerable. There was always the bathroom, but she noted his absence from the small room, marked him down as overdue. Once, when he was concentrating on a cross word puzzle and starting to feel himself again, Lacy had come down the hall, knocked on the door, and mentioned the presence in her medicine cabinet of cures for diarrhea, constipation and piles. He could hardly continue under the circumstances, but had flushed away a wad of empty paper and returned to her unfailing arms.

There were also, he had to admit, advantages to his arrangement with Lacy. She was good company, knew what he was doing and didn't ask for needless explanations. It was almost like being back in Charlottesville. And, she was really very knowledgeable, not only about the Elizabethan Age, but about the various ideas from other departments that needed to be included in his dissertation, the bases that needed to be touched to establish the work as a product of its times, as something of interdepartmental significance. And Lacy was tenured. She knew the shibboleths of academic politics. Her approval gave Aubrey courage to complete what he still felt was a dead work. His ideas flowed again, not from a fresh source perhaps, more from a blocked pool in an old cave, but flowing nonetheless in grammatically conservative and scholastically solid blocks of prose that met the formal requirements of the dissertation committee. It was something. Not life perhaps. But as he watched the footnotes line up neatly on the screen of his Kay-Pro II and sheet after sheet cascade out the back of Lacy's Epson Model 7 printer, "Ancient Scripts In Search of Modern Experience" emerged as an independent creature, something separate from the Aubrey Wythe whose name squatted so irrelevantly on the cover page. Whatever life it had was its own now. It would live or die without him and he without it.

Aubrey placed his weight precariously on his right elbow, wrenched his back counterclockwise and got a foot down on the floor. He paused and checked Lacy's breathing to confirm that he had not disturbed her. He lowered himself gently onto the floor and checked the alarm clock on the bedside table. Quarter past midnight. More than an hour until the bus left for Richmond, but it was a clear night and he looked forward to the walk. He then rose slowly, slipped into a pair of worn off-brand Levi look-a-likes, placed a short note on top of his dissertation, and shouldered the bag that held his few meager possessions. Noticing with pleasure how light the bag felt without the manuscript, Aubrey opened the door and slipped out into the night.

——·19·——

"Lemme get this straight, Henry. You use a bunch of shell corporations. You sell the same piece of property a bunch of times from one shell to another for a lot more money each time. The Rock does the financing every time, getting a big placement fee of about 5% of the face value of the loan, and after you've done this five or six times, you sell it off at some hugely inflated value to some fool of a *bona fide* purchaser?"

"Right."

"It sounds like a God damn daisy chain."

"A what?"

"A God damn daisy chain! You know, when a bunch of people are sucking cock and eatin' pussy in a big ring. I've seen it in some old 9 millimeter porno shows. It was one of those ones done back in the 'thirties when the guys never took their socks off."

"Well . . . call it a daisy chain then if you will." Henry wondered what Vernon meant by "boy" and "girl." He could hardly imagine that Vernon would call himself—sagging jowls and protruding belly—a "boy," but anything else made him wonder about Vernon. Henry's attitude toward child pornography was, as with all ideas, decidedly on the *laissez faire* side, but he wanted Vernon to avoid unnecessary complications.

"Boys like . . . ?"

"Boys like you and me. But with their socks on. In the nude, but with their socks on. Get it?"

Henry did not get it. But he said he did.

"How're you gonna get that old witch Clovis to go along with this? I mean Christ! Fucking Clovis. What a bitch! No offense meant. I know she's still your sister-in-law and your CEO and who knows what else with old Schuler gone. How old was he anyway? Oldest fucker I ever knew."

"She's already gone along with it," Henry said, ignoring Vernon's offensive innuendo. "Like I keep saying, there is no choice except going out of business and losing everything."

"Already started?"

"See our advertisements in the *Journal*. We offer 11 1\8% on six hour deposits. We sold the old portfolio for an average 8% discount and raised $40M. We go public next month. I'll send you a prospectus, but we're already fully subscribed."

"But what the hell are you doing with the money? I mean Christ! That's a lot of shit, you know?"

"We're financing a new development on the Cameron Estuary."

"Who owns it?"

"Pocohontas Development, Limited."

"And who owns . . ."

"I do. One-Hundred-Percent."

"Paying?"

"A placement fee of two-million dollars, and interest at sixteen percent after the first year."

"Sixteen percent?"

"But I'll flip it in a few weeks and make a few hundred thousand. I've already got a customer. I paid $24 Million. I'll sell for $32 Million."

"And you've already got him lined up?"

"Potomac Developments, Incorporated. I own it one-hundred percent."

"But . . ."

"And the Burgh and Tuckahoe will finance the whole deal for another financing fee. Around four-million this time. You see how it goes?"

"But you've got to unload it someday, Henry."

"Sure. Someday."

"But . . ."

"There's one born every minute, Vernon. I think one of your Texans said that, am I not right?"

"Sure. Wild Buffalo Hitchcock, I think, right?"

"Sure, Vernon. Now are you sure you understand everything? We should not discuss this ever again. Not even these pay as you talk telephones can be safe for ever, you know."

"I know, Henry. I've got it. You pay 11 1\8%, then we'll pay fucking 11 1\4%, you got it? Read about the Rock in the *Journal*. We're gonna be hot as a fresh fucked fox in a forest fire! We'll make your Burgh and Tuckafart look like a pile of constipated pony shit. We're gonna . . ."

The voice and the background noise of the Dallas-Fort Worth Freeway went silent. Henry was relieved. Vernon seemed to understand everything. Henry looked up at the Capital dome from the Union Station parking lot. It was too big, he thought, wishing that buildings were as they were in Alexandria, about the same height as a sixty year oak. That was tall enough. Anything taller and you could hurt yourself jumping out of windows, if you were, like Henry, the type of person who sometimes found jumping out of windows expedient.

Henry chuckled to himself as he walked across the Capitol lawn toward the river and his canoe hidden in the shadows of the Washington Marina. Vernon's enthusiasm was more than he could have hoped for. He didn't really know if his strategy to resuscitate the Burgh and Tuckahoe was legal or not, but it was different enough from what Schuler had always done to make him suspicious. And he knew it would be a lot safer if a larger Savings & Loan in a different part of the country did the same thing on a bigger, more flamboyant scale. He could count on Vernon and The Rock to do it up right. Better Vernon Fargoes than Henry Tuckahoe, he thought. There were too many uncertainties. The world had simply become too dangerous, Henry reflected, as several hoboes overpowered a young man out for a midnight stroll across the Capitol grounds, ripped a bag off his shoulder, beat him about the head and left him unconscious. Henry quickened his pace along the Mall and slipped into the shadow of the Washington Monument that led, with a full moon at its back, like a dark carpet down to the river.

——·20·——

Frances Appleby, half asleep under the sheltering boughs of a thick forsythia on the Capitol grounds, heard the cry of a foreign language, high pitched and visceral. She rose up to investigate. There was no telling where you might find a proto-semitic speaker. Washington was filled with wonderful sights, miraculous sounds, and many foreigners. She knew the basic sounds of most tongues. But this was something new, more of a scream, but with a definite pattern, nouns, verbs, adjectives. She crawled out from under the bush and scurried across the lawn with short quick steps that masked her speed. She kept to the shadows and hugged the ground.

At first she found nobody. Then, looking hard into the dark places, she found a body half covered by fallen maple leaves near the front portico. She nudged it tentatively in the ribs, not wanting to waste time on a stiff, or bother a sleeping man, and brought forth the same high-pitched whine she had heard before. She helped the man, a young man she noted, to a sitting position and offered him a drink of tepid tea she had begged from the Library of Congress cafeteria and carried in a Four Roses hip flask. He moaned again.

"You speak English?" She asked, grabbing him by the beard, pulling his eyelids back and peering intently into his unfocused, bloodshot eyes.

"English," the young man muttered. "U.V.A.," he said, trying to square his shoulders, but a deep bruise on the left side of his neck made him wince and moan again with newly discovered pain and the shock of physical violation.

"But what were you speaking right then? It sounded foreign to me."

"Nothing," he groaned. "Mugged." He probed the gash on his head and cringed at the pain.

"It was something foreign. I know you must speak some foreign languages."

"German, French, Spanish, Latin, Anglo-Saxon, Attic and Koine Greek," he said.

"Arabic, or Phoenician?"

"What?"

"Proto-hamitic-semitic-cuneiform?"

"Ugh?"

"You might speak these languages and not even know it, of course. Languages are like that. You pick them up without knowing how you learned them. I hear voices all the time and don't know where I learned the language."

"Don't think so," the young man said, felt his head again and drew away a hand smeared with blood. He swooned, emitting a high-pitched whine as he fell.

"I knew it," Frances said, mimicking Aubrey's fainting cry. "That was proto-archaic-coptic if I ever heard it." You need to look at my manuscript. You'll be able to read it. I know. A night in the summer house will set you straight." And so saying, Frances lifted Aubrey's feet and dragged him to her secret spot in the "C" Street alley. His head bounced as she crossed the First Street gutters, but the resulting sound of old gourds being crushed under foot didn't concern Frances. What harm could come of it, she asked herself as she heard the crisp, empty sound for the third or fourth time. Language was in the frontal lobes. That back part of the brain didn't amount to much. Frances knew. That's where her tumor was.

——·21·——

Lindsay Hayden wiped the surface of the heavily polished Philippine mahogany for a fourth time. The table top was three inches thick, cut in 1905, re-finished in 1952, and polished twice daily. The odor of old wax permeated the heroically proportioned but prosaically named Senate Hearing Room 6 and imbued it with the secure ambience of an old club library on an indian summer afternoon. Shafts of golden haze streamed through Palladian windows. Men in mohair and ladies in silk moved quietly over thick carpet, lifted heavy leather-colored volumes, pointed to underlined passages, nodded tellingly, underlined again and passed notes from hand to hand. Hushed voices discussed constitutional landmarks in soft, earnest tones of intimate familiarity.

From forty feet up in the press gallery, an acre of oak panelling and twelve columns of green carrera marble modulated Lindsay's pointless shuffling into the uniform background hum of Senate business as usual. The scents of furniture polish, scrubbed carpet, Old Spice, Chanel No. 11, and minted breath rose on the hot afternoon air, lodged in the upper reaches of the half-empty chamber and condensed into an irresistibly morphic fug. A cameraman from CNN propped his lens discretely on the worn bronze gallery rail and let his eyelids droop. Stentorian breathing from behind a day-old *Washington Post* merged with the snores of a grizzled veteran from a Chicago tabloid and lulled the cub reporter from the *Boston Sun* into a light swoon.

Lindsay pushed Max's seven notebooks around the desk again and re-settled her laptop computer on an empty chair. All this activity was unnecessary, but it helped her avoid the eyes of a certain Administrative Assistant to Senator Nathan Feaney who was half hidden behind the Committee's dais trying to tell her with crude gestures of the face and hands that the Senator, Chairman of the Judiciary Committee, was through with his lunch and ready to get on with the afternoon's hearing.

The committee members were already settling into their seats, loosening their belts, slipping into the mental shadowland of a three course luncheon and a high blood sugar level.

The witness, or "inquisitee" as he liked to call himself to the consternation of both his supporters and opponents, was already in place, placidly and all too calmly awaiting his third week of questions on abortion, a subject which had, according to media consensus, become the touchstone of his competence.

Neither press nor committee were pleased with the nominee. It wasn't that he was too young exactly. He had some grey around his temples and the promise of a gobbler's fold at his throat. It was more, as the voice snoring from behind the *Post* had shouted over a quick lunch at the Tune Inn only to have it picked up by the network commentators, that he was too boyish, too thin, too loose, too unsoiled, to be an Associate Justice of the United States Supreme Court. "A judge should have grey hair to look wise or piles to look concerned," he had joked, unaware that his comments would be broadcast nationwide.

The nominee's opponents were frustrated, even furious, but more with his apparently blameless personal life than with his obvious naivety on abortion. With no old sweethearts, angry ex-wives, or badgering former employees, they were reduced to talking about the issues and watching their reelection chances drop as they talked.

The nominee's supporters were equally distraught—not with his naivete about abortion—a good thing in their view—but with his disarming honesty and scholarly integrity, uncertain virtues that threw their own agenda into question. But, to their comfort, there were no scandals, no divorces, no choirboys, no unbalanced books, no convoluted stock deals waiting to come unraveled, and, since he had lived at home with his mother or rented a modest flat in Boston all his life, no restrictive covenants against Jews and gypsies in his property deeds. There was that to be said for him.

The press, dragooned from wars, riots, and other more interesting legislative assignments, had already given the nominee up as unnewsworthy. His choices of expression were too well considered, too judicial in tone. His politics were too middle of the road, too thin on doctrine. He wanted to know the facts before he commented on a case. He wanted to research the law. He declined, always too politely for media taste, to be drawn into discussions of judicial philosophy. He was too respectful of precedent, too familiar with the history of the Supreme Court as an institution, too humble, too dull for print. But, as they all knew, unless something unexpected happened, dullness alone, the great cloak of Washington power, would carry the nominee onto the Supreme Court.

The last chance for that something unexpected was the scheduled examination by the attorney for the Wombyn League, the much admired polymath of the law, Professor Aceldama. Senator Feaney would convene the meeting as soon as he arrived. And that was the problem. Max's seat was empty.

Lindsay clicked her computer on and off again to keep from looking at the increasingly dramatic, even obscene, gestures made in her direction by Senator Feaney's aide. The screen accessed a data bank of constitutional law through a telephone modem. It was there in theory if Max's memory failed to retrieve a footnote reference from one of the more than 900 cases he used to argue that the Constitution guaranteed the freedom to copulate without reproductive consequences. But Lindsay knew Max's memory. It would not falter, much less fail. Still, he liked to consult the computer from time to time for dramatic impact. "I believe that Justice Brandeis in the *Hartley* case said . . . ah, yes" . . . punch, punch, flash, flash . . ."there it is . . ." The computer made him look scholarly and kept him from appearing a know-it-all, never a popular figure in the American imagination.   The status of Lindsay's preparation had nothing to do with Max's tardiness. It paid to be the last on stage when the proceeding was being telecast. And that was the problem. By the rules of protocol, Senator Feaney was entitled to make the last entry. And Max had played by the rules. Until now. Now, on the last day of the hearings, Max was obviously playing a new game. Someone had to come in last, and the television commentators were unlikely to blame Max for delay. He was, after all, a hero of the free choice movement, the host of NPR's "National Town Meeting" and a salaried consultant to most of the networks.

Lindsay ducked and bobbed again. The number of eyes to avoid had become prodigious.

Senator Feaney finally gave up, took his seat and asked pointedly if the Wombyn League was ready to examine the witness. The cameras, pre-positioned to cover Max's entrance, swiveled to catch the leather covered doors of the committee room. Max bounded through just as he did for the National Town Meeting. He had the close-ups down pat, the expansive smile, the energetic gestures, the long steps that were meant to say volumes about his youth and the forwardness of his thinking. Max slipped into his chair, smiled into the camera's eye and asked his first question to the television rather than the witness.

"Judge Carroway, I would like to talk with you for a little bit about fundamental constitutional rights."

Karen Moelders, who sat next to Lindsay but did not fidget with computers or flip idly through notebooks, tried to avoid the technicalities of the Constitution. She knew the gist of Max's opening statements, and even admired Max's legal skills tremendously. But she was still appalled every time she heard the thin legal reasoning needed to support the right to abortion. Penumbras and emanations from this Amendment or that had never impressed her. "Ghosts," she liked to call them when she was in a position to be totally candid. And who believed in ghosts anymore? "Soul," as she liked to say, "is for food." It was, she thought, an incisive and scathing criticism of the document by which Americans pretended to be governed. Abortion was not a derivative right, but the essence of female existence. And the right she saw had nothing to do with trimesters. Rather than defend the conservative logic of *Roe v. Wade*, Karen wanted to champion an absolute right of infanticide. It was logical. It gave women total control over their own destinies. Max advised against it. The confused idea of parental obligation enforced by the state—so painfully fascist—could not be challenged. The country was not ready for freedom. But it was a matter of time.

As Karen fumed, Max launched into a short history of the United States Constitution in which he managed to pronounce the word "fundamental" fifty different ways. He said it low and high, broad and deep, tight and crisp, bright and thunderous, dark and mysterious. As he uttered the word over and over again in all its resonant diversity it became, first, a different word, more significant, more important, gathering meanings as he repeated it, appearing as "final, "fulfillment, and "firmament" until it became more than a word and ultimately crystallized into a physical presence grander than the columns of the room and more ancient than the marble itself.

Yet, in spite of his brilliance, Max's focus on the camera rather than the witness detracted from his impact in the chamber itself. Senators fidgeted and doodled on their yellow legal pads, or dozed and drooled the remains of heavy lunches onto starched shirts. The witness looked around and wondered which camera was on, but only as a matter of curiosity, not to enhance his presentation. Jenkin had no sense of media presence, and no intention of altering his personality merely because a black box in the corner panned from side to side and a bank of reporters in a sound proof booth mouthed silent inanities into clip-on microphones. If that were the real world, then he had no interest in it. He worried only that Professor Aceldama would set him to yawning, a serious breach of proper judicial conduct, worse than the many intellectual biases of which he was accused.

"Would you not agree with me, Judge Carroway," Max asked after using twenty of his sixty allotted minutes to summarize the constitutional right to privacy, "that *Griswold v. Connecticut* established a fundamental right to engage in sexual intercourse without reproductive consequences?"

"I don't recall the case mentioning the effectiveness of contraception, Professor, or insuring that intercourse will not result in pregnancy." There were mild titters from the press corps. There always were when Jenkin said "intercourse" or made any other reference to the sex act. And, being fair to a press corps to whom fairness was heretical, there was a certain humorous incongruity between Jenkin's controlled demeanor and the wilder aspects of sexual congress.

"Surely though, the founding fathers could not have been concerned with contraception?"

"Many of the founding fathers were, I'm afraid to say, fathers of foundlings, Professor Aceldama."

More titters from the press were followed by a wave of whispers and a round of quiet sniggers and snorts. "Secondary explosions," the corps of pressmen called it in reference to aerial bombardment, a subject both more familiar and more interesting to them than constitutional jurisprudence.

"Besides," Jenkin continued, "condoms were used by Dr. Gabriel Fallopius in the 16th Century. Casanova used them frequently as did James Boswell during the decades that preceded the American Revolution. I doubt, in fact, if the activities at issue in *Griswold v. Connecticut* or *Roe v. Wade* would have surprised the founding fathers at all, yet the Constitution did nothing to protect the inadvertent father or the unwilling mother from the natural and very well known consequences of their actions." A wild titter and a few random hoots rose from the back of the gallery. The *Post*, whose reporter had long retired to the pleasures of the Tune Inn, attributed a short chortle to a Senator from Indiana.

Max, however, shrugged the remark aside. He was often accused of being humorless. And he had long since given up defending himself. It was, he kept reminding Lindsay, the price of progressive politics. Poverty, injustice, discrimination, even life itself were not funny. Humor was rarely a virtue and pathos was never a vice. Ridicule was the property of the privileged and overindulged, the product of an intelligent but lazy mind. The great humorists—Sophocles, Shakespeare, Swift, Mark Twain, Evelyn Waugh—were all reactionaries, arch-conservatives either starting out or ending up. There was even something in the back of his mind, something he kept trying to suppress, about Groucho Marx voting for Richard Nixon.

Still, as much as he denied the humor of righteous causes, Max took personally his inability to turn the pro-choice position into light repartee. "Founding fathers\fathers of foundlings." The phrase hung around Max's neck like a decomposing albatross.

"Judge Carroway, do you have any particular thoughts about the tri-mester approach of *Roe v. Wade*?"

"No. None in particular, except as I pointed out, Justice Blackman's opinion makes the legal status of the fetus subject to technological re-definition."

"So, if in vitro fertilization techniques could assure the survival outside the womb of any fertilized egg, you would think that the woman's right of privacy might legitimately be contracted?"

"I've never thought it through. But you make an interesting suggestion, Professor. I'm sure it will come up some day." The press corps tittered again, a number of octogenarian Senators wiped their chins and sat up in their seats, enticed from postprandial slumber by the promise of a moment in the camera's eye and even a wry remark at somebody's expense.

"Does it trouble you, Judge Carroway, that the *Roe v. Wade* tri-mester approach parallels Aquinas' theory that a fetus lacked a soul until it quickened at about the sixth month?"

"I'm not familiar with Aquinas, I'm afraid."

"If *Roe v. Wade* in fact apes the logic of Saint Thomas Aquinas, would not that sound to you like an establishment of religion in violation of the First Amendment?"

"Being an Episcopalian," Jenkin said "I'm largely ignorant of theology." The press resounded with hacking guffaws and boozy sniggering. Something was funny. None were sure exactly what. The Chicago veteran looked over the shoulder of the Boston cub, and started to copy. She stopped and barked an incomprehensible word. It could have been "religion." She erased what she had written.

Max filled out the remainder of his hour with a lecture on the religious background of abortion rights, taking pains to point out that religious commentators had never agreed when the soul entered the fertilized egg and concluding that any regulation of abortion violated one's constitutional right not to believe in souls at all, an argument never addressed by *Roe v. Wade* or any other court. It was a novel argument. The press lost the train of his reasoning quickly, checked their watches, 'phoned in their stories and left for the day. The witness took a few notes, but when it became apparent that Aceldama was lecturing the public rather than preparing a question, Jenkin wadded his sheet of notes into a small ball and flicked it unsuccessfully at a trash can. When time was up, Max and Senator Feaney thanked each other repeatedly.

"As we appear to have finished the substantive questions," the Senior Senator from a Southern state said straightening an errant lower plate and licking a strand of somatic hair that had been transplanted to the front of his scalp, "I would like to thank you lovely ladies of the Womb League for com'in over here today. It is always a pleasure to see you and to hear your views in support of the family and the American way of life."

It was too much for Karen. All this laughter! All this low humor at the basic nature of a woman's status under the Constitution. All this legal chicanery to prove the obvious. It all came down to whether women had equal rights with men or not. Men did not have to have babies. So women should not have to have babies either. It was simple justice. It was basic. It was fundamental. She shrugged her shoulders and pouted while staring at the ceiling in manifest irritation at the increasingly low level of the discourse and the pathetic ramblings of the Senior Senator from the Southern state.

"Don't shrug, young lady," the Senior Senator from one of the states next to South Kanaska said abruptly. "I get tired of watching you shrug and kind of look up at the ceiling when my southern colleague says anything at all gentlemanly. You should learn to appreciate a compliment in the spirit in which it was given."

"I will not be called a 'lovely lady.' I will not be insulted. The General Counsel of the Wombyn League demands an apology from the Senator . . ."

"Apology! You should be grateful we let you come in here and ask your questions. Your idea of freedom means full empowerment to kill what is alive and growing, which is sick."

"An apology is in order. We will quit this chamber and file a written demand." Karen stalked out. Jenkin Carroway may be confirmed on the Supreme Court, but she was not through with him yet. Nobody was as pure as he pretended to be. He was fucking somebody, she thought. Men always were. Their little egos needed it. She would find out. She would have a detective on him night and day. There had to be somebody.

The *Post* later reported she was miffed at being addressed as "lovely" more than "lady," but nobody in attendance would confirm the story and no byline was used.

Max, more conscious of his future opportunities with National Public Television than of Karen's wounded dignity, left only after shaking hands with the witness and waving into the lens of the camera as the Senators adjourned for the day. He was overdue for his once a week lecture at Georgetown Law School and bolted as soon as the "on air" lights flickered off and the sound booms were lowered.

Lindsay was left alone to pack the briefcases and stow the computer back in its case. The show was over. Max had, as always, been superb as himself. Without announcing his purpose, he had previewed his new book arguing that any government protection of life is void as an establishment of religion. The paperback rights had already gone for seven figures and there was talk of a film deal. Lindsay shouldered her burdens, fifty pounds of legal research and twenty pounds of data base, and trudged out.

·22·

Clovis Tuckahoe prowled through the darkened granite corridors of the Burgh and Tuckahoe Savings Bank. The floors were worn by seventy years of abrasive shoe leather that was, more recently, soaked in acid rain and other pollutants that quickened the erosion of calcium based minerals. The style was an art nouveau egyptian made popular in the 1920's by the Bowery Savings Bank in New York. The lighting was indirect. Long shadows criss-crossed the floor even at noon. The small brass lamps fixed to the desks in the lobby were green with age and unable to illuminate more than a foot or so of the marble and bronze desks.

The bank's deteriorating condition had worried Clovis even before Schuler's death. She had consulted architects and preservationists with grand schemes to renovate the bank, or even have it taken over by one of the many preservation trusts that showed interest in Olde Towne Alexandria. She even had an inquiry from the Rector of Saint Faiths Episcopal Church about re-locating his flock into the bank, but she hadn't taken him seriously as he was one of the few people in Alexandria Schuler had never trusted. Now, of course, none of the schemes seemed to matter. If Henry's new business plan continued according to schedule, the B & T could pay its own way, renovate its own building, or put up its own skyscraper if it wanted to.

Yet, even though so much rode on Henry's new plan, she hated it and almost hoped it would fail. Clovis thought she would die the day Henry sold the old loan portfolio. She fought his plan tooth and nail. In the old days, she knew the properties the bank had financed. Most of the borrowers were people she could recognize on the street. She knew when they paid late, when they paid early, when they re-financed to send a child to college, or bury a grandmother. It was the thing she liked most about the savings and loan business.

She drew strength from knowing the limits of people's lives, who was getting overextended and why. And, perhaps most of all, she loved being able to help people when they needed just a bit more money. People didn't expect it of her. To the public she was a sort of monster, fat, old-fashioned, stand-offish, remote, scrofulous and reeking of bath powder and sweet floral perfume. People laughed at her. She knew it. But returning good for evil pleased her. She thrilled to see the timid, frightened souls sitting across her desk in the B & T lobby, repenting of their many Clovis Tuckahoe jokes, trying to convince themselves that they may have laughed at one or two but that they never repeated such things even when they knew full well that they had. Clovis turned this fear into relief and the simple joy of hope sustained. Clovis' beneficence over the years had created a small army of Clovis Tuchahoe devotees in Alexandria. They were her only friends. And she had hated to sell their paper to less personal banks. She had written many of them personal letters explaining the bank's financial problems. She had cried in frustration and agony. But, finally, she had to go along with Henry. The bank was losing too much money. There was nothing else to do.

So far, Henry's plan appeared to be working. The B & T had grown twenty fold, at least in book value. It paid the highest interest rates on the east coast. The big Wall Street brokerages "parked" funds at the B & T in sums that made Clovis' head spin. The high interest rates were paid from the proceeds of selling the loan portfolio. The short term cash surplus had been splashed across some glossy stock prospectuses, the prospectuses blessed by one of Washington's top law firms, and the stock then sold to investors around the country, the "more gullible the better," the lawyer said, "start with the widows and orphans."

"It sounded wrong, but it had to be legal. The lawyer was, after all, someone famous, someone Clovis had seen on television interrogating a Supreme Court justice or something like that. That's why she had insisted that Henry use him instead of the local lawyers in Alexandria who were, she had always thought, nice enough, but too slow in a genteel kind of way, and not the type of people one would expect to see on television at all. Not at all like professor—what was his name?—something strange. She tried to look it up in a dictionary once, but she couldn't find anything. Ace. Ace. That's right: Ace L. Domo she called him by way of a mnemonic. Well, if he didn't know right from wrong then who did?

Still, legal or not, Clovis had been uneasy in the beginning. Paying eighteen per cent when you were getting twelve per cent on home mortgages didn't make sense no matter how many times Henry went over the figures. It just didn't make sense. Schuler would have seen that. And even Henry had to dream up bizarre deals to get better than twelve. "Creative" he called them, or "highly leveraged." He assured her the good deals were out there. He could find them. And so far he had been right. Or at least she thought so. She had no experience in evaluating commercial real estate development. All the deals looked good on paper when Henry presented them to the loan committee.

But that was the problem. They were Henry's deals. Like that Indian Head Slough development. Clovis knew all about the property from Schuler even though the other members of the loan committee didn't. It was a swampy sand bar along Pretender's Street and the Wilkes Street Cemetery. Nobody wanted it because it was a snake infested thicket of poison ivy and poison sumac and a noisome fungus Schuler insisted on calling Tuckahoe truffle.

Henry had picked it up at a sale of surplus government land in the month or so of demobilization between the end of WW II and the Cold War. Now he wanted to develop it. His sale to Pocohontas Development Limited looked good. The B & T placed a $40M loan, got a $2M placement fee up front and 20% if the loan was not repaid in two years. It looked too good to be true.

And then, of course, in a matter of weeks, Pocohontas sold the Slough to Potomac Developments Incorporated for $50 M. The B & T took a fee of $3M and the interest rate jumped to 22.7%. Now Potomac Developments, Incorporated had a contract to sell the Slough to H. T. Developers, Inc. for $60.2 M. The B & T could book over $9 M in fees—pure profit—in less than a month. The Slough had become a hot property. Henry knew what he was doing. But Clovis was still uneasy. Schuler never trusted quick profits. And he hadn't really trusted Henry either.

Thinking of Schuler reminded Clovis of the task at hand. The time had come to clean out Schuler's desk. She had asked several old bank employees to do the job for her, but all declined. It was too sacred. Only the widow could handle the mementoes of Schuler's life. She had worked on it a little at a time. She would sort and organize for a while until something would upset her and then she would knock off for the night, go home and have a bourbon and water to calm her grief. Schuler had never been particularly romantic or sentimental, and he left surprisingly few clues considering how long he had lived.

Clovis opened the bottom drawer on the right of Schuler's main desk at the bank. It was an antique English partner's desk, hand carved from gnarled boxwood, scratched during the War Between the States, but otherwise immaculate. The drawer held a mish mash of papers in no order or sequence. It was obviously the odds and sods bin, the miscellany of his life. There were car repair bills from the 'thirties, cleaning bills from a week before he died, tax receipts, reports from various local stockbrokers. And, she noticed, picking up an unfaded slip, a receipt from the Library of Congress: "Received of S. Tuckahoe - Foreign Language Manuscript in two volumes." A shiver mounted Clovis' spine. She knew nothing about a manuscript, much less one in a foreign language. Schuler had not been a collector of books or manuscripts, so far as she knew. But that was the problem. For all their closeness, Clovis realized more and more that she hardly knew Schuler at all. She thought there would be time when he retired to hear the stories he had postponed telling. But now there would be no retirement. She knew everything she would ever know about Schuler Tuckahoe. Unless there was something in this manuscript. But why had he kept it secret? The shiver ran back down her spine and into her extremities. She would find this manuscript. Whatever he had done with it. She would find it.

23

Lindsay knew there was trouble coming when she looked in the mirror of the ladies room and saw Karen emerge from the stall straightening her skirt and clenching the Metro section of the *Post* like a battle axe. She had tried to check this urge to look whenever the stall door opened. It didn't really matter who had been there, or what odd sounds they had been making. It could only be embarrassing to meet their eyes and remind them that their privacy had been violated. And it was doubly embarrassing to confront her boss emerging from the toilet. But, try as she might, she rarely broke the habit of casting her eyes furtively at the opening door, and she invariably regretted it.

As she washed her hands, Karen grumbled for no apparent reason about the sloppiness of the janitorial service and how its inadequate work for the Wombyn League was a form of sex discrimination. She rubbed her hands over and over, flaying layers of dry skin away from her cuticles prematurely, holding the rolled Metro section under her right armpit as if someone would steal it if she put it down, and left without bothering to dry off.

There was something in *The Post*. Lindsay knew it. Or Karen would never have carried the paper away. The newspaper stayed in the Ladies Room. It was more than an unspoken policy. It was Karen's rule not to take a pee without a paper. It was why she used the second floor facility rather than her private lavatory upstairs.

Lindsay's curiosity turned to dread as she saw the headline tacked to the conference room wall. "Raped Nun Says Baby Is God's Will." There was a picture of Mary Scroggins looking brave and holy, eyes rolled upward, chin jutting forward. The story described the gang rape, Sister Mary's prior activist stand against abortion and her unquestioned decision to bring the pregnancy to term and put the baby up for adoption through Catholic Services.

"It could be a publicity stunt," Lindsay said as Karen's firm and still slightly wet hand gripped her shoulder. Without looking she felt Karen's head shake.

"She walks it like she talks it, Lindsay. Mary wouldn't fake it. She won't disappear and say she had a spontaneous miscarriage. I said she's wrong, Lindsay. I never said she wasn't dedicated. Mary is a model to all women, a model to us."

"Oh."

"Do we have that much dedication, Lindsay? Do we?"

Lindsay felt Karen's grip tighten on her shoulder. Her womb contracted involuntarily, much as it did when Max inserted himself before she was fully prepared. She felt Karen's eyes prey across the back of her neck. She started to sweat and wondered what her galvanic skin reaction said to the unasked question of whether she would have an abortion for the cause.

How little space it takes to sell real estate, Esther Anne thought looking around her newly decorated office, a single room on South Royal Street, for at least the thousandth time. No inventory. It was perfect. Back when Jason was alive she used to think of herself as inventory, though never in a way that disparaged their relationship. But now nothing of herself, neither body, charm, nor possessions was for sale. Selling other peoples' property. It was the perfect business.

The plate on her desk said "Esther Anne Hendricks, Realtor and Appraiser," with gold embossed authority. She had added the "e" to her middle name as a concession to "Olde Town." An "e" in the only place she could respectably add one seemed necessary after the Colonial chair rails, the egg and dart crown molding, the Williamsburg colors—Raleigh Tavern Peach and Randoulph Pinckney Green—the natural oak shutters, the ginger jar lamps and the artificial peg marks carved and stained on the floor.

The office had been a modest workingman's cottage of 1917, built for the first migration of Italian emigrants who came to work in the Torpedo Factory on the waterfront. It was narrow, and solid, and its lack of Victorian ornament almost cried out for a Colonial re-interpretation. A change of colors and a little trim aged it a hundred years or more. She was debating with herself about a new pedigree, perhaps some quaint stories, a ghost or two, or a Tory and Patriot Romeo and Juliet. It was entitled to some history now that it was more Colonial than Mount Vernon, and there were really no limits to what people would believe about an old building. The encouragement of Esther Anne's neighbors, an up-scale toy store and a frozen yogurt shop, for "restoring" the building proved the adaptability of Jason's adage that in politics image is always appreciated and rarely questioned. The applicability of Jason's wisdom to her new line of work made her feel even stronger that she had done the right thing.

Jason too, as a long time aficionado of Olde Town's gentrification, complimented Esther Anne's sense of period decoration. He had been there from the first, hovering around as she first visited the place, whispering unheard advice as she negotiated the lease, puffing and gyrating as she dithered over color charts, and nodding with approval as the carpenters hammered the thin strips of historical authenticity into place. Esther Anne Hendricks Realty and Appraisals had been a labor of love for Jason. After soaring over Washington and eavesdropping on the hearings of the Banking Committee grew somewhat tedious, it was the thing he most wanted to do. He found, as the days wore on, that he wanted nothing but to be with Esther Anne. He floated around her office during the day, looked over her shoulder as she reviewed a deed or drew up a contract, darted needlessly up a ventilation shaft when customers dropped by, and went home with her at night to stare benignly at her microwave frozen dinners and curl up against her backside as she slept, playing old scenes of passion through his mind, black and white and somewhat grainy, but free of the guilt and preoccupation with Senatorial business that had overshadowed their relationship.

A silver bell purchased for its resemblance to one thought to have been at Mount Vernon tinkled above the door. Esther Anne looked up from her computer screen of townhomes under $500,000 between West Pitt and South Washington—a commission from some newly appointed judge from up north—and displayed a professional grin, not, Jason quickly saw, unlike the one that had greeted him so regularly during the years when her apartment had been the secret object of his fitness program.

Jason, taken by surprise with his hand on Esther Anne's bosom, darted up the air conditioning duct and turned with a sense of inevitability and horror to see Henry Tuckahoe. Certain that Henry alone among the living might perceive his transfigured form, Jason clung to the thin shadows of the ductwork and struggled to control the noise of breathing even while reassuring himself that he had neither lungs nor form to betray his presence. Death had taught him to disregard coincidence in human affairs. Causality was everything. Nexus everywhere. Henry would not be coming to see Esther Anne without some subtle and undisclosed purpose of his own. Jason did not trust himself with Henry Tuckahoe. Esther Anne, he knew, would not stand a chance. He thought of a ghostly rattle, an auditory haunting from the duct work that might deter Henry. He tried to rumble the thin metal, just enough to set up a high pitched vibration, enough maybe to make Henry think twice about whatever it was he was trying to do, but his powers stopped short of physical manipulation. The world as pure idea had certain conveniences, but there were limitations. He could watch, but not manipulate. Secretly he was relieved at his impotence. There was no telling what Henry would do.

"An appraisal?" Esther Anne was saying. "My experience is limited. I mean I took the course. It was one of my favorites."

"No experience is required. And no diploma."

"But . . ."

"But promptness is essential. I have a buyer for the property at $52M. The B & T will finance it. But the B & T, of course, needs an independent appraisal of the property to support the value of the loan. And in three days. It's asking a lot. I know. But you *are* new. I was hoping that perhaps . . ."

"But commercial property. I don't know. I'm more a residential specialist."

"But it's simple. I'll show you the business plan. The rental projections after completion are supported by comparable rentals at local shopping malls. It's all very conservative. you know the B & T. You simply figure in depreciation and capitalize the income. I can help you if you like.'

"Well . . ."

"And I'll pay a $5000 retainer against expenses."

Esther Anne watched the heavy set stranger peel off five one-thousand dollar bills. Things had been slow. She had to admit it. And there were bills to pay. The return to Colonial elegance had not come cheaply. Five-thousand would pay a lot of bills. And she had to learn commercial appraisals someday. Besides, Henry Tuckahoe was a legend among Alexandria realtors. He, more than anybody, knew local property values. He was on the board of directors of the Burgh & Tuckahoe Savings & Loan. His sister-in-law was the Chief Executive Officer. And the Burgh & Tuckahoe knew its business. It knew Alexandria. There were ways to word these appraisals to avoid any liability. And the way real estate was going up in value her appraisal would be out of date in a week or two anyway. She picked up the money. Jason would be proud, she thought.

"I shall arrange a tour of the Slough, Toughwaugh Slough it is called, for 9:30 in the morning. And thank you, Miss Hendricks."

Henry bowed slightly and let himself out. The bell jingled again. Jason, peeping from around the corner of the grate in the ceiling, was reminded of the poem by Poe. Silver bells. Iron bells. He couldn't tell the difference anymore.

——·25·——

"*L'asperge blanc* should be eaten with the liquid salt that forms between the breasts after twenty minutes of lingual palpitation. As yet unidentified pheromones in secretions of the mammary sebaceous glands enhance the natural acidity of the asparagus and render both vinegar and lemon juice obsolete. It's a quotation from page 107 of *Food As Foreplay*, of course," Max said flatly, staring as directly into Karen's eyes as she would allow, and reveling in her discomfort. "I would, ordinarily, have Lindsay open her blouse for me at this point of the meal so that I could resort to her natural body salts. *Pate*, of course, should be deferred to a later point on the erotic continuum. Any *pate* worth the name needs vaginal condiment, the top of the *mons* if not full exposure to the flavors of the *labia majora*. I never, for that reason, recommend *pate* to start a meal."

"Oh," Karen said gruffly. She was eating a tomato aspic, the only appetizer on the Four Ways menu that Max had not mentioned in *Food As Foreplay*.

"Now you should bear in mind, Karen, that the more muscular lady such as yourself tends to produce a stronger range of flavors than our little wisp of a Lindsay, who while a gift to *poulet* and chardonnay, can easily be overpowered by the more redolent stimulants of meat and claret."

Karen stared into the eyes of a Ming imitation dragon on the bottom of her plate, stirred the remains of the aspic into wisps of red spray on an oceanic background and remained silent.

"You should caution your dining companions that you are a *tornadoes* and red wine type *par excellence*, Karen. You inspire even my overworked palate. You tempt me to order beef against all scientific and moral precepts."

"You've turned eating into fucking, Max, and I don't let men fuck me. You know that." The aspic waves behind the dragon rose to typhoon height.

"But such a waste, I must say. So much lamb, so much garlic, so much thyme and oregano wasted without you. For the sake of your inner connoisseur you should be more flexible." It was, Max knew, the kind of thing Karen Moelders simply did not allow men to say, but Max was different. Max explained early on in their association that he could not communicate with women without acknowledging the underlying sexual tension brought on by their presence, and, Karen, out of respect for his usefulness to the movement, tolerated his flirting.

"I said men don't fuck me, Max. I didn't say anything about having sex. You of all people should know the difference. I can eat Lindsay with asparagus the same as you."

"But there are so many differences. Your chemistry with Lindsay would be wrong. Women taste one way to women and one way to men. The recombination of flavors just isn't the same. By declining men as sexual partners, you limit your taste potential terribly," Max said and then checked himself from going further. His tone, he recognized, had become somewhat close to the edge of the Professor Aceldama pose he tried to maintain with Karen. She was an important client after all.

"Show me a man without a prick and maybe I'll think about it," Karen said pushing the aspic aside and gesturing emphatically for a waiter to remove it.

"Ahh, Karen, so much to learn."

"But for once its your prick I need," she said withholding the word prick until the waiter was within clear hearing distance. "For Lindsay . . ."

"Our Lady of the Delicate Flavors . . ."

" . . . to knock her up, Max, that's what I need you for."

Max started to respond but then paused to savor the last of his asparagus. Talk of Lindsay turned his mind to the perspiration of her breasts again and he wished intensely that she were present. Something was missing without her and it was more than a little salt. The asparagus needed her erect nipples and the soft curves of her breasts for visual harmony as much as for their various and subtle tastes.

"Lindsay has mentioned this recently," Max said finally, licking the back of his left wrist to give at least some somatic piquancy to his last bite. "But I wouldn't say she was truly enthusiastic."

"It's a decision we have to make for her, Max. Lindsay's confused. She's useful to me. She has a competent legal mind. She's fairly aggressive with the religious bigots. But if she's ever going to be more than a fellow traveler she's got to get involved on the personal level. You've got to live the life if you want to lead the movement."

Max sighed. He was all for the radical feminists—as long as they didn't interfere with his own erotic interests—but it seemed a tedious subject in the presence of the veal carbonado that had just replaced his *l'asperge blanc*. He took the first bite and tried to combine the protean images of the restaurant—now quite busy with the lobbyists and attorneys for whom an $80 lunch was a normal expense account item—with the flavors of his food. The Four Ways, a title never explained by the management or questioned by the reviewers who repeatedly rated it the best in town and pushed its prices up to the point where many diners came simply to see whether any food could be worth so much, occupied the Rutherford B. Hayes mansion on the quiet corner of "R" and Connecticut. The spaciousness of the rooms, and the perspective added by arcadian murals in deep perspectives of Washington in 1800 before the Government came, allowed the mixed herbal flavors of the carbonado to expand outward, separating as if they were on a paper chromatograph back into their separate identities. It was a new sensation for Max, the summum bonum of experience, worthy of a chapter in the next edition of *Food As Foreplay*.

"It's really a question of Lindsay's identity, Max," Karen continued. "Who is she? She's lived with you for years. She's apparently monogamous by nature. I mean, I assume she still lets you fuck her. And, for all I know she might have a bunch of kids, leave this work in a few years and forget the need to fight for abortion. I mean who is she? Whose side is she on? Is she really with me, or not?"

God, Max thought, as he barely managed to retrieve the flavors of rosemary and cilantro from separating altogether by a quick sip of an Eyrie Vineyards 1982 Chardonnay, sometimes Karen was too much with all her plotting and scheming for Lindsay. He hated to accuse Karen of trying to seduce Lindsay into her own brand of politics, but her concern for Lindsay did sometimes seem excessive for one who supposedly believed, as he did, in a morality of personal fulfillment.

Max chewed conspicuously several times, sipped his wine and wiped his lips before speaking. "I've done an anatomically annotated menu for the Four Ways, you know, but they won't use it. Some," he said as his eyes prowled aggressively over Karen's bosom, "are still offended by the notion that vaginal mucous is more complimentary to roast duckling than orange sauce."

"Look Max, I know you don't want to talk about it, but it's just something Lindsay needs to do. The Mary Scroggins rape has really put the pressure on us. We look slack, uncommitted. We've got to respond."

"Just open one more button on your blouse, Karen, it inspires me."

"Max, it would give Lindsay real standing in the movement. She could write about it. You could get her on National Public Television. It's a great message for her: Abortion is okay. There is no guilt. There is no post-partum depression. The fetus is part of your body and you can do what you want to with it. What you're free to do must be free of guilt."

Max liked the point and jotted it down on his linen napkin.

"She's bright," Karen continued without noting Max's interest. "She's attractive. She's connected with you. The women's magazines would love her. It's a great career move for Lindsay. But it's got to be grounded in real experience."

Max chewed his veal carefully. Chewing, like everything else in life, was an art form. And there were multiplex ways of prolonging it. There were ways to describe the texture of the veal as it disintegrated and liquified in his mouth, ways to sense it with various lobes of his tongue, ways of cherishing the change in aroma as he exhaled while chewing, ways to revel in the first overwhelming gush of marjoram and then relax as the herbs gave way to the diverse tastes of the meat itself. It was an experience as complex in its own way as orgasm and less draining of the body's strength. Besides, at $34 a serving it would have been wasteful to chew each bite less than twenty times, an affront to the chef's art and a loss of sensual opportunity. Finally, he swallowed the few remaining strands of semi-solid matter. "So why don't you do it yourself, Karen. It would make you more human."

"Because I'm not pretty, Max. You know that. The press will pick up Lindsay's story because of her looks. It's that simple."

It wouldn't be fair to say that fears formed as Karen admitted her own plainness, but a note of sadness entered her voice that surprised Max, as Karen's indifference to appearance, even her rejection of Eve's Mirror as a symbol of the feminine, had been part of her persona for as long as Max had known her.

"You're too hard on yourself, Karen," Max said softly, pausing between bites, even suspending a dripping bolus of veal in mid air, and hoping that she recognized his sacrifice for what it was worth. "You're not a bad looking woman. You're what would have been called handsome even thirty years ago, and that's a compliment given the alternatives. But I take your point. Lindsay is rather a glamour puss with those wine dark eyes. And the media is fickle."

"Then you'll do it?"

"Do what, Karen? I mean I fuck and fuck and fuck," he said gesturing in repeated futility with his knife, "but Lindsay's on the pill. It's not like I use a rubber."

Karen reached down into a shapeless canvas sack from Hudson's Bay Outfitters, rummaged around with her left hand while keeping her eyes fixed on Max, and deposited a thin, flat box on the table. Its cheap vinyl covering looked out of place amidst the polished cutlery of the Four Seasons.

"Pills," he said, recognizing the unique shape of the box, and wondering as he did whenever he saw Lindsay's own personalized pill box, whether it didn't have the same aerodynamic lift as a frisbee.

"Placebos," she said sounding strangely confident, even proud. "Pure sugar."

"So I'm to make a little substitution, is that it?"

"And keep on fucking her, of course." Karen beamed and pushed the package across the table. Max picked it up idly and ran his thumb around the sharp edge.

"There's another technical problem," he said smiling wryly, "but before I get to it, we might discuss something else."

"Like your retainer from the League?"

"Five-Thousand a month is pitifully below market, Karen. You have to pay for what you want."

"It's the Amerikan way," she said. "But you're right. Even at Ten-Thousand a month you're a bargain, Max. I'll recommend it to the Board."

"You are the Board."

"And the Board will approve it," Karen added.

"Then I believe we have an agreement."

"Contingent on performance, of course." She pushed several more packages of placebos across the table.

The waiter averted his eyes from the flat boxes as he cleared away the remains of Max's veal and Karen's fruit salad, the only entre not mentioned in *Food As Foreplay*.

"Which brings up the technical difficulty I mentioned earlier."

"Tell me about that." Karen said as she peered over the rim of a Spode coffee cup. The confidence of ownership suffused her face. Since the first time since the lunch began, she appeared to relax.

"It's the sperm count," Max said lowering his voice. "it's not very high, I'm afraid. Doctor's have told me I could save it up through abstinence, but it could take years."

"So no pregnancies in your three marriages was . . . ummmm . . ."

"No accident."

"Right."

"But . . ."

"I'm not surprised. Three childless marriages usually means something."

Max shrugged helplessly in the face of irrefutable facts and ineffable emotions. It was a low moment in his career of intellectual supremacy.

"But we still have a deal, Max. I'll need your help even if your balls are no good. Talk her into going off the pill, or substitute the sugar drops, and then we'll see what happens." If you can't get the job done, I've got some other ideas.

Max tried to respond. But he was confused. He had trouble visualizing Karen's "other ideas." He needed to do something to re-establish his old dominance. He was so much smarter than Karen. It had to count for something.

"Pay the bill, Max. I'll explain it later."

——·26·——

Henry Tuckahoe stood knee deep in municipal effluent under 806 Pretender's Street. He rotated the new master valve to the clinic easily from left to right and back. Plastic. Teflon. Polystyrene. He wasn't sure what to call it, but exact names weren't necessary to support his contempt. It hurt him to see that the original brass was gone and irritated him to think that he had been responsible, even though, he thought by way of consolation, the way white men overreacted to every little hitch in their over organized way of life was hardly his fault.

Henry's last sales call on Karen Moelders had not been encouraging. She had forgotten the humiliation of feces and fetal debris cascading down the sagging stairway into the main hallway, and dismissed the cost of the plumbers. All that seemed part of a different world now, she said. Something more important was on her plate. She was hot on the war path about a Supreme Court nominee. Henry showed little interest. He had never paid much attention to the Supreme Court, didn't understand it and didn't want to. He'd gotten what he needed out of Washington in more direct ways. The Supreme Court, all those lawyers, all the arguing, he saw as more white man's nonsense, incomprehensible rituals of another tribe, preening and strutting without meaning to the uninitiated, like all their pretended differences in a religion that always struck him as basically the same.

Henry considered simply shutting the valve again, but the idea seemed uninspired. They'd spot it right off this time and with the new plastic parts it would be too easy to fix. He put his nose in the air like a wolf, inhaled deeply and held his breath. The odor of blood was strong. But the odor of bone was strangely absent. He held his hand in the stream pouring out of 806, let the dark fluid filter through his fingers. A few turds wedged between his fingers. Vegetable based, he thought contemptuously and let them plop into the quiet sewer. But there was more. A white granular mass, the consistency of runny grits, had accumulated under his fingernails. Henry cleaned his nails with a knife. He struck a match. A large bit looked suspicious. It was round and pink with five minute protrusions webbed together. Henry knew without sniffing that the fetal hand was about six weeks old.

An eerie whine filled the vaulted sewer. Henry looked over his shoulder. He knew the howl well, the cry of souls dead before their time. He had heard them before, calling his name, demanding their due revenge. His heavy frame shook with deep chills

Henry screwed the plastic pipe shut quickly, took an old Zippo lighter from his coat pocket, and held the flame to the joint until the plastic began to melt. If this didn't move Karen to reconsider his option, he would try more creative solutions. There were floor boards to loosen, foundations to crack, mildew to plant. But the sewer was worth one last try, if for no other reason than to have the brass fittings returned. He finished the work quickly and fled toward the river.

Jason Potter laughed as Henry's bulk disappeared down the sewer toward the light. He uncupped shadowy hands from around his formless mouth. The moans and screams, he knew, couldn't be heard by ordinary mortals. But there was something different about Henry Tuckahoe, something that made him hear these other worldly tunes. He hadn't planned on meeting Henry here, but he was delighted to see what Henry was up to. Shutting off people's plumbing didn't bother him exactly. Living people seemed stranger to him all the time. But Henry could only be up to some real estate hanky-panky, and Jason had seen enough of that. He chuckled to himself, collected a band of small glimmering fetal souls in his hands and escorted them to the luminescent streams he now found everywhere.

27

Ancient Texts in Search of Modern Experience. Lacy read the final page again, turned it over and put it face down on the seven inch stack that comprised the totality of Aubrey's work. It wasn't exciting, she had to admit. But the scholarship, measured by sheer volume, by numbers and density of footnotes, by the names of scholastic giants strategically placed, was not bad at all, everything, in fact, she had come to expect from Aubrey after her short but intense acquaintance with his techniques of love making, mechanically sound but imaginatively limited.

No complaints though. Aubrey had done what was necessary, completed the male's evolutionary function, spraying sperm as required. His unannounced departure had been a shock, of course. One was, she had to admit, culturally conditioned to expect a more than transitory presence from the seed bearer. But it wasn't strictly necessary. And no promises had been exchanged. The opportunity hadn't arisen. Aubrey, so conventional in his Charlottesville tweeds and his Mr. Jefferson gentility, would certainly have done his duty if he had known of the pink swab that had emerged from a vial of Lacy's urine only two days before he left. She had planned to tell him, of course. But later. When she was sure. When it had all been confirmed by a doctor, when an abortion would have presented insuperable moral hurdles even to an unformed, inexperienced, conscience like Aubrey's.

Lacy rose from her desk chair and turned her electric room heater up a notch. A glorious Indian Summer had faded into a chilly November and the five week old fetus in her womb demanded more heat than she was used to. She bundled herself in a shawl knitted by her grandmother, and wrapped a plaid blanket around her thighs. Everything was perfect, she thought. Everything that mattered. She missed Aubrey sometimes. She'd gotten where she could listen to him ramble on and on about his dissertation without really hearing much besides the tone of his voice, the self-fulfilled tune of the scholar at peace, and she'd gotten used to the thought of his continuing presence.

She rubbed her abdomen smugly. Three months until the kicks started, she thought. What she really needed of Aubrey was still here and would always be here. It was enough. She felt grateful to the poor confused boobie. He was such a queer duck, she thought, so out of place, so naive, so vulnerable. Academic life, the tenure track, the politically correct and incorrect do's and dont's, were deeper, wider, wilder than he imagined. And his dissertation was so old fashioned, so one dimensional, that even if it was accepted, it doomed him to small college teaching. It's dullness even started with his name. Aubrey. It smacked of frilly handkerchiefs and rose perfume. She crossed it out on the title page and wrote in "A. Congaree

Snopes Wythe." It sounded more ethnic, more complex, more Faulknerian, a name deep in old blood and pristine truths. She continued into the text. There was a lot she could do. Elizabethan drama without Elizabethan music struck her as odd, even unscholarly. A cross disciplinary approach was so much stronger, so much more fashionable. And re-writing the dissertation was little enough to do for Aubrey, she thought, after what he had done for her.

28

"You must have been on television," Esther Ann said. "Are you sure you aren't an actor?"

"Positive."

"I watch a little television in the afternoons, you know. "Edge of Life" is my favorite. And, of course, I sometimes watch the news."

"Well," the young man grumbled, acting, she thought, so much older than he really was, "it could have been one of the news programs, I suppose. It may have had something too do with that judge thing I was telling you about, the job that brought me down here from Boston."

"Oh yeah. The judge thing." She hadn't really believed him the first time. He looked too young to be a judge. He was so thin and light on his feet, and even though there was some grey around his temples, anybody younger than Jason struck Esther Ann as too junior to be very important.

"This one's only a door and a window wide," she said, fiddling with the awkward lock box on the front door. "The previous owner replaced the bathroom and put in a hot water heater that you wouldn't believe—400 gallons so you never have to wait for a bath when you have visitors—but its still got a lot of the federal period feel to it, don't you think? I mean look at the crown molding."

"Built in 1919, you said?"

"That's what the listing said. 1919. Late Federal." Esther Anne opened the front door and switched on a light. "It's been empty for a couple of months," she said, "and of course the heat hasn't been turned on."

"Who owned it last?"

"A congressman from Ohio," she said. "He didn't run last time. It's a little overpriced at $225—thousand I mean—but he'll take less. All these congressman start high, like someone was going to put one of those little brass plaques outside to show who lived here, you know, like they were George Washington or Robert E. Lee, but in a week or two after they're gone nobody around here cares, you know?"

"Living room, dining room, bedroom . . ."

"I mean there're so many of those congressman! And such a turnover every two years! It's a wonder anyone cares."

" . . . study, bath and a little garden?"

"Right. And a half potty down in the basement. It's a narrow house, but good light from the south and lots of room along this wall for all those books you were telling me about. Plenty of room for a single man with books."

"I take it, then, that the congressman was unattached?"

"He wasn't. He had another house in McLean and used this place to meet people, you know? I think that's maybe why he didn't run again."

"You think I would purchase a house riddled with scandal?" The young judge struggled to show some sense of righteous indignation, but Esther Anne wasn't impressed, indignation being in her experience merely a literary devise.

"Oh, people around here forget that sort of thing real quick," she said. "You'll get used to it . . ." She nudged him in the ribs. "You judges must'a heard a lot of hanky panky sitting up there on that bench what with all the divorces and everything . . ."

"There were rumors that my great uncle Daniel Mather Carroway kept a woman in Alexandria when he was in the 47th Congress, of course. He was on the periphery of the Henry

Adams circle, you know. But mistresses were more common in the 1890's, I think."

"Why yes! I read one of the best Veronica Holloway's called *Sins of the Senator*—maybe you've read it?"

"You really read those romance tinglers, Miss Hendricks?"

"It was the one with the girl on the cover in the red dress looking oh so longingly at the senator in a handsome cab driving in front of the Capital with his grumpy old wife, while she—the girl in the red dress I mean—was the one who had all his babies because his wife was frigid."

"I haven't read it of course."

"What do you like to read Jenkin? May I call you Jenkin?"

"Law, Miss Hendricks. I read law."

"Oh."

"And sometimes fiction. Dickens. Tolstoy. But not the romantic genre writers. Never. I can't even imagine what those books are like."

"Well, all that congressman's carrying on might just drive the price down a little, but not too much. Nothing drives real estate prices down too much around here, Judge. Nothing."

"Oh," Jenkin said, flushing the toilet and counting the seconds as the water swirled and gurgled away. There was no heating vent in the head. He liked that.

"Why just yesterday, I did an appraisal on some undeveloped land over by the creek, just the worst looking piece of no count scrub land you ever saw and about half under water, and that price just keeps going up and up."

"I'll need to stand here in the study to see if the lighting's right. Is that okay? I do a lot of my writing work at home."

"That old slough—that's what they call it—slough—but I'd just call it a swamp—sold for $44M only a week or two ago and I just appraised it at 100 million dollars, can you believe that?"

"I have a desk, you know. It belonged to grandfather Hollyfield. It would have to fit through this door," Jenkin said to himself, removed a tape measure from his coat pocket and began measuring the door jambs from the staircase into the study.

"It all has to do with the income stream from the projected development, you know, all that rent that the tenants are going to pay when it's all finished. That Henry Tuckahoe figured a way to add part of Pretender's street to the Slough parcel, work the historical buildings into some really nice high rises and boost the rentals way up. He's a genius. Everybody says it. A genius."

"The desk would just fit, you know. And I can see book shelves all along that wall, just like you said."

"It's because I have so many books myself, all the Veronica Holloway's in hardback."

"Hardback? Is that right?"

"I don't like that cheap, high acid paper in the paperbacks, do you?"

"Well no, now that you mention it. I have a real thing about cheap paper. Even the law books aren't as well printed as they used to be."

"And you could put books right here in the kitchen, along this old wall, see?"

"You're right," Jenkin said, seeing his books everywhere.

"But I could show you more Olde Towne properties. It's tight now, but there're always new things coming on the market."

"No. I think this is it. It never pays to be too picky, you know."

"Yes, I know."

—— 29 ——

"Counting front and back," Aubrey said, "2,727 pages. Over a million words in gothic characters, longer than the King James Bible."

"With or without the Apocrypha?"

"With the Apocrypha."

"Count 'em again," the old woman said.

"Granny!" Aubrey complained in a voice that was a few notes higher than before he was mugged on the Capitol grounds and dragged head down and bouncing for three blocks.

"Remember, I've got this bologna! It's been dried out for a week. Just the way you like it!" Granny Franny took an assortment of crisp, meat-colored discs from her carryall and waved them at Aubrey. "No counting, no bologna."

Saliva formed on Aubrey's lips. He licked it away and started turning the pages carefully. Some were two-hundred years old, he figured, but the last pages were new, a month or two, no more.

Aubrey counted the pages again. He hadn't shaved in nearly a month. The gash on his forehead had healed into a broad angry scar. He had gone from thin to emaciated. His eyes bulged. Yet, he seemed happier than when he was working on his own dissertation.

Re-counting the pages took over an hour, but the time passed without notice. Aubrey found the task strangely interesting. The feel of the paper and the mystery of its unknown script challenged him. And the changeless surroundings—a forgotten nook amidst the library's periodicals—seemed to be all the peace he had longed for—as much as he could now remember longing for anything—when he left the Folger Guesthouse for the D.C. bus station.

The number came out the same. That made three times in a row. He wrote 2,727 on a scrap of yellow paper and handed it to the old woman. She nodded and gave him an apple. It wasn't whole, but there was some edible flesh left near the stem.

"You said bologna."

"Bologna's for later, when you can read it."

"But . . ."

"Later," she said, dangling the meat high over his head. Light shown through it, revealing the thick blood vessels of an alley cat's placenta rather than the ground up homogeneity of processed meat.

Aubrey ate what was left of the apple quickly and slipped the core into his pocket, a little bite against the hunger that he knew would come back all too soon.

"I'm going to pick up my social security check," Francis Appleby said, checking the shackles on Aubrey's legs. She had fashioned them carefully from chains and locks from the custodian's closet in the basement.

"Nobody will hear, you know, even if you shout and scream."

"I know."

"And I'll be back before supper."

"Take care."

"The chamberpot's behind the 1952 *Intertestamental Archeologist*."

"Okay."

"And I brought you all those dictionaries you wanted."

"Good."

"You're sure it's gothic script but its not German?"

"I'm sure."

"Well it's got to be something. Something important. I feel it. It's like a code, isn't it?"

"All language is a code, Granny."

"You'll get it boy. You'll figure it out. And I'll give you full credit on the translation, you'll see. It'll make your career at U.Va."

Aubrey turned to the manuscript as Granny Franny's worn heels shuffled down the circular iron stairs. He adjusted the lamp she had brought him and copied the first word, apparently some kind of title, transposing the Gothic characters into Latin. Toughwaugh. It wasn't a word he knew. He went to the stack of dictionaries, looking for an ancient root. He eliminated Old Russian and Sanskrit. "Toughwaugh." It wasn't even an Indo-European word. Aubrey's interest rose. He tried the next word. It looked oddly familiar. Papyrus. Of course. He read on. The words flowed. It was Greek, the *koine* version used in the New Testament, but transliterated into a version of Gothic script popular in Muenster in the late Seventeenth Century.

Aubrey read slowly but steadily, stopping from time to time to consult a fat Lexicon.

The Toughwaugh Papyrus: I, being the man indentured once to Johannes FurchteGott Schulerburgh of the Kingdom of Niedersachsen who dwelt among the barbarian Quohee west of the Great Falls, hereby call these papers Toughwaugh in memory and commemoration of my native people now so sadly dispersed and destroyed by the ravages of white Wa-shun-toine people and rum traders who came up the River Potowatomack by sailing vessels in the time of our great-grandfathers. I write these papers that the truth may be known of my people and my family and of the people who removed them from the face of the earth forever and in gratitude to my master Herr FearsGod himself for teaching me the language of the Gospel Matthias he carries with him and reads to me every morning after chores are done and the fast of the night is broken. These things I say are true and worthy to be remembered by all men. Read of these things and weep, for the ways of men are wicked and the ways of the Lord hard to fathom."

Aubrey worked on and on through a night he could not see, forgetful of the world by which he was forgotten. But his imprisonment didn't matter any more. A new world had opened, a new past and a new future. It was a scholar's dream of a fresh source realized at last. He was beyond pain, beyond hunger, and when Granny Franny, her mind compressed by swelling growths and increasingly forgetful, found him three days later, he was ready with two-hundred pages of full idiomatic English.

30

The cloister gardens of the Convent of Holy Desire in northwest Washington emulated the *giardini tutti fiore* at Assisi. Weathered marble saints and worn granite tile reflected the early

November sun, oblique but still warm during the middle of the day. A few hollyhocks and black eyed susans bloomed at the top of overgrown stalks. Banks of withered veronica waited to be pruned. And Sister Mary Scroggins sat doubled up on an imitation DaVinci bench vomiting over the thighs of a Donatello puto donated, a small plaque said, by Riccardi Brothers Pontiac.

It was really too much, she thought, having laughed at morning sickness until it was her own and lingering far beyond the two or three weeks allowed by the textbooks. She stretched out on the bench, waiting for the nausea to pass, marking her place in Thomas á Kempis' *Imitation of Christ* with the brown leaf of a dying sunflower. She closed her eyes, winced, involuntarily wished her condition away, and then immediately prayed for forgiveness and repeated the four things that bring peace: to do the will of others, to choose less rather than more, to take the lowest place, to pray always that God's will may be perfectly fulfilled. She had prayed it many times in the last month, ever since the euphoria of publicly doing what she had always demanded of others ended and she was ordered into seclusion. A pregnant nun, even one who had been raped and was resolute in bringing her baby, God's baby, to life, wasn't considered an acceptable public sight. Mother Superior was right, she admitted, as much as she wanted to be out on the abortion clinic picket lines flaunting her big belly at the Lindsay Haydens of the world.

Only six more months to go, she thought. One could bear anything for six months. There was nothing to it. And then it would be over. Arrangements had already been made for an adoption. She needn't even see the baby. And then back to work with a martyr's crown. It sounded good. Many of her sisters seemed to envy her. And she wished it could be that simple. But there were problems, fears and phantoms she had never expected.

Sister Mary rubbed her abdomen slowly. The nausea was passing. She would be showing in another month. But none of that mattered. What scared her was the first kick, the undeniable sign that there really was a baby inside her and the knowledge that half, or more, of the baby's genes had come from that cretin moaning and slobbering on top of her as the others watched, the one who had been in mid-orgasm when the others discovered her religious status and started to back off. He was the father. She was sure. The doctors said there was no way to know without tests. But she was sure. And the thought of that person—his vacuous stare, his rank breath, the way he kicked and bucked—the thought of his continuing inside her for another six months, continuing to kick her and humiliate her—turned her ill.

The nausea passed. It was probably a subliminal effort to vomit the thing up, she thought, and if so then a sinful response to the trial God had chosen for her. She should confess this vomiting, unintentional or not. It was wrong. But she knew she couldn't. Not yet.

Mary opened Thomas à Kempis again and reviewed the headings. "On Learning Patience," "On Control of the Heart," On the Secret Judgements of God." She'd read them all before. They had never failed her. But they looked different now. She hardly knew where to start. She put the book spine down on the bench and watched the pages part. Well worn and marked, it fell open to "On Purity of Mind and Simplicity of Purpose." She read it three times. "A pure heart penetrates both heaven and hell." The line had once filled her with peace. Yet now, when it came to the vile thing growing inside her, the seed of a violent rapist growing into something she could not control, she felt her own understanding could penetrate nothing. In a surge of hope, Sister Mary resolved to repeat the sentence a hundred, even a thousand, times, until the words alone returned the purity of heart the rape had stolen.

——·31·——

Karen Moelders idled her car outside the Foxhall Fertility Clinic. Frost-rimmed ginkgo leaves blew across the windshield.

Ice clung to the rear view mirror. The heater was on full, its undersized fan chewing noisily on a leaf sucked up from the street. Karen banged on the vent with the heel of her hand. The leaf shifted position. The grinding noise grew louder. Karen rubbed her hands in the air stream. She was still cold. But it was more than the November chill. It had something to do with rising too early in the morning. The circulation was slower. The blood was thin. Metabolism was down. Sugar was depleted. The ozone was higher. Something like that. There was an explanation. And it was gender related. Women felt the chill worse than men. It had something to do with retaining the heat in their bodies ready to warm new life rather than sending it out to the action-related extremities. The theory reduced her to an immobile Queen Bee. It was—considering who she was and what she had done with her life—obviously in error, unworthy of her concern. Still, she shivered, and banged the heater vent again. But, the leaf had done all the shifting it wanted to do.

An all news station played quietly. Wars in the Balkans. Earthquakes in Armenia. Genocide in Turkmenistan. Famine in Chad. Plague in Uganda. Karen paid little attention. World morbidity had to take its place behind what really mattered. She listened only for news of the Supreme Court and its new Justice, Jenkin Carroway. There had to be a way to expose him for what he was before he could decide any important abortion cases. No one could be as sexless as Carroway seemed. He had to have a weakness. It was whores, or it was a married woman, or it was choirboys. There was some way to get him. There was a way to get everybody. It was axiomatic.

Karen turned the radio off and focused on a side door of the clinic, a door most people would never notice, a door the women coming for their little injections of sperm, overwrought with years of longing to conceive, didn't want to think about.

But Karen knew. She had been there herself. Seen it all. Waited her turn, wallowed in impotent shame, begged for the frozen milky goo, the messy stuff that kept women incomplete, reliant on the service of the male. She had dodged the eyes of the other hopefuls in the waiting room, the sellers of their sex and pride, the addicts of parturition dependent on sperm count and organs of intromission for the completion of their little evolutionary function, the end of their breed-and-die lives. She had endured the interviews, the psychological profiles, the pelvic examinations by the well-intentioned midwives, the sociological ups and downs of the sentimental do gooders. She had explained why she, a forty-two year old single woman wanted to conceive at her age—at her age!—and why an adoption might suit her better. And she had lied through it all, spouted the cliches about how it's only natural for a woman to want a baby, a child, offspring, progeny, matriliny to the nth degree, little hands on your shoulders, in your hand, by your side, waiting to help as you age. She'd been a star, won them over, wowed them, in fact, until it came time for the mechanical organ of intromission. Then, the game had gone too far. She explained that she wanted to do it to herself, at home, in private. She wanted to take the thing away—it looked, she imagined, like a turkey baster—and bring it back later, or even buy her own if that's what they insisted on, it didn't really matter to her even though she never planned to use it again. But the request had been too much. Karen refused the treatment unless she could do it at home. The nurses balked at her strange request. A doctor showed up. A male doctor, his natural organ of intromission wadded up in his jockey shorts, curled up to spring, hurtful, mean and violent. He laughed, of course. He had to. It was his way. The cackle of death in the presence of life. And he had refused to let her take the stuff home. There were rules. He said you had to be licensed to handle sperm. She couldn't believe it! Licensed! When half the people in the world sprayed it around, spilled it on the ground, dumped it in places they wouldn't touch with their feet! When the idiots and alcoholics and incontinent dope fiends of the city lined up outside the Foxhall Clinic in the early hours, did they need licenses to beat their meat into jelly jars and take their fifty dollars? Licenses? Licenses to fuck?

They'd shown her out the back door, of course. Some of the wank-for-pay crowd were still around, huddled around bottles, smoking fresh gaspers, saving strength for another pull on the pud. She hadn't spoken to them. They were the wrong type. Uneducated. Unsympathetic. Reactionary. And they stared at places they shouldn't, wondering perhaps if she carried their genotype. Karen had brushed herself off and moved on. She was aware somehow that these soiled men, the great unwashed, had exactly what she wanted—for Lindsay of course and never for herself—and that they were willing enough to part with it for much less than she had been willing to pay. But she had been in too much shock simply to ask for it or unsure of how it could be stored for the right moment without the clinic's facilities. Besides, even with a pot full of the stuff, there was still the intromission problem.

Karen had solved all these problems in time, of course, as she solved all problems. It was all very simple. There was an obvious solution. And the sperm itself was easy enough to come by. There was, really, not much most men wanted to do but part with it.

It only took the right candidate, she thought, watching a group of men huddle against the cold. She wasn't exactly sure what she was looking for, but she had to be fair to Lindsay, and to Max. Not just anyone would do. The thing was to become part of Lindsay's body after all, even if just for a little while.

Karen watched closely as the men started out the door. It didn't take them long to do their business and take their money. It was all over in an obscenely short time, she thought, considering what it was that they were putting into glass vials, what it was the stuff could do, the damage, that is, it could do to a woman.   A dirty man who looked as if he had slept under the ginkgo tree stood stiffly when the clinic door opened. He pawed a bag-wrapped bottle hidden under a pile of wet leaves, poured a ruby fluid into the bottle cap and then threw his head back. He choked violently, coughed, wretched, poured another bottle cap and sipped at it desperately until his spasms subsided. A red residue from his eructations clung to the grimy sleeve of his sweater and caught the low rays of the morning sun like dewdrops. He lapped them up, thrust a purple tongue into the neck of the bottle, replaced the cap and buried it again as if he had been all alone instead of in the middle of a staring mob. He then opened his coat and started rubbing the outside of his Salvation Army suit pants, working what the pants concealed into a state of reluctant excitement. A few of the men stared. Some grabbed their own crotches to make sure the stuff they hoped to be paid for was still available. Masturbation without production for more than fifteen minutes was grounds for disqualification. It was one of the rules. It was posted on the door. It made the old and drunk wary, put them on their toes.

Finding no reaction to his hand through the thick wool, the old man opened his fly. Karen saw a nubbin of flesh. A red tumor, bulbous and fleshy, grew on the tip. His motions were rough and determined.

Karen watched the old man placidly. It was what she expected, of course. She'd known men were like that, living for a drink, a little friction on the penis and nothing else. She wondered briefly why their craniums hadn't atrophied back in Neanderthal times, back when it was obvious that the penis and not the brain was to be the male's contribution to the species. But she didn't waste long on conjecture. Defective as they were as a class, one individual was necessary for her purpose. And, disgusted or not, she had no intention of repeating the effort. It wouldn't do for Karen Moelders, President of the Wombyn League, to be seen stalking fertility clinics.

Karen scrutinized the men as they shuffled into the clinic, telling herself all the while that their looks, even their health, didn't matter. The thing was to be aborted as quickly as possible. Paternal origins were irrelevant.

But it was more in line with the sisterly ethic she preached to use the least offensive male she cold could find. It wasn't, after all, a totally impersonal transaction. A rape—as Karen broadly construed the term—was involved, and, while in purely abstract terms she conceded no qualitative distinctions between one rape and another, the marital rape and the violent wilding being one and the same, Lindsay hadn't come round to her way of thinking yet, and would, if their roles were reversed, prefer a fertilizing partner with as few physical problems as possible.

Karen raised a pair of World War II surplus Zeiss binoculars— the "Feldmeister" model favored by Rommel and Kesserling— and surveyed the line of men. There was one who didn't look too bad. He was thin and pale, perhaps, but from the height of his forehead and the set thin line of his mouth, somehow intelligent, even spiritual. He read aloud as he stood in line from a sheaf of photocopied pages, and he mumbled to himself, taking notes from time to time on a small pad. Karen tried to read his lips. His words were distinct, articulated with considerable effort, but she couldn't understand them. A foreign language obviously. Karen drew no precipitous conclusions. It could be, she thought, a sign of intelligence, or merely a sign of distant— perhaps even humble or embarrassing—origins.

The door opened. The line started to move. The shabby old man struggling to keep his penis erect pushed in front of the young man reading from the copied pages. The young man looked surprised, observed the demeanor of his assailant with some detachment and then gave way with a high pitched, resonant "sorry," that forced Karen to recall the ubiquitous and to her mind inappropriate apologies of her student days at Oxford, the British apologizing so mechanically and so universally that even she, when mistakenly interrupted on the toilet by a charwoman, had used it herself. The universal anglo "sorry" was hardly a virtue as she now construed the world, but it was the kind of educated English touch, not unlike the tony expressions cultivated by Max Aceldama, that endeared men to Lindsay. He might just do, she thought, looking at the young man's hands, searching for dirt under his fingernails, checking the front of his pants for stains of incontinence or signs of unseemly enthusiasm.

The men shuffled into the clinic. Karen waited. It didn't take long. Nothing associated with procreation took long. Short of inception, long of duration, eternal in shame, she thought, fueling the old fires of indignation so effectively that her car heater became unnecessary.

The men walked out. Some, it seemed from their expressions, had been rejected, unable to produce, their sperm count low, or too much whiskey in their seminal fluid. Others—the young man she had started to call the Oxford scholar in her own mind and the scrofulous beggar with the rosy tumored penis included—seemed happy enough, pleased to have pocketed the fifty dollars they were paid for a simple act of self pleasure, an act for which women, unequal as ever, would never be paid.

The Oxford Scholar took a number 57 bus. Karen followed it across Washington, down Foxhall Road to Wisconsin Avenue, over Massachusetts to Pennsylvania, around the Mall and up Constitution to the Hill and the Library of Congress. The young man stepped off. Karen stopped her car, ignored the honks and abusive shouts of the turbaned cabby behind her and watched the Oxford Scholar submit his sheaf of papers to inspection at the main door of the Jefferson Building. He seemed to know the guard. They used first names. The young man was a regular, a professional academic of some sort, perhaps even an impecunious graduate student selling his sperm for a higher cause, even, perhaps, an enlightened person, someone who could understand and would sympathize with the peculiar project Karen had in mind.

Karen made a rude gesture at the cab driver, backed hard into his front bumper, forcing his engine to stall and his passenger to flee, and then drove slowly back to the Wombyn League. She knew enough. She had the right man and she knew where to find him. Max would have to cooperate now. She chuckled, thinking of Max with as much fondness as she could muster for a man.

· 32 ·

"This one—*The Young Laird's Daughter*—was my favorite for—well it seemed forever, you know?"

"Yes," Jenkin said. He eyed Esther Anne warily as she patrolled his newly filled bookshelves.

"When Dramorga takes on the cloak of her fallen brother, hoists his dirk, finds it strangely suited to her grip and goes to serve the bonny young Prince . . . well . . . I wept . . ."

"Yes," Jenkin said and immediately wondered if his note of panic had been too apparent. "Of course, the ceiling cracks you came to see are just here, radiating out from the dining room chandelier. I could have the work done myself, of course, but the seller did promise." Jenkin pointed to the small cracks and then, failing either to silence or to distract Esther Anne from his bookshelf, took her by the shoulder and turned her toward the dining room. She was heavier and stronger than he expected of a woman so much shorter and the tension in his arm and hand lingered after the initial effort, creating a momentary sensation of continuing contact.

"But you have them all," she said. "In hardback. In order of publication. *Amour at Ashley Plantation* all the way through *Zanzibar Bride!*"

"Not that I've read them, of course," Jenkin said pushing her now into the dining room, wishing that he had ignored the cracks altogether, passed them off as signs of wear in the original plaster work, a monument to the quality of colonial workmanship. "The author—Veronica Holloway's not her real name of course—is a friend of mine from Harvard. I might have mentioned that?"

"No . . ."

"I haven't read them, of course. Nobody . . ."

"I'd never noticed before that they went all the way through the alphabet, had you?

Bartered Woman of Buthan, Captive Heart of Cyrenaica, Damascene Damsel in Distress, Empress of Egypt, Slave of Passion. It's incredible! I've read them all and never know they were published in alphabetical order!"

"A cheap alliterative trick, really, not something to be proud of, surely."

"It must all mean something, don't you think?"

"Mean something?"

"I'll bet if you took the first word of every title and . . ."

"You can see how the cracks came right through the paint," Jenkin said diverting Esther Anne's attention away from the bookshelf for a second time. "It happened overnight. Really. One night it all looked fine and the next morning the cracks had appeared. Well within the warranty period."

"And *Gaelic Goddess of Galahad*," she said fingering the spine of a thin volume. "I was still back in West Virginia when I read that. Checked it out of the library. It must have been read by twenty or thirty people before I ever got it. The cover was all worn and some of the passages were dark with coal soot from people's fingers. Especially the parts right here around page 72 where Brownwyn first gives herself to Galahad, the night before their wedding, and he cries when he has taken what isn't his because he knows he has ruined his wedding night, and hers, but he knows that she loves him and will love him forever."

"But, of course, there is no wedding night."

"The Ethelrings come in the night and carry her off, to sell her to the Bey of Algiers and he doesn't see her for twenty years. I know." Tears formed in the corners of Esther Anne's eyes.

"Until he finds her during the Third Crusade and takes her home."

"To be his forever."

"Yes."

"Then you have read them."

"Well . . . Veronica is an old friend. And they don't take long to read."

"You must need something to take your mind off your Supreme Court work. All those long hours and briefs and arguments and such."

"Of course. Everyone needs an outlet."

"And you don't have . . . ?"

"Well . . . ?"

"You don't have anyone do you? A Brownwyn of your own?"

"Only my mother. But, of course, she's up in Boston. I asked her to move South, but, the climate is pretty horrible and very few of the people down here have been to colleges one has ever heard of . . ."

"I know what it's like to be alone, you know."

"You, Miss Hendricks? I would have thought that a young lady like yourself would have had her choice of men in Washington, or anywhere . . ."

"It was a star-crossed thing," she said slipping the Veronica Holloway volume back onto the shelf, lining the bindings up, running her fingers along the row from A to Z. I met a very special person when I came to Washington so many years ago now. He was older and wiser and—I blush to say it—married to another at the time."

"Well . . . it happens . . . I know . . . one can't control . . ."

"The late Senator Jason Potter of South Kanaska. You may have heard of him?"

"Of course. A household name."

"We were lovers."

"Lovers?"

"Platonically speaking, of course. Nothing else was possible. What with his wife still living off in that mental hospital where he paid so much to keep her and all."

"Yes."

"It seemed so unfair at the time. And then him dying before her and us not ever getting to . . . well, you know."

"The Equilibrists," Jenkin said, starting to recite, "by John Crowe Ransom . . ."

"But now I know it was for the best. The purity of what I felt for Jason and what he felt for me has survived his passing, you see, just because our feelings were never consummated, never burned up in the fires of our passion."

"Of course," Jenkin whispered, all thought of the cracks on the dining room ceiling having passed forever from his mind.

"Of course," the late Senator Jason Potter, a dark shadow no bigger than the cracks on the ceiling and easily confused with them, muttered. He spoke only to himself, envisioning in his cloudy intelligence a purer passion and a more consuming ardor than he had, in fact, every known for a living person. He choked with emotion, feeling no embarrassment in showing strong passion as he would have when alive. Esther Anne was right. There really had been something wonderful between them, something he had never seen or felt before, something that had survived to grow stronger, more beautiful, in spite of his death. Tears flowed for what he could have been, for what he might still be.

"I'll drop in and see you sometime, Jenkin, sometime when you are working late in your Supreme Court office . . ."

"It's called a chamber."

" . . . and offer you a little word of cheer. Would that be alright? Say it would. Please."

"Well, Miss Esther . . . of course . . . if you wish."

——·33·——

"You can see it? Really see it?" Lindsay asked. She sat on an oversized, overstuffed pillow of antique Mongolian silk in the Russian sun room Max had added to the upper story of his mansion. Cold light from the Tiffany patterned windows swirled around her body in time with the boughs bending in the rough, rhythmic sway of December winds coming down the Potomac.

"Yes. I see it," Max said. "Faintly, but it's there, a column of light, yellow light like the sun through daffodils, spiraling through your ovaries, through your pancreas, your adrenals, thymus, thyroid, and up, up . . . well it gets lost in your neck somewhere. Something in your head seems to block it out." Blue lavender bouquets from bonsai wisteria and the heavy sweetness of a winter blooming iris (*I. unguicularis*) added a summer fragrance in contrapuntal afterthought. The Allman Brothers' 'Eat A Peach' reverberated with Pachabel's Cannon across floors and walls of green Carrera tiles in an arrangement Max had commissioned from the London Symphony Orchestra.

"Your brain waves are in Theta," he added. "Deep relaxation. I can tell. Even though you're still blocking it with your higher intelligence, not letting something go. You must work past the orgasmic response into ecstasy, Lindsay. It's the only way."

"But I'm doing what you said, Max, visualizing my heart pumping, not blood, but, what was it you said?"

"Phlogiston."

"Phlogiston. Right. Pumping liquid fire. I see it. In my mind's eye. I see it," Lindsay said opening an eye surreptitiously, seeing that Max was in full ecstasy himself, eyes glazed over, looking beyond her into the moment of eternity that was the object of all sex. A gob of Astroglide, a sexual lubricant, had hardened uncomfortably on her left nipple. She flicked it away secretly, guiltily.

"Orgasm isn't something you *do*, it's something you *are*," Max said, "the transformation of genital pleasure into whole body ecstasy."

"Chills and thrills up and down the body," Lindsay said. "I know."

"The flapping overlapping of soft flames."

"Yes."

The two were several yards apart now, each pursuing, or in Lindsay's case pretending to pursue, the ecstasy in their own way, at their own pace.

"Breathe deeply, Lindsay, all the way down to your sex."

Lindsay inhaled deeply and let the breath out slowly. "Did you come Max?"

"For the last two hours. I'm still coming. I'll come for another hour. Or more."

"I mean ejaculate. Did you? You know I'm off the pill this month, ready to conceive, ready to abort. Isn't it what you want?'

"Of course, Lindsay. You know it is. It's what we both want."

"But I didn't really feel it squirting up inside me."

Max shuddered. "Such an offensive word," he said. "I didn't 'squirt' as you say. I let it flow naturally. You wouldn't feel it like you did with younger men. But it'll do the job. Trust me."

Lindsay peeked from behind her mask of ecstasy. Max's penis was as hard as ever, as clean as ever, as free of tell tale semen as ever. She wondered if he had it in him anymore, or if maybe the full body orgasms had robbed his system of its vital essences, turned all his sperm into backbone tissue and spinal fluid.

"I counted them as they left, Lindsay. You've got four million of my seeds inside you now, swimming into your womb to make a pregnancy, okay?"

"Okay, Max. If you say so."

"I do," Max said. He looked at her cautiously to make sure her eyes were still closed. He hadn't come, of course. It was so tiresome, and with his low sperm court he knew it wouldn't have mattered. Better to save himself and leave it all to Karen. She had surprised him with her plan. It would almost certainly work.

"But your temperature wasn't up tonight, was it?"

"No. That should come next week."

"We'll give it another try then, okay?"

"Okay," Max.

"Maybe have a little dinner before hand. Just you and me and Karen."

"Okay." Lindsay didn't think it would matter. There was a reason Max's wives had never conceived. She'd called them up and asked them. And, she wouldn't have agreed to go off the pill—even out of curiosity to see what would happen—if she'd thought there was a realistic possibility of it actually happening.

· 34 ·

Aubrey groped his way with seasoned and sensitive fingertips to the thin work desk under the back issues of *The British*

Israelite, settled into his thin metal chair under the bare florescent bulb, muttered *fiat lux* under his breath, flicked the
switch and heard the pop and hum of purple light as if it were
the familiar wheeze of a long-time bed companion. It was the
only light on the 18th floor, or half-floor as the layers of stacks
inaccessible to the public were called. Neither sun, nor moon,
nor streetlight could penetrate the limestone cave. And the
random flashlight of the underpaid, two-years-from-retirement,
security guard never reached above the third level.

Aubrey checked his watch. Half past four. In the morning, he
thought. But he couldn't be sure. Afternoon or morning made
no difference to him now. He had given his money—the $50
from the sperm bank and the $250 from the eccentric wom-
an who had followed him back to the Library of Congress and
promised him a job if he didn't masturbate for a month—to
Granny Franny. She went out from time to time and bought the
few things he needed to keep body and soul together, sparing
him the need to leave the Library and the manuscript at all.

He looked affectionately at Granny's sleeping hulk perched
easily, even naturally, on the edge of the shelf where *Chlorine
Studies*, an industry magazine discontinued in 1928, sat un-
dusted for fifty years until they had sent its 20 volumes off
forever to a Senator from Nebraska through the pneumatic
tubes that connected the Library with the Congress. Except for
the little sleep he needed, sleep he used only to dream of the
manuscript, visualize it, talk face to face and man to man with
its 300 year old author, he wanted nothing more than to read
and translate the vital words in the odd but regular mixture of
Greek language and Gothic script.

Granny slept soundly. Her breathing was hard. She rolled on
her perch, shifting her buttocks and shoulders unevenly, yet
naturally, the space of woman in repose accommodating itself
to the volume of a few books, tucked, as it were, in the only
space it would really need, the space of a person being so much
less than the beds, rooms and houses most people claimed.

Aubrey opened the manuscript and read:

By the waters of Little River, by the little big creek waters that flowed in sluggish imitation of the sky into the broad Potowatomak through seas of reeds and muddy flats, my family of families, the western, below-the-rocks Tuckahoe people, lived free of the long rifle white face full beard Jamestowne folk and free of the wild mountain Quohee, trapper of bird and hunter of deer, eater of human flesh, cannibal of their own kind. In the year of the white man's God 1690 or so as Herr FearsGod Schulerburgh reckoned it, three Sundays before Pentecost, my father, Slow Beaver, chief of the people and hero of the land, a man of full belly, laden with pride of life, convened the monthly feast as always since the world began, by harvesting the oysters from the low tide mud, heaping them up around driftwood fires and eating them hot when the shells popped open with a squirt of bear fat and hot swamp herbs soaked in paw paw vinegar.

I, called by my mother Silent Otter, and my younger brother Shining Kestrel, played in the coals and grabbed the smaller oysters out of the hands of the elders, hearing their stories and filling their gourds with spring water. They told the same stories we had heard before and which never tired us, like the story of Danoah the sea snake who made the Great Falls to keep the Quohee away, to let us know where we were to stop, to put borders between men. Men danced slow and men danced fast. Drums beat many rhythms. Maidens beckoned from the shadows. Bucks and braves lifted their loin cloths and ran after them. Oysters made the sex grow big and wanton. The moon was full and it was the time of courtship and marriage, the time of putting babies into the wives, and the time for the boys like me and Shining Kestrel, who I called Dung-Crow so he would know I was the bigger brother and he the little one, to eat our fill and keep out of the way of the bigger boys who would marry in the spring.

It was then that a white man named Wa-shun-toine came. My father, Slow Beaver, bade him welcome, gave him a clay pot of the biggest oysters, showed him how to shuck, how to eat and where to pile the shells in mounds 20 feet high or more, the mounds my people had been building for ages. Slow Beaver called him Big Wa-shun-toine because there were some other Wa-shun-toine tribesmen there too and they called the big one Au-gu-soon-toine. He was a big man with white hair and bad teeth. He wore too many clothes for the warm season as the white men always did and he and his Wa-shun-toine tribesmen drew Slow Beaver off to a separate fire they built out beyond the circle of our camp, in the low part of the swamp where my brother and I didn't like to go because of the snakes that hung in the branches and snapping turtles that lived in the mud.

Big Au-gu-soon-toine had a brown jug with him. He poured something from the jug into Slow Beaver's calabash. Slow Beaver drank it, choked, spewed a little bit back, grinned, and then drank off what was left in his gourd. He asked for more. Big Au-gu-soon-toine gave it to him readily. This went on for some time. I lost interest because our tribal priest White-Owl-Knows-All was telling the story about the time he wandered away from our Potowatomack people up North to the Algonquin and saw the big forts the French had built. He didn't think much of the White Tribe or the Wa-shun-toine tribe. He said they ate their own people just like the Quohee and buried their dead under ground, which Dung-Crow and I thought was horrible because the body needed to be eaten by birds or fish or at least burned so the soul could rise up to the Sky Spirit or hunker down with the water sprites and tormenting a soul by putting it in a box underground could only mean that you hated that person a lot and wanted to keep him out of the Sky.

After a while, Slow Beaver and Big Au-gu-soon-toine Wa-shun-toine came out of the dark swamp. They both seemed happy. Big Au-gu-soon-toine had something white and flat that he held up and showed everybody, pointing to a mark on the bottom that looked to me and to Dung-Crow like nothing more than a little map on the ground of two trails crossing. *Slow Beaver announced that he and the White Man had agreed to share the oyster beds, but most people didn't hear him because his voice was slurred and after speaking he fell face down into the succotash pot. Big Au-gu-soon-toine Wa-shun-toine's tribesmen led a couple of mules into the camp. They were horrible smelly things. White-Owl-Knows-All said they weren't natural but had been invented by the White Man's bad juju. The Wa-shun-toine tribesmen unloaded more of the brown jugs from the mules and left. The bucks and braves started drinking the clear white liquid but they wouldn't let me or Dung-Crow have any because we were underage. Dung-Crow caught me eating his oysters and I had to beat him and chase him into the dark swamp for punishment. When I got back, someone had taken the white juice into the maiden's lodge and they were all coming out giggling and swaying in the moonlight. The braves danced for hours, drinking from the brown jugs, eating more oysters raw and cooked, boiled, stewed, baked, daring each other to eat five, six raw peppers at a time, belching, vomiting, chasing the maidens behind the bushes, singing, calling war taunts to the Quohee, baring their backsides in the direction of the Quohee, boxing my ears, rolling me and Dung-Crow in the low tide mud flat, pulling the deerskins off the maidens. Finally, when they were all occupied with the maidens, I drank the brown jug juice myself and passed it to Dung-Crow. It burned and made us dizzy. We fell asleep, half buried by the warm shells that were now steaming in many piles along the river beach.*

The next morning brought chaos and remorse. The old wives said there were no maidens in the Tuckahoe tribe anymore and blamed Slow Beaver. The braves who had violated the maidens said the girls had been so slutty the night before that they would have to marry Quohee. The girls said they were full of babies and needed husbands right away to take care of them. They all demanded that Slow Beaver provide husbands, even if they had to marry me and Dung-Crow which we thought was a real bad idea. Everybody had headaches and bad wind like we had all eaten long dead possum like the Quohee. White-Owl-Knows-All had disappeared. It was a bad time for the Tuckahoe.

Then, when it seemed things couldn't get worse, Bug Au-gu-soon-toine came back with his Wa-shun-toine tribesmen on horseback and ordered us to get off the land, which he said was his land, as if land could belong to only one person, as if he could put it in his leather pouch and carry it off to his big White Man's house, and he kept waving that flat, white thing with the cross trail map on it and pointing it directly at Slow Beaver who didn't know what to do. Nobody understood the White Man's word, really, except White-Owl-Knows-All and he couldn't be found. After about an hour, one of the bucks threw a war club at one of the White Men's dogs. The White Men let off their fire sticks and wounded some of the braves. Big Au-gu-soon-toine's horse panicked and he ran over some of the little Tuckahoes and then a real battle started. The braves were groggy and didn't do too well against the firesticks and the iron rods the Wa-shun-toine tribesmen had so it was over pretty quick.

Slow Beaver led us into the forest. The White Men charged after us picking off the slow ones, all the women and the little children. We hid for a night at the Great Falls on the Potowatomack and the next morning Slow Beaver made a several hours long speech to the wind and threw himself over the falls in remorse for being a bad chief. He told us we would have to follow him, but once he was gone and we saw his body floating face down in the river gorge, it didn't seem like such a good idea. Dung-Crow, who even then was overly dogmatic and stubborn, wanted to go ahead and get it over with, but it just didn't seem like a good idea to me. There was some of the brown jug juice in a gourde so we passed it back and forth and thought it over. We didn't have many options, but the brown jug juice helped us think. Going over the falls after our father, duty or not, just didn't seem like a good idea to me.

Aubrey arched his back and stretched his arms. The translation was tedious. The writer's vocabulary was antiquated and eccentric, and his Greek was rusty. Every fourth or fifth word sent him to the massive Liddell & Scott next to his right elbow.

Aubrey was hungry but he hated to wake Granny Franny. She slept more and more these days and even when awake, her lucid moments were less lucid than when she had first rescued and then abducted him. Aubrey stroked her thin grey hair. He'd grown to care for the old bird. And he knew she was dying. She'd told him about the tumor, made him feel the urgency of the translation. And, then, once he had broken the simple code and seen for himself that many academic careers would be built on the *Toughwaugh Papyrus*, that it could, in fact, re-write the last three hundred years of U.S. History, if not also turn religion and science on their ears, he needed no further encouragement. The manuscript was more important than food and drink he thought and renewed his transcription. Besides there was the Karen Moelders job coming up. He needed the money, but he hated to lose the time away from his work. He'd done what she asked. But playing with himself had never been one of his serious vices. And she should be calling in a few days. He put hunger aside and lost himself again in the 1690's, on a river unspoiled by habitation, in a valley of tall oaks clogged with creepers, loved by a tribe to whom it provided an easy subsistence and haunted by only a few white men who had come to see it as their own.

It was dark in the sewer under 806 Pretender's Street, dark with the eyeless wonder felt in caverns 150 feet below the surface when the lights are turned out and the tourists gulp and gasp, pretending that they can control emersion in the pre-creation gloom by whistling a little tune, when in fact they see ugly forms of their own creation in the palpable obscurity that send them in reversion back to the child in the dark bedroom calling for a parent and no parent is coming. Henry preferred it that way. He knew the sewer and the foundation of 806 purely by the touch of his bare feet now, from the junction off the Prince Street connector to the Northwest corner where there had been a sump pump before he clogged it with sand. He knew the large limestone blocks that had been quarried in New England and brought up the river on mule-drawn barges. He knew the feel of the soft mortar joints, how to slip his fingers in, work a slot free, insert an awl, a diamond tipped rock saw, a crow bar, and loosen them up a little, not enough for permanent structural damage, but enough for a major crack or two in the interior plaster, enough to tip the scales against keeping the place. He'd have to lower his price a little, start to make Karen panic. News of a crumbling foundation might hurt prices in Old Town for a week or two until he had an engineer in to put it all right, understate the cost of repair, reassure the community, maybe even have the B & T lower its rates for a week or so to fuel things up again.

Henry stood thigh deep in sewage, braced himself against a corner of the foundation, and put his full weight against the crowbar. The block moved with a deep sucking sound and slid into the sewer. Henry knelt immediately to thrust his hand into the cavity.

"Shells," he said out loud but not in a European language, and held the object of his attention closer for inspection by touch of all ten fingers and the soft skin at his throat. It was a bivalve mollusk, but larger than the fresh or even salt water muscles and oysters one finds in the mid-Atlantic states today. It was large and crude, the home of a tough, meaty creature used to protecting its own territory.

Henry sniffed and tasted the shell. He tucked it in the black pocket of his trousers and dug further into the layers of silt and crustaceans under the foundation, well beneath the water line. He dug up more shells until he found one that smelled still of drift wood smoke. He polished it on his shirt and found room for it in a sagging coat pocket. He dug further, through the residue of old charcoal, fires that had burned centuries ago against clear dark skies, fires that had shimmered off dusky naked skins dancing by moon and stars. He made a mewing sound like a kitten separated from its mother and sat down to think.

The shells, the smoke, and the embers brought on intense visions of his brother. Schuler's death had affected him more than he had cared at first to admit. Oh, he knew it was coming, even that it was inevitable, and even in a way that it was Schuler's own doing, but they had been together, brothers, partners, survivors, for so long that nobody else knew him that same way anymore. And, there was the burial. He told Clovis to have the body cremated. He'd pleaded, begged, but to no avail. She was adamant. Still, he'd fixed Clovis already with a revenge so appropriate that he marvelled sometimes at his own sense of moral poetry. She had loved that little Burgh & Tuckahoe Savings and Loan too much. It didn't pay to love any one thing that much. You got too tied up with it. It got to you. You were at its mercy.

The B & T was the tenth largest savings and loan in the country now. Clovis had fought him hard, but she'd had no choice. They'd sold the loan portfolio, jiggled the books to show big profits, gone public, sold lots of stock and they were now taking in big deposits on an overnight basis from the New York stock brokers. It was an electronic dream. But it could only work as long as Henry produced the big placement fees on high profile developments like the Toughwaugh Slough. He had to keep spiraling and daisy chaining it up and up in an inflationary cycle and then unload it on a bona fide purchaser, someone who would really develop the land and pay off the accumulated loans. It was the only way a daisy chain could work. And it was risky. Vernon, whose Rock of Ages was the second largest S & L in the country, had already gone too far. He was in trouble with the regulators, being sued by unhappy investors, and subpoenaed before Congress to answer questions about his lobbying activities. Henry was glad he'd kept his distance from Vernon.

If Vernon didn't move out of his daisy chains pretty soon he was going to be headed for jail.

Henry felt queasy for the first time in decades. The Tough-waugh Slough project was risky. Things were happening so much more quickly than Henry had intended. The day of reckoning, the day when the B & T missed a payment or had to cut its rate wasn't far off. The regulators were starting to ask questions. And Clovis was starting to probe. But Henry had a long term purchaser on the string, a real live one in the language of the trade. But the sale would go a lot quicker if he could speed up Karen's decision to sell and consolidate the properties. 806 had something the Slough needed to make it really valuable.

Henry pocketed a few more of the old oyster shells and waded down toward the river exit where he knew the moon would just be coming up.

—— · **36** · ——

The heavy wood door shuddered as it fell back into the old brick archway. Sister Mary turned the ringbolt carefully to prevent any unwanted noise, heard the metal pieces lock together with considerable relief and then hurried noiselessly along the darkened street toward a bus stop. She'd just have to find another place to live for a while. That's all there was to it. A convent was no place for a pregnant lady to live. No place at all. The other nuns had no idea what was going on inside her body, or why her moods shifted unexpectedly. Some of them thought it was all a big spiritual thing, her face glowing and the spirit of the Lord coming on her and all, and they loved to get together with her to recite the Magnificat, or to pretend they were right there with Saint Elizabeth herself when the babe leapt in her womb. But Sister Mary had grown tired of the Magnificat. She knew that the babe, barely big enough now to make her belly swell, was not divine, no light to lighten the gentiles, no glory to his people Israel. When she thought of the baby at all, she saw the face of the boy called Ramone, the most determined, most desperate of the rapists, the one whose seed seemed endless, the only one who actually seemed to enjoy her pain and humiliation.

The nuns knew nothing about Sister Mary's true feelings, of course. There was no point in trying to explain to them what a rape was like. Most of them really were virgins. They'd joined the Order as girls and hardly seen a man for ten, in some cases thirty years, years spent in the convent, behind the high brick walls, closeted in communion with God.

They meant well. They hovered and clucked and tried to comfort her when the crying jags started. They talked politely about hormones and depression, but none of them saw Ramone kneeling in diabolic ecstasy over her thighs, revelling in her blood, savoring her despair. None of them had to feel the rapist's flesh growing inside their own bodies. And there was nothing she could say to make them understand how much she alternately wanted to destroy the baby and to keep it forever as her own. Best not to mention how thoughts of sweet abortion had crossed her mind, entered her dreams. Or how the thought of giving the baby up to an anonymous family for adoption made her skin crawl. Best to leave for awhile she thought again. Money was no object. And she could go back when the ordeal was over.

37

"I'm looking for a book," Clovis Tuckahoe, decked out in a black feathered muu muu that looked alternately green and purple in the florescent light, said to the grey haired clerk at the reference desk.

"Most people who come here are," the librarian said kindly.

"It's something my husband donated to the Library about six months ago," Clovis said showing the receipt dated and stamped by the Library of Congress. "He gave away this manuscript—I believe it must have been a diary of his entire life—shortly before he died." She daubed at her heavily made-up eyes with a peacock-patterned hanky.

"I'm afraid it wouldn't be in the card catalogue yet," the librarian said without interrupting her search for some quaint and curious megabyte of forgotten lore on a video monitor. "Even if the Library kept it, it takes about six months for the cataloguing service to catch up, at least six months."

"What do you mean 'if' the library kept it? I thought the library had to take everything."

"Not everything. The building would have sunk into the ground a hundred years ago if we'd kept everything."

"I thought it was law."

"A lot of people do, but the law never is quite what one thinks it is. There should be a Latin maxim to that effect, maybe there even is, but I'm not . . ."

"But the receipt . . . ?"

"Yes, a receipt. But that's all it is. Look, I'm really sorry, it'll be another six months until we know anything down here. There's a whole staff of people on the fifth floor who review donations and come to decisions about what to keep and what to discard."

"But . . . I had so hoped to read it myself . . ."

"And, say, aren't you Mrs. Tuckahoe of the Savings and Loan?"

"Yes, but . . ."

"You wouldn't remember me, but your husband was the dearest man, saved our house back in '55 when my first husband had leukemia. I probably didn't make a payment for a whole year, and he never once sent me even a nasty letter, let us get back on our feet, waited until I finished my masters and got this job. I never thanked him properly. He was a saint if ever there was . . ."

"Thank you so much. I can't tell you how many people have told me stories like this since he passed away."

"Everybody in Alexandria was so broken up by his passing. It was like he was older than the town, like he would live forever . . ."

"Yes . . . thank you . . ." Clovis withdrew her hand from the clerk's. "But the little Burgh & Tuckahoe isn't what it once was, I'm afraid. My brother-in-law has made it so big now one can't know the customers the way one used to."

"I'll be looking out for Mr. Tuckahoe's book though. And I'll give you a call."

"Thank you so much," Clovis said again. She didn't see it herself, but at the mention of the word Tuckahoe, a woman who she took for a cleaning lady over by the bank of elevators picked up her ears and came in her direction.

"I work on the fifth floor," the woman from the elevator said. "I couldn't help but overhear. And I'll be on the look out for your husband's book. You said Tuckahoe?"

"Yes. Tuckahoe. It's not a common name. But I'm not sure what he called the book."

"Just give me your address and 'phone number dearie and I'll be in touch."

Clovis did as the woman asked.

Granny Franny tucked the note in her purse and headed back to the twelfth floor to warn Aubrey that rival scholars were afoot, ready to stop at nothing, pretending even to have been married to the author of the *Toughwaugh Papyrus*.

— 38 —

"It's going numb in my left hand," Granny Franny said.

"Just that tumor thing again," Aubrey said without looking up from the *Toughwaugh Papyrus*.

"No," she said faintly, "this time its really numb, no feeling at all and getting number, going up my arm. This is it, Aubrey. I know it."

"This isn't it," he said severely. "You're always saying this is it and then it isn't it. I know you Granny. When it's it you won't know it."

"This is it," she said. "My face is growing numb."

"Let me read you some of this," he said. "It's the best part yet. And interrupt me if your condition gets any worse, okay?"

"Okay."

We watched Slow Beaver's body going round and round in the whirlpools below the falls. It was sort of sickening really, not what he had wanted at all, almost as if his journey of release from this world into the next had been suspended.

Dung-Crow decided it wouldn't be right for him to jump until Slow Beaver's body moved on, so we sat down on the boulders at the top of the cliff and watched. A long time passed. Bustards circled and watched the body floating and bloating and getting nibbled on by the minnows in the river. An otter swam up against the current and bit at Slow Beaver's hand, took off a few fingers. One of the bustards went for his eyes, but a carp chewing on his foot rolled him over and tipped the bustard in the drink. Slow Beaver's face had gone the color of the ploof mud further down river and Dung-Crow and I were both starting to cry when this shadow appeared over us and we looked up to see White-Owl-Knows-All. He was wrapped up in a shawl of hummingbird wings and pike scales we had never seen before and his face was painted blue. He said something banal—which is how he always talked even when he said the weirdest things—about how it sure was a sorry way to go.

"How come Slow Beaver doesn't float away," Dung-Crow asked and White-Owl-Knows-All said it was because he had put a spell on the whirlpool a long time ago to make it trap fish and corpses and other things he liked to eat.

"Then take the spell off," Dung-Crow said.

White-Owl-Knows-All waved an old carved stick and threw some powdered stuff at the water that drifted away in the breeze long before it got to the bottom. But Slow Beaver's body floated downstream. The bustards and the otters left. The carp swam away.

"My turn now," Dung-Crow said. He stood up to jump. He was stubborn. But White-Owl-Knows-All stopped him.

"Why jump?" he asked. "What's jumping going to do for you?"

Dung-Crow mumbled something about how honor and death couldn't come soon enough to suit him.

"Says who?" White-Owl-Knows-All asked.

Dung-Crow spat his contempt on the ground.

"And what honor is there in death?" White-Owl-Knows-All asked.

Dung-Crow said nothing and stared into the foam at the bottom of the falls. "I'd live forever if I could," he said, "just to get revenge on Big Au-gu-soon-toine Wa-shun-toine and his descendants forever."

White-Owl-Knows-All said he sort of knew how the young man felt and thought he could help, living forever being one of the spells he had learned on his last big trip up north in Iroquoisland.

"This is it, Aubrey. I know it now. My lips are numb and I can hardly talk."

"You're sure?" Aubrey asked, putting the manuscript aside reluctantly.

"Sure. And you've got to do what you promised. Promise me again."

"I promise. I've got the letter in my coat." He pulled a yellowed envelope out of his pocket and held it up for Granny Franny to see and touch with her one good hand.

"Promise me you'll mail it and I'll go a happy woman."

"I promise."

"Mine has not been an ordinary kind of life, you know."

"I know," Aubrey said, stealing a glance at the *Toughwaugh Papyrus*, wondering what happened next.

"You probably would've croaked if I hadn't rescued you," she said. "And there wouldn't have been a manuscript to make your career."

"You're the best thing that ever happened to me Granny."

Unable to speak any longer, Francis Appleby puckered her lips at Aubrey and then lay silent. Aubrey listened for a heartbeat in the silence of the twelfth floor. The silence was total. He removed his glasses and held a lens up to her nose. There was no mist.

Aubrey returned to the *Papyrus*.

You could make me live forever for revenge on Wa-shun-toine and his descendants?" Dung-Crow asked. White-Owl-Knows-All said "no big deal" and did it right then with some more of his powder that blew away into the wind so easily that it hardly seemed real. "You, Shining Kestrel of the Tuckahoe people and the Tuckahoe land," he said, or something like that as best I can remember now because it's been a long time and, frankly, I was in a state of heightened emotion and didn't think too clearly at the time, "will live forever, or until you have grandchildren, with power to sell the Wa-shun-toine land provided that you never live under a roof. You understand?" Dung-Crow said he did and then White-Owl-Knows-All put the same spell on me except he forgot the bit about never living under roof.

"Come," White-Owl-Knows-All said then, "let's celebrate with some body and blood." We said, "what body and blood?" And he said, "you know, body and blood like the white priests, the England Church fathers, do, with a little wine into blood and a little bread into body and a little he who eats of this flesh shall never hunger," which he said was a mistranslation from the Greek and really meant you would never die. He explained that the powder he'd thrown around was dried up communion host he'd stolen from the French Fathers. And then he put a towel out on a rock and made us eat some stale bread and drink some rot gut rum out of a gourd and then,

after a few swigs on the rum bottle which he said all priests had to do, he wandered back toward the Wa-shun-toine land to learn more of the way of the white Church of England priests, maybe even become one someday if they'd let him.

Night came and Dung-Crow wondered if he could even sleep in a wigwam or a bark lodge again. I said it didn't sound safe to me unless he wanted to break the spell, which he immediately started calling a curse. I got tired of listening to him whine, set up my lean to and went to sleep.

Aubrey read through his translation, checked a few words in his lexicon, and then turned his attention to Granny. She looked alright really. Her hands were folded across her chest. Her eyes had closed naturally. She could be asleep, he thought. She certainly looked comfortable enough where she was and there was plenty of room on the shelf. He took some back volumes of *The British Israelite* and saw that they fit neatly in front of the body. He arranged the books, spread them out, closed ranks here, made room there, and then looked at what he had done. It was perfect. Granny had disappeared. The books were in order. They wouldn't be bothered for years, decades, centuries even. Granny would be pleased. He went back to the manuscript, wondering who Dung-Crow really was and whether he had lived forever after all.

—— •39•——

"It's just that I'd never thought of it," Jenkin said, "never thought of it at all."

"But surely," the priest, an almost round man with an irregular bald pate and piggy eyes encased in folds of fat, said in a professional tone of comfort and confidence, "back when you were in college, you must have wondered what you would do if one of your girlfriends got 'in trouble,'—that's probably how young men of your generation said it—instead of pregnant, a word that even I didn't use regularly until the last sixty years or so."

"No. I didn't have intercourse with the girls I dated in college."

"No? Well, you must have known some boys who did.'

"They married the girls in question, I believe."

"Married them perhaps. But for how long? That's the question for those marriages. How long?" Father White, rector of St. Faiths Episcopal Church in North Alexandria laughed knowingly, as if he were looking for winks to share and ribs to nudge.

"Oh, as long as most I think. Divorce wasn't the option then that it has become. Life was, I think, somehow more serious. Do you know what I mean?"

"Oh, life? Serious? Well, I mean, nothing is more serious than life to the church." Father White squirmed on his red velvet chair and tried hard to anticipate the questions of this thin, intense, man.

"Would you say life is sacrosanct then?"

The priest choked. "That's not a word we use in the Episcopal church anymore," he said. "There are too many things that have to be considered. The life of the fetus and the autonomy of the mother have to balanced. The very meaning of being a person is to be an agent of action. To deny this in others is to deny their very humanity. Very important this autonomy. Very important."

"Life isn't sacrosanct?" Jenkin looked disappointed, confused. He had come to his local parish church hoping for some guidance in his first ever abortion rights case.

"Human life is good, now, I wouldn't deny that, but it isn't an absolute good. Well, maybe to the pacifist, but how many pacifists are there? I mean *real* pacifists?"

"But you can't say killing a fetus is an act of self defense."

"Well . . . it all gets back to the autonomy thing, you see. It's so important."

"I've never felt very autonomous. Or wanted to feel very autonomous."

"Now there are support groups here in St. Faiths for people who . . ."

"And what about the Bible? Doesn't that figure into how you approach the problem?"

"The Bible . . . well . . ."

"Wasn't there something in *Jeremiah* about being called to be a prophet when he was still in his mother's womb?"

"It could be, you know, there's so much there . . . but we have to consider reason and tradition along with scripture, you know. It's all part of our Anglican tradition. All three are important . . ."

"And God? Where does God figure in . . ."

"Well, it depends on what you mean, of course. God—immortal, invisible, God only wise, you know, that kind of thing—isn't quite on the cutting edge of our church now, I'm afraid. You must have been out of touch for quite a while with mainstream Episcopalianism to talk about God in such bold terms, as if there really were such a construct."

"There's not?"

"Well . . . not quite God in the sense of GOD THE FATHER, you know. We now think of God more as the sum total of all our uncertainties, the reification of our collective consciousness. It's easier for people to relate to."

"Oh."

"Well . . . is that really all you . . . ?"

"That God's not much help on my little abortion problem is it?"

"Autonomy. Think of all our God-given autonomy."

"Autonomy."

"Right."

"Well . . ."

Jenkin got up to go.

"We usually have a quick eucharist after these little one on one sessions. It's the way the church is going. Less God and more eucharist. I don't suppose you . . ."

"Sure. Love to. I was afraid you'd . . ."

"Oh, no, the eucharist is still the same. Jesus Christ the same yesterday, today and forever, you know."

"Right," Jenkin said and gladly knelt in the gloomy gothic church. The words were familiar. But the wine tasted strangely like cheap rum.

—— ·40 · ——

"You're sure she's your sister?" Aubrey asked. They certainly didn't look related, the one heavy set and pale, the other passed out on a camel-backed sofa, so thin, delicate and dark, her skirt pulled carelessly up around her thighs, her arms sprawled in heavy sleep.

"Same mother," the woman who had paid him the $500 said, "different fathers."

"And you?" Aubrey asked the man who hovered ingratiatingly.

"Her husband," the man said pointing to the heavy set woman.

Aubrey looked at the woman again. She didn't look married. She wore no ring. She lacked the proprietary air of her husband, and didn't, in fact, seem to know her way around the house very well. And, he noticed, she had a strange smell. Not at all like the smell of the well-scented, even ambrosial mansion she claimed as her own. There was something raw about her that clashed with the setting, something of the abattoir that had crept uninvited into the parlor. Aubrey couldn't stop himself from wondering—rude as it was even to raise such a question in the privacy of his own mind—how long it had been since she had washed properly.

"And you're sure she's asleep?" Aubrey asked, trying to focus on the job at hand.

"Drugs," the man said. "In her wine." He pointed to the remains of a Paul Prudhomme concoction of veal and oysters and creme de menthe parfait in the adjacent dining room. "She's out until morning. Trust me."

"How do I know she consented to this?"

"She signed this," the man said holding up a piece of paper.

Aubrey looked it over carefully. The signature "Lindsay Hayden" looked alright, but he couldn't tell whether it was real or not.

"I mean I don't want her accusing me of rape or anything."

"She won't," the woman said. "She wants you to do this. She picked you out from the line of men at the fertility clinic. She wants this to happen. Believe me. She just can't face letting a man do it to her, or going through the artificial insemination thing. She just can't face it. But it's the only way to have a kid."

"Well . . ."

"We paid $500 for this," Karen said. "I don't suppose you want to give the money back."

"No."

"Well. Staring at her's not going to get the job done is it?"

Aubrey looked the strange couple over once again, one so dapper in silk smoking jacket and the other in a grey dress he might have called hopsacking as a compliment. Their eagerness surprised him. The man, who had never introduced himself, kept a hand in the pocket of his jacket. As he moved the hand stayed in place over his crotch.

"I don't want anyone watching," Aubrey said defensively.

"Oh, no, we trust you," Karen said. "You can use the downstairs bedroom."

"Help me with her feet," Aubrey said to Max, picking up Lindsay's shoulders, but it was Karen who responded while Max watched. Karen lifted Lindsay easily, letting her skirt ride up above her waist, exposing pink underwear. Max's hand stayed in his pocket.

They stretched Lindsay out on a double bed. Karen turned on a small bedside ginger jar lamp. Max stripped Lindsay's pantyhose and stood back to admire her legs and mons veneris. He walked awkwardly from the room no longer trying to mask his full erection. He took Karen, who had been staring at

Lindsay's nakedness, by the hand and led her out. They closed the door silently.

"Are you sure about her temperature?" Karen asked Max after they had retreated to a back room overlooking the garden.

"Sure. It's perfect. If you could see inside, you'd see the ovum in place, a relaxed cervical opening and channels opening in the vaginal mucous. It's awesome, Karen, truly awesome how a woman's body opens up for conception."

"What day is it in her cycle?"

"Eight. She felt some *mittleschmertz* this afternoon. It's perfect. I never knew procreation was such a turn on."

"What are you doing?"

"Turning on the television."

"Why?"

"I had a camera put in behind the bedroom mirror. You didn't think I was going to let this guy impregnate Lindsay without watching, did you?"

"It's rape. How can you watch?"

"You can leave if you want."

Karen folded her arms across her chest in defiance, but she didn't leave.

The television flickered. Aubrey, black and white and somewhat fuzzy on the small television screen, opened Lindsay's legs, and, staring at her crotch, removed his own trousers.

"He's not even hard is he?" Karen said, the tone of her voice showing an ignorance and wonder Max had not expected. He stared at her, as if for the first time.

Aubrey rubbed his penis until it was hard and then knelt between Lindsay's thighs. He felt her briefly and then looked around the room, found a tube of KY jelly next to the lamp and anointed first Lindsay, then himself.

"Oh, God," Max said staring at the television and opening his robe.

"What are you doing?" Karen demanded rhetorically. Max exposed himself fully and assumed the lotus position. His eyes rolled upward, looking intently at the screen and beyond it. "It's a spiritual moment, Karen," he said. "Please."

Karen watched Aubrey try to work his penis into Lindsay.

Max moaned.

Karen stared at the screen. Aubrey was on top of Lindsay now, starting to move back and forth. She looked again at Max. His penis was longer now, redder, harder. She'd never seen anything quite like it, so intense and determined.

"It's, it's so . . . unusual," Karen said, unable to take her eyes off Max, "so unlike the rest of you . . . I wonder . . . I know it's not like me . . . but I've never . . ."

"Touch it," Max said.

" . . . just once. I've never . . ."

The effort took Aubrey longer than he had planned. The young woman was so beautiful, so frail, her sleep so complete. His purely business-like approach proved ineffective. He hated what he was doing. It didn't feel right. It was so strange. His erection began to slip. The act itself, so cold, so mechanical, was foreign to him. He couldn't go through with it. He withdrew from Lindsay, lay next to her, kissed her, hugged her until he felt he knew her better and then, excited again by the novelty of the situation, entered her, this time more easily. After a few minutes of gentle motion to let her body adjust to him, Aubrey began a quick friction that drained his testes rapidly and without much of the pleasure he knew he would feel guilty about later. He dressed himself and then put Lindsay's feet back in her pantyhose. They were awkward things, bunching where they shouldn't, knotting and twisting in the most unlikely places. Aubrey tried to get the garment back up but it stuck at her knees. In frustration, he left the pantyhose for Lindsay's friends.

Aubrey looked around the house. It seemed deserted. He started to leave, but he wanted to let the strange couple know he had earned his money. He wandered through the living room, into the kitchen toward the back of the house. There were halls and alcoves, loggias and curtained passageways. He couldn't tell where the couple could be. Then he heard something, first breathing, then panting and feral grunts from the very back of the house. He walked through a dark corridor until he could see a light. The strange couple, sources of the barnyard racket, were too busy with each other to notice him. The heavy set woman was on top of the man called Max, whose pale rump was pumping like a steam engine, his thin, dry skin crinkling like parchment as it thrust back and forth. And he was coming, groaning like he hadn't come in a long, long time. The woman raised her head to the ceiling, eyes closed, and bellowed. The man sighed, went rigid, collapsed. The woman fell off him. White semen lay in gobs on her heavy thighs. Another wad of spunk shot belatedly out of the man's still potent phallus. He moaned again, rolled over on the woman and started over.

Aubrey let himself out, his mind turning quickly from the perversions of the rich to the wonders of the *Toughwaugh Papyrus* and the pleasure of reading the next chapter to Granny Franny, who now that she was dead and encrypted behind the *The British Israelite*, seemed to Aubrey to be more interested in the narrative than ever.

——·**41**·——

Back on the twelfth floor of the closed stacks, Aubrey counted his treasure again. The $500 for the act he intended never to mention to anyone was enough to keep him in writing paper and his other few necessities for three months, even six, he thought, if he stretched it. There was so much for free in the Library. People threw away perfectly good ball point pins, note pads, bond paper, yellow legal pads. It meant that his transcription of the *Toughwaugh Papyrus* was a rag tag affair. The sheets were of different sizes, different colors, different types and grades of paper and he had bound them all together with string so they looked more like a bundle of scrap rather than a

serious work of scholarship, but Aubrey liked the idea of cam-
ouflaging his work, especially since Granny Franny had told
him about the spy in the library, the big woman with the black
dress and the plaster of paris face.

He was sure he had seen another woman looking at him oddly, someone who looked familiar, but whom he couldn't really
place. She too had been large, perhaps even pregnant. She had
hallooed at him from across Constitution Avenue. She seemed
to be saying something about 'manuscript' or 'dissertation' or
something similar, and Aubrey had slipped into a side door of
the Madison Building to escape. He knew tunnels and passages
that not even the janitors knew and could appear and disappear
where and when he wanted now. There was reason to be afraid.
The *Toughwaugh Papyrus* was more important than even he
had imagined. It was the secret. The big secret to just about
everything. Nothing would ever be the same after he published
it. He thanked Granny again for making it his life's work.

He checked her face behind Volume 36 of *The British Israelite* again. The mummification process of the Library's naturally
dry, mold-free environment was working well. She'd gone puffy
and smelled like a bad pile of raw hamburger for a week or two,
but that was over now. When she dried out the enteric bacteria
had to give up, go into dormancy, float off in search of another
body to inhabit. She looked a little thinner than she had in life,
but there hadn't been much flesh on her bones to lose. Her col-
or was no worse. And her expression had remained kindly, concerned, even grateful. Aubrey replaced the book, careful not to
disturb the dust, and continued with his work of translation.

*I camped with Dung-Crow by the Great Falls for several
weeks, feeding on rock fish that got trapped in the eddys and
small birds that we caught in nets made of vines and creepers. Dung-Crow slept outside, afraid of the curse, sure that
even one night in my simple lean-to would finish him off. I
laughed at his petty superstition at first, but then the implications of the spell we had requested and received started to*

come home to me too. What, I thought, could it really mean to live forever as long as you don't have any grandchildren? It sounded simple, but at the same time complex. Having children was one of the things Tuckahoe tribesmen were proud of. The more children you had, the more oysters you could gather, the more deer you could hunt, the more Quohee skulls you could bash and the more Quohee maidens you could ravish, not to mention what a nice little band of brothers and sons could steal from the White Men downriver. It meant we couldn't live forever to get our revenge on the Whites unless we gave up the best parts of our native way of life. What had seemed like such a good idea at the time gradually started to look sort of gloomy and we took to drinking up the bottle of the God blood that old White-Owl-Knows-All left behind to cheer us up.

"No maidens for you and me," I said to Dung-Crow. And he looked at me stupidly, as if to say 'how can a man live without taking maidens and putting his seed in their bellies.' But I explained it all to him and how we had to just give them up. Dung Crow said that was impossible. A man could not live without the pleasure of maidens to assuage his indignities at the hands of the White Devils. I agreed that it sounded like a bad idea, but it was the bargain we had made.

'Bargain with the devil,' Dung-Crow said. 'Have you ever noticed the skin on that old White-Owl-Knows-All? Its grey, not brown or red like real people's skin, like he doesn't really have blood in his veins, like he wouldn't bleed if you cut him. And how old is he? And has he ever had any wives or children? And does he sleep at night or turn into a bat and fly around in the trees eating mosquitoes and beetles?'

I didn't know the answer to these questions, of course, and I wished that Dung-Crow, who had grown strangely articulate and confident as he drank the God Blood, had raised these questions before we had taken the pledge.

'There's a way,' he said, waking me up in the middle of the night once after it had rained and the roar of the water

coming down the Great Potowatomack Falls was too loud for
him to sleep anymore. 'There's a way we can still put our
roots into the squaw's bellies for our own pleasure.'

'Have you ever done that?' I asked incredulously. I thought
maybe he had done it with one of our cousins, little Possum
Tail, who seemed precocious in that regard and had been
married off early and obviously pregnant to a partially blind
old Tuckahoe down in the low country who lost his wife to
snakebite. 'Just with my hand,' he said, showing me what he
meant, 'but Slow Beaver said the hand is nothing compared
to the pleasure inside a Squaw's belly. I've dreamed about it
for years. Possum Tail once agreed to let me do it. We met behind the thousand year oak and she lifted up her skirt. I was
just getting it in when a bear scared her away. She left to get
married to the thin legged blind man after that. But it was
wonderful and I can't give it up. I can't.'

'Then die like everybody else,' I said. 'Die, if that's what you
want.'

'I'll do both,' he said. 'There're ways. There're herbs and
roots and juices from the big trees that kill the babies while
they're still inside the squaw, even before the squaw knows
for sure that the baby is there."

'But what about the baby's ghost,' I asked. 'Aren't you afraid
of the spirits?'

'Where were the spirits when we needed them against Big
Au-gu-soon-toine Wa-shun-toine,' he demanded to know. And
I had no answer, the ways of the spirits to Tuckahoe being
hard to justify sometimes.

'I'll find an old woman to teach me these things,' Dung
Crow said.

The next day, as we were drying our buckskins out on a
bush and roasting a box turtle, we heard a White Man on a
horse riding through the brush, beating around like he was
lost. It was Big Au-gu-soon-toine again, with his sons L'ence
and Ge'ge this time. We thought for a minute that it was our
chance for revenge, but then we thought better of it, because

the White Devils never travelled alone and if the others caught us bashing them up and throwing their brains over the falls then it would go badly for us and the promise of eternal life didn't, we concluded, necessarily protect us from bullets and knives made of steel.

Au-gu-soon-toine saw us hiding by the river and called out to us for direction back to the big lodge he called Mount Vernon. We couldn't believe he didn't know he just had to follow the river, but these White Men were odd about direction, looking at the stars when they needed to look at the earth. So we pointed out the way as if it weren't the most obvious thing in the world, something squaws and littlies would have been ashamed not to know. He then asked us if we knew the country thereabouts and we said we did. He had evidently forgotten that he had killed all our people and taken the land from us by deception and under false pretenses and duress in a way that was entirely voidable under his own law, which I admittedly didn't understand for another hundred years or so.

But, getting back to the story, Dung-Crow volunteered that he knew all the Tuckahoe land from the salt sea to the Blue Ridge, and Big Au-gu-soon-toine asked him to be a guide for some Englishmen—investors he called them—who wanted maybe to build a canal to the Pacific Ocean, a place Dung-Crow immediately said he had visited only a week or so ago.

Big Au-gu-soon-toine was really impressed and asked what Dung Crow's name was. I knew he wouldn't say 'Dung-Crow,' because it was only a little boy family nick name, but I was shocked when he said his name was Henry instead of Shining Kestrel, Henry Tuckahoe, he said, the last of the real Tuckahoe people and that he would sell the White Man's land for him forever, just like old White-Owl-Knows-All had promised, provided he got a sales commission. Au-gu-soon-toine said he was sure something along a commission basis could be worked out if Henry could really get any money from the Englishmen for all this worthless forest land that Au-gu-soon-toine was sorry now he had bought.

Henry, as he had now become, went off to the Wa-shun-toine camp where he has stayed from that time until this time, selling the land many times over to many people for commissions, sometimes making a lot of the White Man's money and sometimes not too much for long stretches of time that upset the White Man but not Henry because he can't live in a lodge and he eats mostly what he catches in the Potowatomack, the rich White Man's food not agreeing too well with him.

I wasn't sure how I fit into this picture of slow revenge, so I wandered west, over the mountains and into the Great Valley of the Shenandoah where I met a simple man of the Moravian religion named Schulerburgh, who taught me what I know about writing. I lived there until Old Herr FearsGod Schulerburgh died and left me enough money to start a small bank. But that is another story for another chapter.

The page was dated June 17, 1808. Aubrey put his face down on the table, turned his study light off and went to sleep.

——·**42**·——

Henry put his full weight of over 300 pounds against the crowbar and felt the casket lid open. Weight was such a useful thing. He had seen it come in and go out of fashion many times during his long years. It was decidedly out of fashion now, but still, it was so much more practical than mere physical strength. It was so easy to use. One little step up onto the crowbar was better than all the muscles in his arms and back combined, muscles that needed a rest after digging the 84 cubic feet of clay, heaping it carefully on a canvas tarp so the brown and frosty grass would show no signs of an exhumation.

He pried the lid open. It wasn't much of a lock really, considering what Clovis had paid for it and all the things the salesman at the funeral home had said about waterproof, burglarproof, airtight and hermetically sealed.

Schuler didn't look any worse than he had at the funeral. Henry loosened his brother's tie, opened his collar and then wiped the make-up from his cold stiff face with a large cotton handkerchief. Henry then checked Schuler's hair and nails. He'd heard rumors about these things growing after death, but he didn't know whether there was any truth to them. There wasn't.

Henry ran his hand into Schuler's coat pocket and retrieved a small envelope. He wasn't surprised. Schuler had promised some final note and both the suit in which he was to be buried and the exhumation itself were matters on which they had agreed several weeks before Schuler died.

Henry blew on his cold hands, slipped a ten foot length of hemp rope around Schuler's neck, braced himself at the foot of the grave and then pulled his rigid brother upright. He then got beneath the body and pushed it up onto the frozen ground, threaded the rope under the armpits, and pulled it downhill to his Jaguar parked on Timber Branch. Schuler was too big for the boot, too stiff to sit in the back. Henry folded the passenger seat down and put Schuler in a reclining position. He thought of covering the face, but decided a fully covered body would draw more attention than one that looked merely worn or, at worst, a little done in after a long ride. He then trudged back up the hill, refilled the grave, rolled up the tarp and then drove westward out of Alexandria, around the Beltway, onto Interstate 66 exiting at Culpeper, through Sperryville, following the signs to Luray Caverns, and then onto the Blue Ridge Parkway. He stopped at the Forest Service turn off for Stony Man Mountain, checked to be sure the parking lot was deserted, and began dragging Schuler toward the summit. It was only a mile and a half according to the conveniently located signs, over easily graded trails. Tourists were encouraged to wear appropriate shoes and clothing. Another sign warned of bears.

The summit was a rocky outcrop overlooking the Valley of Virginia. From certain angles, the rocks appeared, to an active imagination, like a human profile. Henry lay Schuler out in a recess above the stony man's left ear and retreated behind a blackberry thicket. Crows and buzzards circled, hovered, dipped, and circled again in the early morning light. Some landed at Schuler's feet, pecked at his shoes, took small bites of his clothing, and then flew away. Word seemed to get around quickly. All the birds left. Henry had been afraid of that. The odor of formalin was too much. It probably would have poisoned the birds anyway, and that wasn't what he wanted. He was doing the birds a favor, inviting them to play their part in a Tuckahoe ritual that hadn't been performed for 300 years. But if they'd forgotten their role, or simply couldn't stomach embalmed flesh, he bore them no ill will. He had another plan.

Henry found some rocks to serve as andirons, cut a pile of dry blackberry branches, broke several dead saplings at mid trunk and piled them under and around Schuler. He poured a quart of kerosine over Schuler and the wood, muttered an incantation in the ancient Tuckahoe prayer language, and ignited the pyre with a match. Schuler was pretty dry and the fire burned well. The clothes went first, then the skin. He watched the fire climb higher into the rising sun and saw Schuler's skull appear where his hair had been, then the bony orbits that had held his eyes. His lips burned away. The teeth turned black. The soft parts crinkled, burned, exploded in little gasps of white light. It took about an hour. Henry ached to see his brother's form disappear, but, at the same time, he felt Schuler's presence around him and sensed Schuler's gratitude at being released at last from his body.

There were things Henry wanted to discuss with Schuler, last minute advice he needed that no one else could give him. Vernon's Rock of Ages was in big trouble. Some of his big daisy chain deals had fallen through. His stock had dropped right off the board. He couldn't pay his depositors. They were making claims on the Federal Deposit Insurance Corporation. The Government didn't have the money to pay. Vernon's corporate jet and vacation palace in the Bahamas had been attached. The FBI was involved. There was talk of a Congressional inquiry. Savings and Loans all over the country were getting bad publicity. The bank examiners were looking more closely at the B & T books, some were questioning the appraisals on the Slough. Clovis was acting suspicious. Henry had doubts about where it was all going, about whether yet another banking scandal was the kind of revenge he really wanted on the White Man, especially now that there was nobody he could talk to, no audience to appreciate his secret manipulation of markets and laws to ruin the people who had stolen his family's land. He had to find a real purchaser for the Slough soon, or he'd be joining Vernon in one of the Federal Farms for white collar crooks. It was not a pleasant thought.

As the last flames collapsed over Schuler's ashes, Henry remembered the letter. He took it out of his pocket, opened the envelope and read.

I should have done this years ago. You won't believe this, I know, but the best years of my life were the last ones, after Daphne was born and I had decided to leave her alone, to let her marry and have her own children if that's what she wanted. It was the best thing I ever did. If a good woman will ever take you, Henry, you should do the same.

As you may know, I kept a diary. I left it to the Library of Congress. I doubt anybody will ever read it, but I thought you should know.

See you later. And thanks for letting me out of the box. Clovis just didn't understand.

Henry put the letter in the dying embers, raked Schuler's bones together, crushed them between two stones and threw the powder into the wind.

·43·

"So this is your office?" Esther Anne asked, awestruck by the high ceilings, the mahogany furniture, the piles of briefs, the leather covered volumes of reported decisions, the aura of importance that permeated the marble walls.

"Chamber really," Jenkin prompted. "Judges offices have been called chambers since, oh, since the time of William the Conqueror, I guess." Jenkin looked embarrassed by her presence, but it had been his idea after all. She had followed up on the cracks in his own dining room ceiling so effectively and reminded him with such touching delicacy of his tentative invitation, that it had been the only thing, the only chivalrous thing that he could do. And this way, having her shown in so late, nearly midnight in fact, her visit wouldn't detract from his work schedule or come to the notice of his generally discrete, but callow and sometimes imprudent, law clerks.

"Senator Potter used to say being on the Supreme Court was the best job in town. He knew all the Justices when he was alive," Esther Anne beamed, running her eyes over the volumes open on Jenkin's desk.

The remark caused Jason, who had been sound asleep, if that's really the right word for the half waking, half sleeping, always dreaming state into which he had lapsed, to rouse himself out of Esther Anne's handbag and take a look around the room. He didn't recall the remark, and writing legal opinions had always struck him as too much like real work compared to what he did on the Hill. But he trusted Esther Anne. If she said he'd said it then he probably had. His thoughts turned quickly to Jenkin Carroway. Something was fishy about this man, and it was more than the natural suspicion of the heartlander for the Yankee that came so naturally to the South Kanaska populist.

"Well, we don't have to be re-elected. That's probably what he was thinking about."

"You probably don't have constituents looking over your shoulder at your private life either, do you?"

"Well, the press gets interested in us from time to time, but I'd hardly call them a constituency."

"Exactly. I could tell you some things Senator Potter used to say about the Washington Press Corps that would singe your New England ears!" Jason fled back into the handbag, covering his ears, hoping that she wouldn't. He hated hearing about his past now. Nothing that had happened, nothing that he had ever done, or said, or been, seemed entirely real. The happiest days were when he forgot even his name in life. He couldn't bear the details anymore.

"I'm sure he did," Jenkin said, trying to move Esther Anne away from his desk.

"But what's this?" Esther Anne asked, uncovering a manuscript beneath an 1897 volume of the Supreme Court Reports in the center of Jenkin's desk. She read: "Her fingers played with the curls that lapped like soft waves across the fine sandy beach of his shoulder. Olwyn hadn't been reared to be bold with men, but this was no ordinary man. The years in the crusades, the years of piety and slaughter, the brutal abduction of his lovely wife Isolde by Viking Pirates, the uncertainty of Isolde's survival that kept him from remarrying, had crushed, changed, transfigured him into priest, saint, and still, before all, a man of such irresistible force that, she knew as surely as the eagles soared over the east face of Tryffn, given even the slightest encouragement, he would take her and cling to her with a power that would shame the heavens into blessing their union."

"Oh, Jenkin," Esther Anne said. "That's so beautiful. I had no idea that you could write anything like that. It never occurred to me that words of such . . . such . . . potency, could come from, from, a man like . . . well . . . you know what I mean . . ." Esther Anne blushed.

" . . . you mean from a Supreme Court Justice," Jenkin said. He tried to slip the manuscript from under her hand but he only succeeded in drawing her hand into his and pulling their chests together.

"Olwyn's heart skipped a beat," Esther Anne read on, turning the page with Jenkin's help, "as she sensed his body respond to hers. She had sensed it as soon as he entered the room in the West Tower above the lake, the room with the evening breeze, where she liked to read as the sun went down. 'Excuse me,' he said. 'I didn't know I was disturbing you.' She turned quickly toward him. The setting sun caught her profile, highlighted her strong features, the curve of her full lips, the outlines of her figure, the topaz sparkle of her eyes. 'You're not disturbing me,' she said. 'I came to return a book,' he said, refusing to meet her eyes even though she could tell from the way he held his hand above his robe that his love was too strong to be denied. 'I didn't know you read Horace,' she said taking the book of Odes from his hand, opening and reading" . . . but I can't read this Jenkin, could you?

"Of course, Jenkin said: *quis multa gracilis te puer in rosa perfusus liquidis urget odoribus, grato, Pyrrha, sub antro? cui flauam religas comam, simplex munditiis?*"

"But what does it mean?" Esther Anne asked.

"There's a translation here in the text: 'What slim boy, Pyrra, drenched in liquid scents presses you in an abundance of roses under some pleasing grotto? For whom are you binding back your blonde hair in simple elegance?'

"Tell me then, Anheld," Esther Anne read on, "have you not noticed for whom I have been binding back my hair in simple elegance?"

'Anhalt stuttered and turned away," Jenkin read. "He was afraid to answer Onwyn's question."

"It was too much for Onwyn,' Esther Anne read. "Where will my slim boy drenched in liquid scents be when all our men are gone to war? And who will press me in an abundance of roses under some pleasing grotto?"

Jenkin read the next paragraph: 'Anheld trembled, wrestling against duty and desire. 'But my wife,' he cried. 'I am a married man. I cannot undo you, Onwyn, for I love you too tenderly . . . '

'Then,' Esther Anne read, 'I undo myself for you, my Lord, and give you all.'

"Onwyn pulled the golden cord that held her scarlet robe in place," Jenkin read, "and stood proud and confident in the last rays of the setting sun as perfect as God had made her. Anheld came to her. And they were one."

"It's Veronica. I know it's Veronica. A new Veronica Holloway," Esther Anne moaned, putting an arm around Jenkin's waist.

"Yes," Jenkin said. "It's called 'Maid of the Hibernian Sunset.'"
"And you wrote it, didn't you Jenkin?"
"I'm writing it. Yes." His voice quivered. He was strangely overcome by passion.
"And you are Veronica Holloway, aren't you Jenkin?"
"Yes. It's a pen name." Not even his agent knew his real identity. He rarely admitted it even to himself. He wasn't sure why he had told Esther Anne. He hardly knew her after all. Yet . . . Yet . . . there were as he had always known, but always confined to his fiction, passions inside him that one simply could not control. He took Esther Anne in his arms, kissed her, felt his hands cup her breasts as if they were some one else's hands and then made love to her on the leather couch by the window that overlooked the capitol dome, the Mall, the Washington Monument, Arlington Cemetery, the hills of Virginia, the Southern Cross and all eternity.

Jason Potter, disturbed by the commotion when Esther Anne dropped her purse, fled to the ceiling and hid behind a light fixture. When he was sure of what was happening on the couch, he was suffused by an ineffable pleasure that made the room glow pink, and he realized for the first time what it was that would make Esther Anne happy, that would undo the terrible thing he had done in taking up her time with his impure passions and low concerns. He felt a purpose and saw opportunities that might still make his haunting of the world worthwhile.

Jenkin drove Esther Anne out of the Supreme Court parking garage at four in the morning. The lowering of the door awakened a short doughty man in a ten year old mustang who had parked, and slept, on the far side of 2d Street for months to watch Justice Carroway. He had never seen anything to report to his boss. Until now. As he drove discreetly behind Jenkin's Volvo sedan, he scribbled in his log, and checked his face book of Supreme Court employees. He had seen the Justice with a woman. That was for sure. And not just a woman. A looker! And how! A looker that sat over on his side of the car and put her arm around him! And she didn't seem to be a secretary or a law clerk.

When they stopped at Jenkin's house, went in and turned out the lights, the man parked, ran around the corner toward a 'phone booth. As he ran, a plastic shopping bag blew against his ankle. He couldn't feel any wind. He stopped to remove it. He ran on. The bag blew back, still without the aid of any wind, got under the sole of his shoe and tripped him. He fell forward, skinning the palms of his hands. He got up, batted the bag away from his eyes, and made it at last to the 'phone booth. The bag had jammed in the door. He pulled. It wouldn't move. He tugged at it and ripped the plastic. He got inside the booth and shut the door. The bag came back to life and, shreds and all, threw itself again and again against the glass. He dialed his employer. She was delighted with the news. As soon as he told her, the bag went away, into the middle of the street and then back to the Justice's house. It was weird, but it was a weird world. He thought about an article for *The National Enquirer*. It was the private detective's dream. His night was complete. If he got a picture of the Justice and the broad coming out together in the morning he got a $5000 bonus!

Jason Potter slipped from what was left of the plastic bag under the door of Jenkin Carroway's house. It wasn't hard to find them. They were at it again. Upstairs. Sounds that he had never heard coming from Esther Anne made him forget his defeat in the street and the peril that the telephone call created for the woman he still loved. He found the bed, occupied a warm spot, let himself be lulled by the steady rhythm, and went to sleep.

——·44·——

Mary Scroggins lay on the sagging mattress of an iron frame bed in a mildewed motel too close for safety to the twelve lanes of traffic and the high ultra violet energy of the Route 1 Strip south of Alexandria, a road that had once been called the Richmond Highway but had now lost even that small degree of distinction. Route 1 never stopped, never darkened, never slowed. It was people and commerce, goods and services, cash and carry twenty-four hours a day, seven days a week and pushing for the eight day week, the forty hour day. The General Lee Motel reflected its surroundings as a place built in the 'fifties that had lived too long. Rooms built for families on the tour of the nation's capitol were now ready for occupancy by the hour. Mary's room was poorly heated, poorly ventilated, not very private, uncared for, used to short term tenants, accustomed to illicit love, a place of promises never kept. Yet, she liked it. Nobody knew her. Nobody cared. Nobody questioned her secret thoughts. Darkness. Privacy. Refuge.

She lay on the sagging bed with her hands folded across her swelling abdomen. The blood had long since drained from her hands, yet she couldn't move them. She had a cold. Her nose was stopped up and she breathed through her mouth. There was a nose spray on the bedside table. She wasn't to use it because of the baby. Birth defects. The doctors had laughed. It was easy for them. They didn't have to breathe through their mouths for nine months.

Something was swimming through her abdomen. It was remote at first. She tried to pretend it was wind, an unwelcome but natural product of digestion, yet she knew that none of the ordinary bodily discharges would free her of this twisting squirming sensation, this worm beneath the skin. She tried to picture it as God with the face of God, with the golden features, the innocence, the purity. But the faces that came to mind were all wrong. Faces of salamanders and toads, faces of serpents and lizards, faces of devils, wolves, insects, sharks, faces of Ramone and his gang of jolly boys out for a good time, stabbing, hurting, laughing, planting their seed where it wasn't welcome, making things grow that were meant to die. It was wrong. Ramone's violence had upset the natural order violated her virginity, desecrated her marriage to Christ. Nothing conceived of that act could rise any higher than the act itself. The rape was evil and the thing conceived of rape was evil.

She felt the thing swimming again in her middle and saw in her mind's eye the cruising shark, the malignant hunger, the shredding teeth, the restlessness, the gills panting, panting, never stopping, looking for blood, her blood, new blood, future blood. She rolled over and blew her nose, eyed the nose spray and thought that if she could be sure the spray would rid her of the thing then she would do it, pretend to the doctors, to her mother superior, to her conscience, that it had not been intended, that she hadn't known the consequences. But, with her luck, the nose spray wouldn't have put an end to anything. It would make the thing more deformed than ever, cut its already small intelligence quotient in half, warp its already twisted personality.

And then the thought hit her. Deformity. It was the only reason for abortion that she'd ever had any sympathy with. She'd never accepted it as morally justifiable, of course, and it was still a mortal sin, but still, practically speaking, it provided some justification. But, of course, you had to know ahead of time. There was a test. Amniocentesis. There was no problem in having the test. If the thing was kin to who she thought, then something was bound to show up and she could then decide what to do about it. If not . . . well, if not, she'd just have to decide what to do, that was all. She'd just have to make up her own mind. The faint glimmer of an option seemed to open Sister Mary's sinuses. She called her obstetrician and made an appointment. She sat up, drank a hot lemonade, and turned on "General Hospital." There was a lot to be said for hanging around a television in the afternoons. And the idea of a choice, not big, not very probable, still there, put her back in charge. She felt thankful, started to offer up a little prayer and, then, at the last moment, stopped short.

——·**45**·——

The envelope Granny Franny handed Aubrey shortly before she died contained a letter to be delivered to an address in one of the Capitol's Maryland suburbs and a stock certificate made over to him. He was to sell it when the time was ripe, give half the proceeds to the recipient of the letter and keep the other half himself. Granny left no instructions about who the other beneficiary was. If the beneficiary didn't contact Aubrey within a year he was to keep the money himself, get the *Papyrus* published, do some traveling, have some fun. Aubrey posted the letter as directed and then checked the value of the stock in the *Wall Street Journal*. It was a mutual fund. A hot one. "The Savings Fund" it was called. It invested in shares of all the high flying Savings & Loans, the fast ones like the Rock of Ages down in Dallas that were driving the economic boom. As the stock went up and up day after day, he took a certain pride in Granny's perspicacity. The certificate for five hundred shares hadn't cost her more than a few hundred dollars when it was first issued. Now it was worth $75,000 and growing all the time even though some Savings & Loans were failing and their officers were going to jail penniless. Aubrey was happy for Granny and her beneficiary. He was happy for himself. He used the stock certificate as a book mark in the *Toughwaugh Papyrus*.

Aubrey dreamed daily of the beneficiary's appearance. In his own imagination he turned the recipient into a daughter of etherial beauty and deep convictions about the origins of the Tuckahoe Tribe who would appreciate his work. He would take her to Franny's final resting place. The daughter would be so grateful. She would see the beauty of the twelfth floor. She would love the manuscript as her mother did. She would take up caring for him the way Franny had. They would marry each other in silent prayer with the lights out. His life would be complete.

Aubrey turned on the light and started another chapter:

Johannes FurchteGott Schulerburgh was not like any white man I had heard about before. He didn't want a lot of land he couldn't use. He wasn't interested in tobacco as a cash crop. In fact, he didn't use tobacco at all, considered it a vile, nasty, unhealthy tool of Satan. And he had little use for cash, preferring to raise his own vegetables and kill only what little meat he needed to keep him through the winters. His wife had died in his old country and he lived all alone. He had been a soldier once in the army of the Great King of Prussia, but then he saw Jesus face to face one day on the battlefield, picking up the dead, caring for the dying and he gave up the soldier's life to seek solitude and communion through study. He sometimes called himself a monk, sometimes a recluse, sometimes a hermit, sometimes a desert anchorite. I never knew exactly what he meant by these words because the tradition was unknown to my people at the time. Alone wasn't where we sought the Great Spirit at all, really, our theology, as much as our system of beliefs could be called a theology, pointed to God in the life of the tribe, and the children of the tribe, in the life of the fish and the oysters and the water and the trees, rather than in something that a man on his own was likely to find by renouncing all society and commerce. But Herr Schulerburgh's ways were his own and I came to respect them, because he was kind to me, thinking, as he told me, that the Indians, as he liked to call us for no reason I could ever understand, were innocents not knowing good from evil, children of the Garden, models of prelapsarian virtue. I tried hard not to disillusion Herr Schulerburgh. I made up stories about our simple lives and our good and kindly ways. But then, one day, after he told me that I was his best friend on earth and the closest one to Jesus, and that I was to have something from his estate when he died, I had to tell him the truth about my hatred for the Washun-toine tribe of White Men and the curse I had accepted from White-Owl-Knows-All. He listened silently and then got down on his knees for the longest time, until I thought he had

*gone dead, and then he told me I needed the Gospel after all
and that I would have to learn to read.*

*Every day, sometimes for hours and hours without a
break, Herr Schulerburgh sat alone reading his book. I had
seen men of the Wash-un-toine tribe read their little pages—notes or directions or deeds probably—but never whole
books. Herr Schulerburgh said the English weren't very
studious people, good horsemen, but not good thinkers. I
told him I liked the Germans in Quoheeland better than the
English in Tuckahoeland because they hadn't cheated my
people out of their right to live by the great Potowatomack
waters. He frowned and asked if I knew what the Germans
had done to the Quohee. I told him that nothing was too bad
for the Quohee because the Quohee were cannibals. But he
told me I was wrong. He said that the Quohee were poor
gentle people who swore that the Tuckahoe were cannibals
and even ate their own children. He told me that he had
paid a fair price for his land and that he still let the Quohee
hunt there as long as they didn't step on his squash vines
or steal his goats. Later, I saw that he was right about the
Quohee and I started to feel sorry for them and guilty that
I, along with Shining Kestrel, had spread such evil gossip
about them for so long.*

*Herr Schulerburgh told me that his Book held all the secrets
about God and life and how I could be saved from my fool-
ish bargain with White-Owl-Knows-All. I asked him to teach
me how to read it. He did. He taught me the Greek of the New
Testament and he taught me German so I could read the ser-
mons of Martin Luther. I learned them both well, and later,
when I learned English, and realized that nobody in America
spoke the koine Greek or used the Gothic Alphabet, I decided
to write my diary in this special code: Greek words in the
Gothic script. It's not hard for a real scholar, but it would deter the casual reader or the fainthearted. And, since the truths
I disclose here are not for the common mind, I wanted to dis-
courage the former and intimidate the latter.*

Herr Schulerburgh lived a long time to be full of years and taught me well to read and to keep my own council. The war between the Wa-shun-toine tribe and the British came and went but left us alone in peace with Herr Schulerburgh nursing the wounded of both sides and preaching a peace that nobody wanted to hear. I lived with him for thirty years. As he grew frail with years he told me he was growing closer and closer to God, but I had my doubts and every time he made me pray for the curse of White-Owl-Knows-All to be lifted, I crossed my fingers or just put a note of true insincerity in my voice to let the Lord know I wasn't serious. But during all those years when Herr Schulerburgh was growing older and turning into the Godhead and I was getting thick-skinned with immortality, I couldn't quite face my brother Shining Kestrel who had changed his name to Henry Tuckahoe. I hoped that maybe he had broken the curse, married, bred, become a happy grandfather and been gathered to his ancestors. But I was wrong. He lived even as I did with the old revenge festering.

When Herr FearsGod Schulerburgh died he left me his land and his money and told me to use them to build the new land, to lend the money out at fair rates. He taught me that a modest amount of capital honestly managed will bless both lender and borrower and quoted Martin Luther to that effect. He was right, but he did not foresee how I could twist that kindly platitude into the revenge I longed for, or how Henry and I would conspire to combine our talents to the discomfort of our enemies and our enemies descendants.

So, Breaker of the Code and Reader of Greek in the Old Gothic Script, read on if you will, and learn of the great financial panics and scandals of American history and marvel that they were all acts of revenge by the brothers Tuckahoe on the people of the Wa-shun-toine tribe, may they be confounded for ever, acts of justice by Young Henry and Old Schuler Tuckahoe, for I took part of the name of my patron and mentor for myself and gave the other half to my company because I loved him so, may he forgive me for turning good into evil. God rest him in peace and light shine upon him and AMEN forever until the world is set right again and the Tuckahoe return to the waters that the Lord God gave them before anybody else was there.

—·46·—

Aubrey showered in a janitor's closet on the 17th floor of the stacks. It wasn't really a shower, but there was a large wash tub in the corner that he could stand in, and he had scavenged a short length of hose that made washing his long hair easier. He hadn't cut his hair, shaved, or trimmed his beard since he slipped out of Lacy's bed into the night, but he no longer remembered that event or connected himself in any significant way with the memories of life before Washington. He hadn't quite forgotten himself as a clean shaven, well groomed young teaching assistant in Charlottesville, but so much had been erased between the memory and the present that he more and more frequently refused or failed to connect the two as bearing any relationship to each other at all. His life was so simple now, so pure. There was the *Toughwaugh Papyrus*. There was Granny Franny's place behind the *The British Israelite*. There was the hairy figure he saw reflected occasionally in the library's marble surfaces. There were the dark halls he prowled for exercise in the night when the casual readers and professional scholars had gone for the day, places the night watchmen ignored, dark places he knew by heart and by touch and which he loved as he had loved only his boyhood home in Richmond and the lawn at Charlottesville.

Aubrey emptied the wash tub slowly, to avoid unnecessary noise. He knew he was trespassing in someone else's work space. He had seen the janitors going in and out. One of them left him a note once about the ring around the tub. It was addressed to "Night People," and Aubrey knew he wasn't the only person who lived in the library on a permanent basis, particularly now that it was so cold outside and nearly Christmas. But the stairs and halls of his world, from his shower on the 17th floor to his "carrel" as he called it on the 14th, down to the basement kitchens where he could always find leftover scraps to eat, were uninhabited and he knew them perfectly with the heightened sensations of the blind.

Aubrey closed the maintenance room door carefully and started down the circular stairs that connected the stacks. He knew the feel of each step, some worn, some recently painted, some loose and likely to squeak. He knew the odor of each floor as he descended. There was an acrid pungency from the unpublished Korean War memoirs on the 16th floor, no odor at all from the theology journals on the 15th and a new, fresh scent on his own level that came, he knew, from the *Toughwaugh Papyrus* itself. He hurried back to it eagerly:

Henry was all grown now, of course. Thirty years make a big difference in the life of a man. He had grown enormously tall, taller than the General George Wa-shun-toine he worked for. His skin had gone grey and thick, like mine, the mottled grey that comes with living too long. Henry had sold a lot of the Wa-shun-toine land already and the rest he knew by heart, land that went from the white encampment at Fredericksburg all the way to Fort Pitt in the West, the very end of Potowatomack headwaters. And Wa-shun-toine paid him commissions in gold that he wore around his neck, but didn't know what to do with because he couldn't buy houses or squaws and eating deer and pig fat had made him uncommon fat like he was out of the feeding pen and off to the sausage mill himself in a few weeks. A more rich and miserable sod I never met in all my days, I tell you. I hadn't called him Dung-Crow all those years for nothing, you know. Once a Dung-Crow always a Dung-Crow. But he hadn't been totally idle. He'd spotted the General George as an up and comer a long time ago and I have to give him credit for that because I never saw much to the wooden toothed stiff myself. But then we all have different gifts of the Spirit as Herr Schulerburgh used to quote from Saint Paul and Henry's great gift was to hide in the dark and listen to people.

Now, to get on with the story I promised, Henry was hanging around Mount Vernon after the Revolution, still working as a guide and land agent for the Washington family, when he overheard George arguing with Thomas Jefferson about getting the new national capitol located in a district to include both Georgetown and Alexandria. His chief opponent was Governor Robert Morris of New Jersey, the richest man in the country and the banker of the Revolution, who had offered to give land on the falls of the Delaware near Trenton for a new capitol. There were a lot of competing interests. The northerners didn't want to go south. The southerners refused to go north. They couldn't stand the climate in New York, and they couldn't take their slaves into Philadelphia. Trenton wasn't a bad compromise, but it was still too far from Charleston, and there was no money in it for Washington or any of the Virginians who thought that their prominence in the war entitled them to some personal reward. Washington, already the first president and starting to be called the father of his country, didn't see a way to stop Morris and it didn't seem fair.

Jefferson, though, hit on the crux of the problem and a solution. Morris was rich beyond the imagining of the land rich but cash strapped Virginia gentry, true, but his money was all in Continental Dollars, paperbacks that had given rise to the rude expression "don't give a continental." Morris had factored all his continentals to Dutch bankers promising that they would be redeemed in full and he had put up many businesses and all of his land as collateral. If Congress repudiated the continentals then Morris was bankrupt and the offer of land on the Delaware was off the table. It was up to Congress, and the southern delegation had no interest in ratifying the continentals because they had already paid off their foreign debts and didn't favor taxes to relieve the Yankees of their

financial profligacy. All George had to do was to delay rati-
fication of the continental until after the Dutch foreclosed on
Morris.

Washington called for a third whiskey and thought it over.
He'd never been a man of many words, and since the adoption
of his oak teeth, the stingy flow had just about dried up alto-
gether. Finally, he proposed to think it over some more, which,
Henry knew from his long association with the man and his
blood-thirsty family, meant that Morris was finished, bound
to go the way of the Tuckahoe. Henry slipped away from his
hiding place and sent word to me up river to see if I had any
money to invest in some swamp land south of Georgetown.

I had just buried Herr Schulerburgh and was wondering
what to do with my money. So, I did as Henry suggested. Our
reunion was awkward and strained. We were both now past
the age when Tuckahoe warriors had gone to the sky in the
bellies of birds, but neither showed our age in the usual ways.
Instead of grey haired and stooped, our skins had the feel of
thick felt, and we both noticed that various senses were grow-
ing more acute.

Aubrey closed the book and rubbed his weary eyes. It hurt to
read for so long, but he couldn't wait to see each word resolve
from Gothic/Greek into English under his hand and continue
the most incredible autobiography ever written. It's publication
would, he knew, make him as famous as Champolion, Howard
Carter, John Lloyd Stevens and the moon landing astronauts.
He turned out the light and went to pee down the closest ventilation shaft.

But Aubrey sensed something wrong as soon as he returned.
Somebody else was there. There was a moldy odor he hadn't
smelled since Granny Franny had finally dried out. There was
a movement in the air, almost a breeze, hot and moist like the
breath of a bear over his shoulder. Aubrey froze. The air trembled, pulsated. He sensed a mass of darkness darker than the
darkness of the unlighted stacks. There was a hulking blackness

right over the *Papyrus*. Aubrey waited for his eyes to adjust. He had been in the library so long now that he could almost read in the dark. Almost. And that is what it appeared the black form was doing. It stood above the *Papyrus* looking down, turning the pages without reading, confused apparently by the antiquated script and the unexpected vocabulary. It muttered something. Aubrey couldn't hear it at first, but as the word was repeated, he heard it first as shoal, shoo, shooter. Then he heard it clearly as Schuler, and he knew intuitively who it was who had located the manuscript. Henry Tuckahoe! It had to be. No one else could have found it. No one else would have wanted to. Granny had warned him. And Henry had secrets to protect. Two-hundred years of secrets that now belonged to Aubrey.

Aubrey threw himself bodily at the darkest spot in his field of vision. There was a jarring contact above his work area. A large animal fell and groaned. Aubrey grabbed up his notes and the manuscript, fled down the stairs into the basement, through an emergency exit that tripped fire alarms and turned on every light in the building. He looked to left and right, picked an alley and lost himself in the shadows of the night.

——·**47**·——

Henry took the loss of Schuler's manuscript stoically. It had been easy enough to find it once he knew about it. It had a scent that could never be hidden from him, the strong odors of rag paper, lampblack and boiled linseed oil combined with the distinctive odor of Schuler himself. He knew from the down-river breeze that the manuscript was still in the city. It had been taken over into Georgetown, up into Rosemont Park, and down into Foggy Bottom by the mouth of Rock Creek. It wasn't being taken in doors at night and the odors were growing stronger rather than weaker. The person who stole it must have been a street person, some crazy interloper who could never read Schuler's code. Henry had never bothered to learn *koine*

Greek either, much less the peculiarities of Gothic script. He fully expected the homeless person to forget his heavy burden soon enough and throw it away, or leave it somewhere where it would be forgotten and rot. That was alright with Henry. He would never know what was in it, but he didn't need to know the details. Whatever Schuler said could only hurt his present plans.

Henry was back under the foundation of 806 Pretender's Street. This visit, however, was unrelated to the condition of the building itself. He had already taken enough action to assure that Karen Moelders would sell within a few months. Cracks were appearing up the walls to the second story windows. The floor boards were creaking loudly. Some of the floor joists were pulling out of their sockets in the walls. The structural integrity of the building was badly compromised. Any engineer would condemn it without a second thought. 806 was hardly worth the price of the lot now. Henry expected to get it dirt cheap and then sell it along with the entire Slough project for enormous profit.

His digging was well below the water table now, assisted by sump pumps he kept running 24 hours a day. He was down to a level of oyster shells he dated about 1601. There were graves and artifacts, potsherds, arrow tips, animal bones mounded up and carved like scrimshaw. Some bear and deer bones were inscribed with religious symbols, marks of gratitude to the spirit of the beast that had provided the feast for the Tuckahoe, signed with the mark of old White-Owl-Knows-All. The signature made him think. This meant that White-Owl-Knows-All was over a hundred when he put his strange spell on the boys Henry still called Silent Otter and Shining Kestrel in his own mind. He was a strange one that White-Owl-Knows-All, Henry thought, and decided to have a word with him someday, find out the truth, learn when he had the spell put on him, and who had done it. The old shaman was still in Alexandria, of course, as that seemed part of the supernatural bargain, and still practicing his mystic arts. He had shortened his name though, anglicized it to keep up with the times. But there was no rush in having that talk, not when they were both going to be around for . . . well who could say . . .

Henry tagged some human bones covered in the same talismanic scribble, wrapped them in plastic and put them in a duffel bag. They were enough for his purpose. They would complete the daisy chain in a grand flourish, make him a hero, give him the clout to buy Clovis out of the B & T so that he could get back to the routine gouging of the white man, selling the same land over and over at ever higher prices and larger and larger commissions. It was such a perfect scam. So perfect that the whites had been doing it to themselves for hundreds of years and no longer remembered that it was, in the beginning, purely Henry's revenge and that, for him, it would always be the most satisfying retaliation for his people's eviction.

Henry had gone too far with the daisy chain. He saw that now. With Vernon's Rock of Ages in federal receivership, his investors and depositors suing for billions and Vernon himself in jail for making false statements about the value of the Rock's collateral, it was easy to see that the whole scheme had limitations. And involving Vernon as point man had probably been a mistake too. He was too greedy, too much the cowboy. Well mistakes were nothing new to Henry. He'd inflated and deflated the market before, not always at the right time or to his own advantage, but always in a way that satisfied his sense of revenge. This was no different. If it worked, fine. If not, he could drop out of sight on the river, catch up on his fishing and laugh while Clovis and that young fool Esther Anne what's-her-name tried to answer the questions about the obviously phony appraisals on the Slough.

But, while Henry saw that he couldn't lose, there was a way he saw of increasing the vengeance of his scheme beyond what he had first envisioned. He hugged the duffel bag and shuffled out into the biting December air. It was easy. There was one buyer who would take the Slough at even Esther Anne's appraised value. It was his favorite customer. The U.S. Government. Uncle

Sugar himself. The bones would do it. He'd include 806 in the Slough development based on the option he had with Karen Moelders, show the bones to the Smithsonian, threaten to put up massive, vulgar, condos that would obscure the indian burial ground forever and force Congress to buy the whole thing, at his price, for a National Park. It was a stroke of genius. Henry decided on a midnight snack to celebrate. He put the bones in his Jaguar, tested the points on his spear against his thumb and chuckled as thick, oily blood popped to the surface of his skin.

·48·

"You have to look down here where the plaster has pulled away from the shoe molding," Karen said. She was down on all fours in her office, behind her desk. "And shut the door. I don't want anyone getting suspicious."

Lindsay had been looking at an obviously pregnant teenager on the street staring up at her window, knowing she should be out there encouraging the girl to come in, and wondering why the will to intervene had fallen so flat. She was glad, therefore to have an excuse to abandon the problem. She squatted next to Karen, and then followed the beam of Karen's flashlight carefully into the dark crack. "I don't see it," she said.

"There," Karen said wiggling the light for emphasis. "It's that little black line. You shouldn't be seeing anything there at all. It means the floor joist has pulled out of the wall socket."

"So?"

"I heard it fall out about a week ago. I was working late and I heard a grinding noise like the beginning of an earthquake and then there was a plop and a thump. So I got down here and looked. It still makes a grinding sound, but not as bad as it used to—the joist has pulled so far out it hardly touches the brick wall anymore. Sometimes—especially late at night—it starts banging and clattering. It's awful. I'm, surprised the patients downstairs haven't complained."

"Can it be fixed?" Lindsay asked. She got up slowly, held her head, put her arms on her hips and breathed heavily.

"Are you all right?"

"Yeah. I got up too quickly is all. I do that a lot lately."

Karen looked at Lindsay carefully. "Are you taking care of yourself?"

"Sure. As much as ever."

"You've been looking a little pale to me lately."

"It's the cold. Last winter I went to Max's tanning clinic, but this year I just can't seem to be bothered, you know?"

"I thought maybe . . . well . . . with you and Max trying to . . ."

"I'm not pregnant, if that's what you're asking."

"You're sure?"

"Well . . . my period's late, but that's nothing new."

"You don't think you might want to see a doctor?"

"No."

"Of course, I don't really know anything about all this first hand . . ."

"No. Me neither."

"But I've heard of these kits."

"Home pregnancy tests."

"You don't want to try one?"

"No."

"Well . . ."

"They're degrading. Peeing in a jar and seeing if the dipstick changes color. Really!"

"Well . . . I see your point. It could be something worth writing an article about. Another way women are exploited."

"And Max hasn't shown much interest in that sort of thing lately anyway."

"Really? From that book he wrote I thought he couldn't get enough of it."

"His mind's on other things now. It started right after you were over for dinner. Since then he just hasn't shown much interest. Works all the time on his legal projects. And he is fifty, you know."

"Men really are pathetic, aren't they? Like eels spawning and dying."

"Sort of."

Lindsay turned her attention back to the state of the building. She thumped Karen's office wall, listened for hollow spots, checked for new cracks, tried to look intelligent. "You could call an engineer, I guess."

"No. No point in engineers. They all want a fortune to put these old places right. I've already called that Tuckahoe man. I told him he could exercise his option now as long as he stuck to the price and accepted the building as is. He put up a fuss, but I was tough, wouldn't budge. He agreed. I knew he would. I've had him over a barrel for years."

"But . . ."

"We'll take space in a modern building down by the river, something further from the street, more defensible when the crazies come around. I've seen that Sister Mary hanging around in her maternity dress, you know. Disgusting. She just won't quit. Besides, it makes financial sense right now. The commercial real estate market is glutted with new construction. All that cheap savings and loan money chasing not enough demand for offices and condos. There's going to be a depression. Believe me."

"But is the place safe now?"

"Yeah. We've got a few more months before we can move."

"Because now that you've shown me that loose floor joist, I remember hearing some really loud creaks on the stairs."

"They've always creaked."

"I mean really loud."

"Show me."

The two women started down the staircase slowly, shifting their weight tentatively. Lindsay's steps caused a mummer of creaks in the woodwork. Karen's heavier tread caused tremors and aftershocks. She found one particularly loud board and moved from side to side.

"It's worse," she said to Lindsay. "You're right. The place is coming down on our heads."

"Then you did the right thing with Tuckahoe."

"Absolutely." Karen held onto the bannister for balance, pulled a plain handkerchief from her sleeve and wiped her brow. She was breathing heavily.

"You know, you've been looking a little pale yourself lately, Karen."

"It's the strain. I've been sort of sick at my stomach lately too. The problems with the building have really put me over the top."

"You don't think you need one of those tests?" Lindsay laughed.

Karen laughed too.

But there was no mirth in 806 Pretender's Street.

——·49·——

"It's hardly been a week since the last appraisal. How could the value have doubled?" Esther Anne asked Henry who sat like an immovable Buddha in her small reception area. "It's just a bad time," she told him and repeated her reasons for haste and hesitation, the difficult closing going on right that minute in her small conference room, the buyer's expiring loan commitment, the shaky market, the banks and savings and loans going to hell in a hand basket. Good manners learned from the years with Jason and the new rapture with Jenkin kept Esther Anne from adding that she didn't need Henry's appraisal fees anymore, and that his elusive habits, odd requests, and souring reputation had started to frighten her.

"The development has an historical dimension that it lacked previously," Henry said without noticing the confusion in the conference room or the tension in Esther Anne's eyes. "Plus, with the Slough property and the 806 property combined the value easily skyrockets," Henry pointed to a sepia plat of East Alexandria and traced the boundaries of the new consolidated property with yellow transparent ink. "We'll gut 806 and use it as a facade for the sixty-two condominiums in the Slough."

"Do you own 806 Pretender's Street?"

"Soon. Very soon. The closing is set for early next month."

"What's your client's name again?"

"Kestrel Development Limited. I told you. It's a Delaware corporation."

"They all are. All Delaware corporations."

"All the best ones."

"But why would they pay that much? There're already a bunch of lawsuits. There's no guarantee they'll ever be able to develop it."

"Because they know what I know about the property." Henry spoke more softly even than usual.

"Which is?"

"That vast and strange Indian artifacts are below the surface at 806. When excavation begins, there will be a great public outcry such as Washington has never heard. The Park Service will be forced to buy the development at a fair price . . ."

"Fair price?"

"Fairness under the circumstances being determined by the most recent appraisal."

"Isn't that some sort of conflict of interest on your part? I mean that Kestrel Development knows what you know?"

"No. I am Kestrel Development. President. Chief Executive Officer. Stockholder. It and I are one."

"But . . ."

"And perfectly legal I can assure you. Perfectly."

The assurance would not have affected Esther Anne very much had it not been for the singular manner in which it was spoken. Henry had a certain regal loftiness that reminded her uncannily of Jason in his Senatorial splendor and Jenkin at his judicial finest. The effect of men in power. It was irresistible. It had the same effect on her independence of thought as the tug on a kitten's neck.

"Well," she said to get rid of him as much as anything else, "I'll come out tomorrow and look at 806."

"I shall meet you at ten," Henry said, rose to go and rolled his plats and maps.

Esther Anne completed her closing, collected a fee of $40,000 for three days work and then thought of calling Jenkin about her latest deal with Henry Tuckahoe. Taking the commission check to the bank, however, she hesitated. She didn't know of anything really wrong in what Henry was doing and she would be embarrassed to complain about how other agents made their livings. Some people would have scoffed at one who picked up $40,000 for a few days effort whining about Henry's loan practices. Putting it all in perspective, Esther Anne had to wonder why she had thought about calling Jenkin at all. He was, after all, in court, on the bench, up there in his robes and backed up by velvet curtains and all that marble. It was heady stuff. And more than heady. She'd known men before. But never a virgin. And never like this. Never when there was so much to say. So many plots to unravel. And nobody else had ever encouraged her to speak about the things she loved the most.

——·50·——

Jason Potter nestled quietly in the top of an eighty foot black locust in the middle of the Indian Head Slough. The tree was a hundred years old at least, perhaps twice that much. The bark was deeply pitted, the few dead leaves that remained after the deep February freezes turned in the dull light of a starlit night from old silver to pewter and back, rustling and swaying in a multitude of rhythms that could never be reduced to time signatures. Jason was immune to the physical power of the wind yet he played in his mind with a rocking motion that matched the gentle sway of the treetop in the breeze. He missed the physical intensity of life, the total dependency of life on the real world, the surrender of mental presence to winds and slopes, the power of gravity, the blindness of night, the necessity of sleep. All the demands of an overpowering world, freedom from which had once seemed a deliverance, were now too precious to abide. He longed for someone to see him again, to call out to him from afar, to renew the importunate demands of the campaign contributor, to drag the freedom that follows death back into the tyranny of life. But there was only the cold steady wind heading down river, blowing from west to east, from the mountains to the sea.

The sun peeped tentatively over the eastern horizon, casting a thin shaft of grey light across the broad Potomac, turning the treetops into a golden yellow, and forcing the blue streams of eternity into pale green.

Jason looked heavenward and saw again the fiery rimmed chariot and the golden headed Apollo. He waved. Apollo waved back and dipped his chariot down toward Jason, closer and closer, until Jason could see him more clearly than ever before. There were six matched arabian stallions, black, white, paint, roan, red and appaloosa. There were wheels of gold and studs of diamonds, reins of gossamer, and a chariot of emeralds covered in mosaics of all the creatures of the earth, from trilobites to dinosaurs and man himself. The creatures were all wiggling, squirming, doing whatever it was that they did best, from ripping antelope flesh to selling mutual funds. And the Man himself, Apollo of golden mein that flowed in a celestial wind, eclipsed any image of man ever made. He was a different species, the perfection of all species, the summation of all life, the ideal of existence. And when he was as close to Jason as one standing on the platform waiting for a Metro train, Jason waived him away, hid behind a locust bough, and closed his eyes in denial that a vision of loveliness and perfection could ever want a man of his own painful nature and pitiful achievements. The light swirled away, continuing on its heavenly track. As it left, Jason opened his eyes again and saw for the first time that the figure he had called Apollo was clothed in white linen robes. He wore a gold belt. His eyes flamed like torches. His arms and feet sparkled like discs of bronze. And on his head was a crown of thorns. The Man smiled at Jason, not an ordinary smile, but a smile of light and time beyond time that transformed everything in its path into a stillness that Jason had once called death but which he could not now describe. The Man reached out an arm and beckoned to Jason and then disappeared beyond the blue haze that protected the world as he had known it from the infinity beyond, the continuum of everything and the end of nothing.

Jason waved the Man away as he had before, but with less conviction. The Man's proximity could mean only one thing. The same thing that was meant by the deepening color of the blue streams that invited him in with their cooling ethers. The time was up for him to hang around the world and pine for the pleasures he had misunderstood, to love the slavery of life he had chafed against so belligerently for so many years. The time had come for him to part with the pleasures of trees and water and air and the company of women and Esther Anne's romance with Jenkin Carroway, the pleasures she felt in his embrace, and the novelty of her new career.

Jason made up his mind to call Apollo back. He cupped his hands around his mouth to shout, but before he could make a sound, rude mechanical noises distracted his attention back to the Slough. There were roars, coughs, rumbles, the clatter of steel treads over frozen clay and the blast of hot diesel fumes into quiet air. Bulldozers from the Pretender's Street side advanced in military order, each aimed for a separate part of the Slough forest. Eleven trees and countless low shrubberies fell together. The mechanical monsters backed up for another assault. A wail of sirens filled the morning air. A dozen squad cars from the U.S. Park Police, the City of Alexandria, the Secret Service and the F.B.I, descended on the marsh. Uniformed officers with M-16s and shoulder mounted anti-tank missiles took positions behind opened car doors, pointed their weapons at the hard hatted men on the dozers and demanded that all destruction of timber on the Slough cease and desist at once. And it did. The construction crews seemed to have been alerted ahead of time to the police raid. They turned their machinery off and dismounted before the charges could be read.

No sooner were the dozers shut down than a hundred or more protesters from Friends of the Earth with anti-tear gas suits emerged and began a medley of protest songs from the '60s. They lay down in the access streets. They put their bodies in front of the dozers and in front of the police cars. Some threw mud balls at the police, water ballons at the construction workers. But while they were busy, a dark complected giant snuck out of a leafless sumac grove and stuck a sign in the ground: "Indian Head Slough Condominiums—Financing by Burgh & Tuckahoe Savings and Loan. Lots from the low $350,000s."

Sirens wailed. More police arrived. The protesters were quickly dispersed and a court order served enjoining further construction pending hearings into the historical and legal status of the property.

Jason, who had fled upward at the first sign of physical danger, was relieved to see the police go, and, at the same time, troubled by the peace that ensued. He had noticed Henry on the scene, and it made him uncomfortable. Henry had a kiss of death—no worse than death, a kiss of chaos—for everything that he touched. He schemed and plotted and chaos followed where he went. Jason had almost forgotten him. Apollo would have to wait a while longer. Esther Ann might need him yet. Jason settled back into the locust tree, and wondered what the Slough, garbage yard of Alexandria for as long as he could remember, had to do with Henry.

Max Aceldama lay back against a mound of lavender pillows, his peacock robe open at the waist, and watched through half closed eyes as Lindsay rotated her tongue around the tip of his penis and pumped rhythmically with her left hand on its root.

"Please, no . . . ," Max groaned. Lindsay had never gone this far before. For years he had begged and pleaded with her to complete the act of fellatio, but she had refused. Now she seemed to have changed her mind. Max tried hard to hold back his orgasm, fearing the lower back pain that had plagued him for so long after his incident of ejaculatory excess with Karen. But it was impossible to resist. Fully half of his shaft was now sliding in and out of Lindsay's mouth. Her hand gripped him tightly, moved in time with her mouth. He felt a slight suction that took his breath away. The thought of Lindsay, so thin, so elegant, so dark, breaking this taboo for him was too much. The suction increased. He heard her saliva bubbling. He felt it drip over his scrotum. The friction from her hand took on a new, slippery sensation. She sucked again, hard, pulling him up and out of himself. Max felt his prostate kick, fought back, felt Lindsay's fine white teeth and then let himself go with a groan that shook the chandelier. He collapsed into the prenatal position and yielded to sleep.

Lindsay disentwined herself from Max. She turned out the bedside light and stepped down the hall and into a bathroom that was usually reserved for guests. She locked the door, retrieved a black leather pouch from under a stack of towels, opened it, and placed a small microscope on the marble topped vanity. She took a glass slide from the case, spat slowly on it, slipped it onto the stage of the microscope and focused the eyepiece. She looked into a foggy mass, a thick cloud settled on a dark road. She shifted the slide from right to left. Then up. Then down. She cleaned off the slide, spat again and repeated the process. Then, satisfied, she brushed her teeth and washed her mouth out with a mild antiseptic. Her jaw was sore. Her neck was stiff. Her eyes were puffy from virtually standing on her head to perform the act. But she knew what she wanted to know. Nothing swam in Max's spunk. He was sterile as a mule.

There was nothing to worry about. Just another late period. Just one of those things.

Aubrey wiped the top of the bottle with his sleeve. Not that a wipe really mattered. His own sleeve was none too clean now. And it seemed rude to question the hygiene of people so willing to share what little they had. Still. He wiped again, half-heatedly, barely cuffing the bottle, put the Thunderbird Wine to his lips, drank sparingly and passed it on to his neighbor of many names, none too rational, none consistent from week to week, but who had landed on and stuck with Immanuel for the last few days.

"My own dissertation," Immanuel said, "started with the distinction of all objects into phenomena and noumena."

"A useful line to draw surely," Aubrey said taking the bottle back after Immanuel had finished drinking his fill.

"'The Noumenon of Physical Excellence.' That was one of my working titles. I began by refuting once and for all the old Platonist doctrine that perfection and existence cannot be properties of the same thing. My argument relied on the socio-theological implications of Wittgenstein's metaphysical paradigms, of course, but its implications for quantum physics and practical cosmology were glaringly obvious, not to mention revolutionizing Durkheim's concept of the *conscience collectif* and the entire nominalist dialectic."

Aubrey passed the bottle back to Immanuel and turned he *Toughwaugh Papyrus* toward a dawn to dusk light on the Whitehurst Freeway overpass. It was four o'clock in the morning. It was snowing, not unusual for Washington in early March. The two men sat with twenty or so other homeless wanderers on a vent in the heating lines between the White House and the Georgetown Power Plant. Steam condensed around hem in swirling clouds. Traffic—exhausted survivors from

Georgetown's nightlife—stopped reluctantly at the light on M Street and endured the outstretched hands of the seasoned panhandlers. Aubrey found he never got much this time of the morning. People who had just paid their bills at Blues Alley were unlikely to feel generous. Better to beg from the morning rush hour folks, fresh, hopeful, filled with liberal sentiment from National Public Radio.

"Of course," Immanuel continued through a beard so dense and matted that it seemed made of fiberglass glued onto his face, "noumenon as object of intellectual intuition devoid of all phenomenal attribute should never be confounded with that old bogeyman, the soul, specter, ghost, haunt, banshee, or lemures as the Romans called the spirit of the dead exorcised from homes in early religious observances."

"Of course," Aubrey said, ignoring an act of petty vandalism by one of the homeless wanders against a *Washington Post* reporter who had come to live on the steam grate for the sake of experience. He wrapped the sheet of clear plastic he had taken from a construction site more closely around his head, used it to protect the manuscript that was now his only possession and continued to read. Schuler had just started to describe how he and Henry had personally caused the 'Potomac Bubble' of 1792. Governor Morris was running out of time with his creditors, and Washington was holding his feet to the fire: If the federal government ratified the debt then the capital went to the Potomac. The Tuckahoe money was on Washington. Henry set up an office in Funkstown, across the river from Alexandria and gave tours to British investors. Schuler was buying Continentals at half a cent on the dollar and storing them in clay pots calabashes, anything he could find. Henry drafted descriptions and swamp reclamation plans and sent them to everybody who had any money. He had clients and options and land futures He sold and re-sold deeds everyday on the same property as national confidence swayed back and forth between Washington the sentimental favorite, and Morris the man with the money Congressional parties came up the Potomac in barges, then

as rumors shifted, toured the Delaware Valley. Someone proposed the headwaters of the Susquahanna as a compromise.
New speculation was rife. The Congressional parties were fer-
ried up the Chesapeake Bay and money left Funkstown to go
north. Fortunes were broken. But Henry stayed firm. He knew
George Washington personally. He knew Washington's plans for
a canal that would connect Harper's Ferry with Pittsburgh, the
Atlantic with the Mississippi, Alexandria with New Orleans. He
had heard Washington, Jefferson and George Mason planning
out the streets of the new Capital even while they complained
about the mud and the mosquitoes. And Schuler held on to his
Continentals, picked up more by the bushel load. They were
betting all, but it was hardly a bet. The fix was in. It was the
revenge they had been promised, to be traders in their family lands forever. They bought up land and dollars cheap and
waited, careful to keep away from women.

Immanuel interrupted Aubrey's reading of the *Papyrus*:
"Right before my dissertation defense, news came out about
the grand unification theory, the union of quantum mechanics,
the calculus and the universe. I had to withdraw my topic naturally. Overnight, it had become too narrow in focus. The theory
of Social Transcorosity meant nothing without the integration
of Sysmogenesis and psycho-anthropology. And I thought then
that I saw the way. My advisor agreed. We found a new grant
and I came to the Library of Congress to push it on through to
perfection."

Aubrey took the Thunderbird back from Immanuel, more
as a matter of courtesy than actual desire. He'd heard of these
wandering scholars like Immanuel, first down at U.Va. where
the dropouts were pumping gas and parking cars, carrying
L'Etre Et Le Non wistfully as existentialism faded into cliche,
as their classmates matured, moved on. Some went to Law
School. Some sold insurance. It wasn't a pretty scene. But it
was nothing compared to the stories reverberating around the
Library of Congress. The failures there had risen higher and
fallen farther. Boosted from the provinces to do great work,

they found it impossible to accept the disgrace of returning to their origins and chose, instead, the life of wandering and talking, reading and re-reading their still unfinished dissertations, basking in a glory whose potential had long faded but which they could not forget. Aubrey realized that he had been on a razor's edge of joining the street scholars himself and that the mugging and Granny's rescue were all that had saved him. He hugged the *Papyrus* tighter. It was his salvation. That and Granny's mutual fund stock.

But as long as Henry Tuckahoe was chasing the manuscript he needed to hide out with Immanuel and his like. There was no need for money now. When he published the *Papyrus* there would be money galore, more than he had ever expected from an academic career. Then he could sell the stock, find Granny's beneficiary and give the money away. Of course, the stock had lost some of its value lately. All banking stocks were down. But the stock would go back up. The Government guaranteed it. He knew that. And then the *Papyrus* would stun the world. He would be sought after for tenured positions. Everything would work out.

"But the chapter on the phenomenology of feminist symbology was—quite rightly I may add—thought to contradict my original rejection of the synthetic *a priori*. I'd come full circle without going anywhere, so to speak. Or, to put it another way, the tail was wagging the dog. So to speak. Or, from yet another angle, I did an Indian rope trick without the rope. I forget now which it was my advisor said when he sent me back to Washington—without any more money, of course. I mean who'd ever heard of four grants in a row? Still, when my brain subsides, when my mind collides, when my muse provides, when my hand subscribes . . ."

Immanuel was interrupted by a middle aged woman wrapped in many layers of old rags. She danced and weaved in the rising steam. Flush from some minor act of philanthropy, she poured methylated spirit into Immanuel's Thunderbird bottle. The volatile aroma hit Aubrey's nose and he realized with shock that what he had been drinking was not wine.

"Meth, Meth, glorious Meth," the woman sang, "nothing quite like it for bringing on death." She kissed Immanuel on the mouth, stuck her tongue into Aubrey's ear and moved on. The odor that lingered on his cheek reminded him of dead garden slugs decaying in a beer trap.

"Judy, from the music department at Fresno State," Immanuel said. "She's been on chapter 2 for sixteen years."

Aubrey turned back to the manuscript with a shudder.

53

Esther Anne lay next to Jenkin Carroway and listened to him read from a Veronica Holloway novel in progress: "After the thuggee disappeared into the darkness with the stolen horses, Captain Victor Hallam found Miranda huddled over Lord Pankhurst's body. The scar of the thuggee's garrote still oozed blood onto Lord Pankhurst's white shirt. Victor took Miranda to a nearby stream. She was too stunned to move on her own. He washed the blood, her father's blood, from her hands, and wrapped her in his scarlet tunic more against a wave of oncoming shock than the evening chill. He rolled up his sleeve, wrapped Lord Pankhurst in a saddle blanket that had come dislodged during the course of the fight, and then, using the bayonet from a Henry-Martini rifle, he scraped out a shallow grave for the old general who had fought so long and so gallantly for the Empire.

"Victor cocked an ear to the sounds of the night. Bats chirped. Monkeys chattered and screamed. Insects scraped and screeched. And over and beyond it all, thuggee howled in the night, crying praise to Kali the goddess of death and begging for more English blood. He found a cave on the far side of the stream. Moonlight through the banyan forest showed it to be unoccupied. Victor lifted Miranda into his arms and carried her across the water. She clung to him tightly. As he nestled her down onto a bed of plantain leaves, her thin white arms drew his lips toward hers. They kissed. Her breath was hot and sweet as the lotus. 'Oh, Victor, she whispered, 'what if it had been you instead of daddy, what would have become of us?'

Esther Anne held Jenkin tighter and closed her eyes. There was something about his words, his voice that had taught her peace. She lived for its sound, its strange knowledge and rich texture. It had taken over her being, entered her, and, now it was growing inside her. Quite literally. Esther Anne had intended to tell Jenkin about the baby tonight. But his reading was so impassioned, the love he had created between Victor and Miranda so true to life, and her need to sleep so overwhelming, that she chose the luxury of allowing the story to carry her off and to save the news for another day. There was plenty of time to say what had to be said and she knew with certainty that his reaction would be a proposal of marriage. She could feel his longing for a wife, a family, a home. And with these thoughts, she drifted off, rejoicing in her own secret and comforted by hands she could not see and felt only in a metaphorical sense, for Jason Potter, the lover to whom conception had always been a nightmare, had fallen in love with the minuscule fetus in Esther Anne's womb and reveled in the thought of becoming a godfather. He nestled up to Esther Anne's belly and listened to the tiny heartbeat, the heavier, slower, louder cadence of the mother and the tinny stillness that echoed where his own beat would have been in life.

Jenkin continued: "Victor wanted to warn her that the fighting wasn't over, that the thuggee would certainly be looking for them in the darkness, that they could be attacked at any minute, that he would have to fight the villains in the morning with only the bayonet with which he had dug her father's shallow grave. 'Don't leave me, Victor,' she cried into his breast. And he promised that he wouldn't. 'Don't leave me, Victor,' she cried again. 'Don't leave me ever.' And he said that he wouldn't. Ever. Victor took Miranda in his arms and held her securely, letting her head rest on his chest so that she fell asleep. Her even breathing lulled the night to sleep."

Jenkin put the manuscript aside, kissed Esther Anne's sleeping forehead and put out the light.

· 54 ·

"If you've already written the article why bother with the research?" Lindsay asked, looking dubiously at the boxed home pregnancy test kits lined up on Karen's desk.

"Actually doing it might add something. There might be things I missed. I might even add a little "I did it myself" section.

"Karen, I've got a lot of work to do . . ."

"It won't take a minute . . . well four to six minutes according to the directions, see . . ."

Lindsay agreed reluctantly to participate and in a few minutes, both women were standing in front of small beakers of their own urine pretending not to notice the distinctive aroma or the differences in color.

"Now, we want to time them, make sure the package isn't lying about how long it takes. Stick the paper in on the count of three okay?"

"Okay."

"One, two, three."

The papers were plunged in, held for the required time and then withdrawn at Karen's command.

"Red for preggers, blue for not," Karen said. "It shouldn't take but another minute."

In fact, it took less.

Karen's strip turned lavender, pink, then bright red.

Lindsay's went scarlet almost immediately.

Karen feigned an emergency and went into her private toilet. She sat down, looked at the strip again, read, then re-read the directions on the package. She was, it seems, supposed to see a doctor next. Objectively, it was an outrage. She'd only been with a man once. It hadn't been the most likely time of the month for her. And it certainly wasn't something she would have expected. She examined her feelings as she had been trained to do. But they weren't where she expected them. The outrage, the anger, the sense of rape, invasion, the hurt, weren't there at all. She didn't know exactly how she felt. But it wasn't all bad. She fought back at a grin, stifled a giggle.

When Karen flushed the test slip down the toilet and went back into her office, Lindsay was staring out the window at the street looking for Sister Mary Scroggins, longing to ask her about something she had always mocked. The red slip meant only one thing to her. She was to have a baby. Not Max's baby. He had no sperm. She'd confirmed it. And there had been nobody else. That meant . . . it had to be . . . the virgin birth. There was no other explanation. It had happened once. It was going to happen again. To her. To Lindsay Hayden.

"Well," Karen said, "nobody's in the family way around here I guess . . ."

"My soul doth . . , " Lindsay mumbled.

"What? What was that?" Karen asked as she dialed Max's number and shooed Lindsay out.

Lindsay cleaned out her desk and left early in the afternoon without telling Karen.

——— · 55 · ———

Back in Georgetown, Lindsay rummaged through the mail mechanically. Most of it was for Max, but she always looked. And this time there was something from her mother. She knew immediately that it was odd. Her mother only lived six miles away in Bethesda, and she never wrote. Lindsay took the fat envelope into the study. The envelope contained a yellowed sheaf of paper with a cover note in her mother's hand:

Dearest Lindsay,

I have known for years and years that I would someday have to write this letter, yet I have never prepared myself for it, and writing it now is nearly impossible. There are so many things I should have told you before, and so many more things I wish you never had to know. But these things are beyond my control.

Here are the facts I know. Your father—God rest his soul and how I wish he were here to do this himself—and I adopted you as a three week old baby back in 1957. The adoption was handled privately through an attorney in Old Town Alexandria who died twenty years ago, maybe more. We never met your birth mother as these young women are called now. It wasn't done. There was more shame attached to having children out of wedlock back then and for some reason I can't remember adopted children weren't supposed to know about being adopted. Anyway, we agreed to accept a letter from your birthmom and give it to you when we received notice of her death. This we just received and I feel honor bound to send this old letter along. I haven't read it. I didn't feel it was my place or any of my business.

We all have to carry burdens we didn't bargain for, Lindsay. Being barren wasn't my choice, but I wouldn't want anyone else for a daughter because you are and always have been just the most wonderful person. This letter may be more than you can take. I really don't know. But whatever it is, know that I have always loved you and that I always will.

The enclosed letter had no return address and was simply addressed: My dear baby girl: It read:

I will be gone when you read this, so I hope it is many years from now and that you will be grown up and happy, maybe with a family. I hope so.

I was a graduate student at George Washington University in 1956 doing research on the origins of the North American Indians, particularly the tribes in the Potomac Valley. My theory was that the American Indians were descended from the Lost Tribes of Israel. You will remember that after the Assyrian conquest of Israel in 723 B.C., the 10 tribes of the North simply disappeared. There are various theories, of course, but I have always found parallels between certain customs of the Potomac Valley Indians and the Ancient Israelites, like eating a certain fungus that appears in the morning and treating it like a gift from God. Well, in the course of my research, while I was on my toes night and day thinking about these problems, I overheard these two gentlemen talking the language of the Upper Tuckahoe which, of course I had studied, but never spoken because I thought all the native speakers had been dead for hundreds of years. Well, imagine my surprise when I found these two men standing outside of the Burgh and Tuckahoe Savings and Loan down in Old Town Alexandria. I immediately introduced myself. They were quite taken back that I could even recognize their language and even make a few sounds that they could recognize. They were very suspicious and made me promise not to tell anybody what it was they had been speaking, because, they said, they were now a secret society and their indian ancestry wouldn't have done their business any good. I agreed to this provided they agreed to meet with me and teach me their language and tell me what they could remember about their tribal ways. They had a heated conversation, and then the younger agreed to what I asked. He said to call him Henry. I did.

Henry and I met a few times but there was something strange about our meetings. We always met outdoors exactly where he said and there was never any way of getting in touch with him. He would never give me an address or telephone number. But he was agreeable enough. He helped with my pronunciation of words and then I wrote up a little Tuckahoe Gammer which would have been enough for a Ph.D. dissertation in a linguistics department, but I was doing history so it didn't count. Anyway, when I was getting pretty good at the language, I really and truly fell in love with Henry and I think, he with me. He had a real way with women and was very experienced in knowing what women want, which is the kind of man I hope you will marry some day, but he was real skittish about my getting a baby and very careful. The pill wasn't around back then and abortion was a crime, so it really was something to worry about, except I didn't care because I really loved him and I guess I wanted his baby, subconsciously at first and then openly, even more than I wanted him. And that's when he got scared. He made me promise to get an abortion if I got pregnant and I did. He told me that he even knew how to do abortions and had done lots of them on his girlfriends over the years because there was some kind of spell on his people that they weren't supposed to have children. I couldn't believe this. And I wanted to see all the Indian tribes continue in perpetuity, so I decided to get myself pregnant to save the tribe in spite of Henry. This was hard because he either wore a condom or pulled himself out before he ejaculated. But I was tricky. I got him drunk once down under the Memorial Bridge where he liked to take me in the summer and drugged him with phenobarbital in his wine. I then worked him up into a state of erection and forced him to come inside me. Once did the trick and you are the result. I never told Henry. He wouldn't have liked it. So I disappeared from his life. I knew I couldn't keep you. But the Florence Crittenden people find good families and I am sure you will be loved and cared for better than I could. I did this so that the blood of the Tuckahoe would not die out. You are unique and precious and I wish you well.

I gave you a name in that hour or so we spent together after your birth. I named you 'Talitha Cumi.' It means 'damsel arise' and it's what Jesus said to the little girl when he raised her up from the dead, for you are the last of the ten tribes of Israel and you must rise up to be who you are. Whatever your name is now, be who you are, Talitha Cumi.

Now, here is what you must do. Henry Tuckahoe is under some kind of curse. I could smell it all over his person, but back then I didn't know what a curse smelled like. I know now, I'm sure he's got one bad. This curse of his has something to do with having grandchildren. You seek him out when you have children of your own and show him your baby and I'm sure that seeing the baby all by itself will cure his curse and his deep depression. Seek him out. If he's still alive, and for the life of me I think he's got some deal with death too, you can free this man from the devil.

God bless you.

The letter was signed Francis Appleby.

It was too much for Lindsay. First the virgin birth. And now to be mother to the last of the Tuckahoe. And a father to save. A devil to cast out. A savior come from the stump of the last of the native American people. There was a definite ring of theological possibility to it. Talitha Cumi, she thought, handmaid of the Lord. She left the Georgetown mansion in search of her father, wherever he was.

——·56·——

Mary Scroggins watched impassively as the cold metal hydro phone slithered over her swollen abdomen. She looked at the ceiling. The nurse, professionally cheerful, directed her attention to a bedside video monitor.

"Let's see," the nurse said moving the silver disc over the lubricated skin and watching the monitor carefully. "There's the head. You see? Right there." She pointed. "There. And . . . oh . . . he . . . I don't know why I said he . . . the way it's turned we can't tell the sex for certain . . . he's moving . . . there . . . oh, everything looks very normal . . . yes . . . very normal . . . a perfectly normal fetus . . . no problems here . . ."

Mary winced and looked at the monitor. It was like going underwater at the beach. Everything moved. Nothing was clear. Nothing was in focus. Sand got on everything. She hadn't wanted the sonogram. She'd wanted the amniocentesis. She wanted an excuse to justify terminating the pregnancy, not some Pollyanna ooo'ing and ahh'ing over the life to be, a regurgitation of the propaganda she had used herself for so many years on women who must have looked at her the same way she was looking at this nurse. But the sonogram and the amniocentesis were part of the same Blue Cross insurance package. You got one, you got both. She could have objected. But rules were rules and she'd wearied of objecting. It took energy she didn't have. It required decisions she couldn't make any more. Not by herself.

"And here's the face," the nurse, really starting to bubble with enthusiasm now, said. "See . . . a nose . . . forehead . . . eyes . . . see?"

Mary did see. She tried to close her eyes but couldn't.

"It's a perfectly wonderful face," the nurse said. "You're so lucky."

But Mary didn't see what the nurse saw. She saw a face she had seen before. And she heard a grating expression she had heard before: "Ramone, you fuck a nun, man, you know that. Hey! Ramone fuck a nun. Fuck a nun. Fuck a nun." She heard the taunting jeer as she left the clinic in tears. The nurse thought Mary was overcome with joy.

——·57·——

"As dawn filtered through the dense canopy of the banyan forest, and the whimpering call of the coral pheasant replaced the cackle of Forster's hyena, Victor knew that the worst was coming. Ten thugs, maybe more, waited further down the Malabar Road. They were armed with a brown bess or two and their usual assortment of tulwars and scimitars. A vicious breed, Victor could count on them to have a go at Miranda first, outrage her person, violate her even, subject her to unspeakable tortures and force him to watch the whole time, tormented, furious and impotent. The thought made him tremble. He rested the form of the one he had sworn never to desert carefully on a bed of moss and looked for eatable fruit in the jungle canopy. Hindu plum and wild white grapes abounded high in the overhanging trees. He plucked the fruit and ate heartily. His confidence rose. There was a way. The only way. Using the bayonet, he carved straight saplings of native teak into iron-hard spears. He balanced them gently, tenderly in his throwing arm, testing them for weight and balance, remembering his javelin throwing days at Eton, the old school on whose playing fields the battle of Waterloo had been won. The spears were hard and strong. Victor threw one with a fair degree of strength. It flew true to pierce a clump of citronella growing fifty feet away. He threw another with all his might and with all his pent up rage at the crimes of the thuggee. It penetrated a twelve inch sago palm, soft wood to be sure, but harder than a man's body. He retrieved the two spears, sharpened the points again and, with a total of ten weapons altogether, he laid his plans."

Jenkin's voice was hoarse. He paused to sip from a glass of water on his bedside table. "They had the killing power of bullets," he continued, "without the noise of a gun. Provided that he got within fifty feet, Victor was certain . . ."

"Could we talk a little bit Jenkin?"

"Well . . ."

"It's important," Esther Anne said. "I meant to tell you last night, but I dozed off just when Miranda did."

"It is that kind of sympathetic scene, I realize . . ."

"But it's about work," Esther Anne said and then related the entire history of her appraisal services to Henry Tucka hoe including the last appraisal premised on forcing a sale to the Interior Department. "The thing is," Esther Anne said in conclusion," I can't believe what he said is true. I don't believe that there are any real Indian relics down there. I think he's a fraud. Nobody knows anything about him. He just pops up at the worst times and he's got this way of saying bizarre thing and making you think that maybe he's right. He's crazy and he makes other people crazy." She broke down and sobbed.

Jenkin got out of bed as she spoke, a man as terrified as if he had seen a ghost. "You'll have to tell the FBI, of course, it's th only way."

"I can't . . ."

"It's the only way . . . the only way . . ."

"Can't you . . ?"

"I can't do anything. I'm on the Supreme Court. I can't do anything for people caught up in criminal investigations. I can't even be seen with you again. Not now. Not ever."

"Can't be seen with me?"

"Of course not! What did you think?"

"I thought you'd want to know that I going to have your . . ."

"You'd ruin it all. The Supreme Court! Everything! All my life!"

"But . . ."

"Title Eighteen *United States Code* section 371. Conspiracy to defraud the United States and commission of any act to effect the object of the conspiracy means Ten-Thousand Dollars or 5 years or both. Out! Out!" He flapped and fluttered like a rhea caught in a chicken coop until Esther Anne, horrified and sobbing, gathered up her undergarments, slipped on her dress and fled back to her apartment, fighting all the while to make Jenkin calm down and listen to what she had to say about the baby.

Jenkin settled back into bed when Esther Anne was gone. He was too upset to think straight, to distraught to reflect on what he had done. He took up the manuscript again and started to read aloud, as if Esther Anne were still there beside him.

"Keep this, Victor said to Miranda, giving her the bayonet. It the thuggee come here it will only be because I am dead and there is no other help. Fall on the bayonet before they get to you. They respect a corpse, won't touch them in fact. You'll be safe then. But you must promise me. She did. He showed her where to place the point, right under her breast, and how to jump on it so that there would be no pain. She knew that what he said was for the best, that if he were gone she would want nothing but to follow him into the great beyond, his flawless bride unknown to man, gift of perfection for all eternity."

Jenkin read the passage over twice. The first time it sounded weak. The second time it's cloying falseness struck him almost physically. It was cliched. The worst thing he had ever written.

He crossed it out. There had to be a truer ending, something consistent with the characters and the times. He searched his imagination. It was empty. Esther Ann would know how to fix the story. But she was gone He had run her off. Jenkin could never remember such loneliness.

——·58·——

"The subject entered his house in the Old Town part of Alexandria with Esther Anne Hendricks at 9:52 p. m. on the 27th of February. The lights came on in the kitchen of the townhouse and stayed on for 12 minutes. The lights then came on in the front bedroom on the third floor. The enclosed pictures taken through a radio controlled camera mounted on a telephone pole opposite the window show the couple getting into bed. Justice Carroway read from a heavy book for approximately two hours, and then turned out the lights. The light came on again at 6:30 a.m. The couple snuggled and made love (see enclosed photo). Mr. Justice Carroway then began to read from the big book again. After a few minutes, Ms. Hendricks said something that evidently upset Justice Carroway. Their voices could be heard in the street, though what they said was indistinct. At 7:15 a.m. on February 28, Ms. Hendricks departed through the front door and slammed it. She appeared to be crying. She walked to her office where her car was parked and drove to her apartment in the District of Columbia."

Karen put the detective's report aside and looked at the pictures. The faces needed some enhancement, but there wasn't much an air brush and a little imagination couldn't do. Pictures of them both going to bed. Jenkin in his old fashioned flannels. Esther Anne in a short lacy thing that looked like it had seen better days along with its owner. Esther Anne had put on a pound or two since she first started sleeping with the Justice, Karen thought. And it was all just in time.

The first major abortion rights case to hit the Supreme Court since Jenkin's confirmation was about to be argued. It went

to the heart of the issue: the right to copulate without reproductive consequences. South Kanaska or one of the other Mid-
west states—Karen prided herself on not being able to tell one
from the other—had passed a law that free consent to sexual
intercourse constituted an implied acceptance of pregnancy
and childbirth as natural consequences. Any woman who consented to sex therefore consented to being pregnant. It was another way of saying that abortion could only be legal in case of
rape. Defining the act a woman was free to chose as intercourse
rather than abortion defeated the entire free choice movement
and it was vital to the movement to have the law struck down.
Sex had nothing to do with reproduction. It was the keystone
of American jurisprudence. On that, she and Max agreed. After
not speaking for a week or so, they had started putting their
heads together for the big argument. Neither mentioned what
had happened. And Karen certainly didn't mention the red
stain on the test paper, or what she planned to do about it. The
law and the movement had to come first. Once she got Max
through the argument, she would decide what to do. Not that
the argument really mattered. Jenkin Carroway was the swing
vote, and she now owned Jenkin Carroway. The Yankee had
finally found his floozie, a whore recycled from a dead Senator.
Karen laughed. The right to life was dead.

59

Clovis Tuckahoe prodded the spongy ground gingerly with
her toe. It was warm for March, but patches of ice and snow
lingered between muddy rivulets of meltwater. She looked at
the sky, clear with high cirrus clouds forming to the East and
a bank of grey looming over the Appalachian foothills to the
west. It could be an early spring, she thought, or it could be a
false interlude before the worst blasts of winter. She had known
both. One was as common as the other in March. Nothing was
consistent in the Washington area.

She mumbled and then grumbled under her breath and cursed softly as a spiked heel cracked through the hard layer of frost into a clay based mud with the consistency of window putty. She wiped the heel of her shoe on an old tea towel she had brought for the purpose and trudged on into the under-growth of sumac and Queen Anne's Lace.

She was determined to see the Slough from one end to the other, to find out what the flap was all about, to get behind the injunctions and the publicity. She had reviewed all the loan files and was surprised to see Henry's name as chief loan officer on them all, surprised at the number of transactions the bank had financed on the same property, amazed at the amount of loan fees the bank had booked without receiving any interest on the note. No property in Alexandria had ever been in such demand. It all looked above board from the bank books, but . . . well, she hated to admit what she had always known, that with Henry one could never be too careful.

Clovis skirted a deep pool bursting with methane bubbles and found herself on the far side of the swamp facing Hunting Creek. It was nothing but a bar of silt really. No foundation to speak of, no rock, not even any good soil, though with all the organic debris and the sewerage plant discharge it would probably be alright for gardening in the Spring. And there was the view of Pretender's Street to consider. The two were really much closer than she had thought. No doubt the developers were excited about that. But then there was the Old Confeder-ate Cemetery abutting the western edge, so close, so poorly kept up even though the Park Service had owned it for fifty years or more.

The Slough was hardly ideal for any development much less high rise condominiums no matter how one looked at it. Still, there was only so much land inside the Beltway, and this was part of it. With enough pilings the foundation problem could be overcome. And condos high enough above the creek and the river would get a nicer breeze, a less humid atmosphere. Maybe it would work, she thought, turning the possibilities over in her mind. Schuler had taught her long ago never to substitute her natural caution as a lender for the inspiration and gambling instinct that fueled the developer.

Clovis had lowered her eyes and started walking back to the mainland when she detected signs of cultivation. She stopped to look more closely. It was true. Someone had planted a kind of herb garden right in the middle of the Toughwaugh Slough. Purely out of curiosity, Clovis stopped to see what prospered in the silty ground. She was puzzled at first. There was nothing she recognized as kitchen herbs. She stared at the stalks and dried leaves. Some species names slowly came to mind. There was something that looked like the stalk of a truly giant fennel, and Artemisia, the source of wormwood, as well as the African Commiphora known to the ancients as myrrh, common rue and pennyroyal, a kind of mint. Odd choices. But familiar for some reason. And then she remembered back before the birth of her daughter, back when Henry had come to dinner every Monday night. All these herbs, or some of them had shown up in the salads and stews Henry had brought over. Tuckahoe food he had called them. But that had all ended with the baby.

Clovis stooped and plucked a few of the dried leaves and put them in her hand bag. Funny old Henry! Out here growing his own exotic weeds for all those lovely old dishes. She picked a sample of each and thought of a bouquet garnie for Henry, a sort of peace offering. Clovis suddenly thought of him in a new and more friendly light. The development was probably alright after all. Henry the herb man. He was alright really.

—— · **60** · ——

'The Constitutional right to copulate without reproductive con-sequences is, the Appellant argues, derived from this Court's ruling in *Griswald v. Connecticut*, a case in which a state stat-ute banning the sale of contraceptives to married couples was held to violate a right of privacy never explicitly mentioned but emanating, even glowing like a penumbra, from various other rights such as the 4th Amendment right against unreasonable search and seizure and the equal protection clause of the 14th Amendment. Though backed by weighty argument in the law journals, this broad reading of the Constitution . . ." Jenkin was interrupted by the telephone ringing in his bedroom. It was an unlisted number. It had to be Esther Anne. He knew she would call eventually. He ran upstairs, ready to beg forgiveness, ready to promise anything, flushed with the thought of her joining him in bed again even tonight.

But it wasn't Esther Anne. It was a non-descript voice, a voice disguised by a cone or a muzzle. "Justice Carroway," it said. "The South Kanaska abortion decision has been assigned to you and even though we are all your friends, we want you to know that if the pro-life view isn't upheld we will have to disclose certain pictures of you with a Miss Esther Anne Hendricks. These pictures show you in bed with the young lady, sir and I know . . ."

Jenkin hung up and thought of calling the FBI. They were out there to protect him from this kind of thing, and this was the second call. The first had been from the pro-choice people. He had hung up on them too. But he couldn't call. If the FBI knew about the pictures it was only a matter of time until the *Post* put it all on page one and his career on the bench was finished. There was nothing to do but search his judicial conscience, play it straight and take the consequences. There had been a time when he would have reveled in his resolution. But that time was gone. Now he wanted Esther Anne and she wasn't there. He thought of calling her himself. But he couldn't. The Yankee rectitude was too much. He tried to work, but after a few more hours, he retreated to the scene in his latest Veronica Holloway novel where Victor gave Miranda the bayonet and told her how to use it. It had sounded so wrong when he had last read it. It was sounding better now just true to life.

——·**61**·——

Max dined alone in the Four Seasons now that Lindsay had gone. He felt a sense of concern for her well being, of course, but her disappearance itself had not surprised him. In hindsight, a streak of instability had been surfacing for some time. He reviewed the little hints, her declining interest in his new sex positions, particularly the one he called the *Chthonic Interuberall*, several proof reading tasks on his new manual of sex mantras that she had not completed on time, and a lack of zeal for the big South Kanaska abortion decision. All had pointed to psychic exhaustion. He had imagined very briefly that she might have remembered the young man having intercourse with her while she was asleep and born some grudge for that, but he dismissed that thought as too close to a guilt reaction, just the kind of thing that blocked spirituality altogether if one let it get a hold. Still, he thought, it would be nice for her to drop him a line. Just for old times sake. Just to let him know that she had run off with some young Adonis who was really making her happy, moving her along the great orgasmic continuum of life, so to speak.

Dining alone was not the problem for someone like Max who lived so much in his own imagination as it would be for the less gifted. No evening papers or small books surreptitiously brought to the table for him. Instead, Max created a dinner companion in his own mind and then had long, witty, elegant conversations with her that always ended with a seduction, usually in the restaurant parking garage, the dark corners of the smoking lounge or right in the dining room itself. He had come to like the idea of letting people admire his love making excellence. He was considering giving expositions, very discretely of course and only to a coterie of initiated devotees, but still with the basic format of him performing, sometimes with a partner and sometimes not, while others watched and paid and praised.

The dinner of Dover soles and fresh out-of-season hydroponic raspberries complete, Max sipped at an espresso and focused his mind on the old problem of the purely spiritual orgasm. It was all a problem of mind, of course, and that meant he could solve it as he could solve all other mental problems. He first needed the right companion. This was easy enough. By playing with his memory, he recalled every woman with whom he had ever had a sexual experience worth reliving and brought them all into his presence. It was, he saw intuitively, merely a matter of deleting time from memory, treating past experience as the existential present, multiplying himself a hundred fold to embrace all his lovers at the same instant, to feel them all caressing and loving him at the same time. And it worked. His penis reached the state of erection he called Sheffield Steel and the waves of sensation began to approach climax. But then, something beyond his control took over. One of the images, the most recent of the memories, drove the others away. She was real as life and she demanded more than he was prepared to give. She started a contraction in his prostate that he resisted, but to no avail. It was Karen, and without any contact, the force of her remembered form brought on an orgasm that Max could not control. He rocked in the chair, braced his legs, whimpered, moaned and then cried, his face down on the table, and semen flowing slowly down his pants leg into his shoe.

"Are you alright, Professor Aceldama?" a waiter asked. "I'm afraid one of the other patrons has noticed. They suggested that you were having a stroke."

Max looked up helplessly. The need for Karen was overpowering. He lay in a catatonic state until the waiters carried him out to an ambulance.

——·62·——

Clovis sat in a back corner of the Alexandria Public Library with volume six of the *Cyclopedia Herborica*. Volumes one through five, dusty, but hardly touched since they were published in 1872, were piled neatly on her work table, slips of yellow paper protruding at key points. She took notes in a crabbed but legible style, copying everything exactly as it was written.

Artemisia, or wormwood, has many small, greenish-yellow flower heads, containing only disc flowers. The heads are grouped in clusters. The leaves are usually divided and alternate along the stem; they may be green, grayish green, or silvery white. The leaves of tarragon (*A. dracunculus*) are used as a seasoning. Mugwort (*A. vulgaris*) and wormwood (*A. absinthium*) have been used in medicines and beverages such as absinthe. Wormwood is said to induce menstruation and has been used in ancient and folk medicine as a contraceptive and abortifacient. Its efficacy for these purposes has never been proved by science.

Commiphora, or the incense-tree, is the common source of myrrh (from Arabic *mur*, "bitter"), bittertasting, agreeably aromatic, yellow to reddish-brown oleoresinous gum. Myrrh was highly esteemed by the ancients; in the Near East and Mediterranean regions, it was an ingredient of costly incenses, perfumes, and cosmetics and was used in medicines for local application, contraception and in embalming. Myrrh has slight antiseptic, astringent, and carminative properties and has been employed medically in tinctures to relieve sore gums and mouth. Upon exposure to air, myrrh hardens slowly into globules and irregular lumps called tears.

Pennyroyal (*Mentha pulegium*) is a low plant with small, oval scented leaves and bluish lilac flowers common in moist meadows in North America and Eurasia; it reaches one meter (over three feet). Used in ancient and folk medicine for various purposes including control of menstrual irregularities.

Common rue (*Ruta graveolens*) is cultivated as a small garden shrub for its evergreen leaves and dull-yellow flower clusters. The gland-studded, translucent leaves have been used for centuries as a spice and in medicines to reduce fertility.

Fennel (*Foeniculum vulgare*), a perennial or biennial aromatic herb of the family Apiaceae (Umbelliferae) used as a flavoring agent and formerly as a medicine. According to a Greek myth, knowledge came to man from Olympus in the form of a fiery coal contained in a fennel stalk. Native to southern Europe and Asia Minor, fennel is cultivated in the U.S., Great Britain, and temperate Eurasia. The sap of a species of giant fennel known as silphion by the Greeks and silphium by the Romans, now harvested to extinction, grew in the hills near Cyrene, an ancient Greek city-state in North Africa and, according to records of the time, was a valuable export crop worth more than its weight in silver. The ancient physician Soranus wrote most explicitly of the plant's use in a concoction called 'Cyreniac juice': He gave several prescriptions for preparing the sap to be taken by mouth and said it would either prevent conception or cause an early abortion. For further discussion of ancient practices concerning contraception and abortion, *see*, *Corpus Hermeticum* (Sartwell, trans. 1757) and *Asclepius* (Oldfather, trans. 1857).

Clovis closed the books, returned them to an obscure corner of the library and folded her notes into her purse. On the way out, she checked the card catalogue for the *Corpus Hermeticum* and the translation of *Asclepius* mentioned in the *Cyclopedia*.

"Is there any record of when these books were last checked out?" She asked the reference librarian, a grey haired lady with heavy glasses and a broken demeanor.

"Well . . ." the librarian said slipping on heavy reading glasses she wore around her neck on a silk cord, "data on those old books has never been put in the computer. You could check the volume itself. There should be a sign in sheet in the back."

"Could you, do you think . . ."

"Of course, Mrs Tuckahoe, I'd be happy to."

The librarian returned in a few minutes with the books. She dusted them carefully with an old piece of terry cloth and opened the back binders tenderly. "Heavens," she said, "nobody's checked this out for twenty years or more."

"And can you tell who . . ?"

""Yes. It was your brother-in-law, Mrs. Tuckahoe. It was 'H. Tuckahoe.' See?"

Clovis looked carefully at the signature. There was no doubt. "Mrs. Tuckahoe," the librarian said, "I hate to bother you about this. I know its only been eight months since your husband, Mr. Schuler, died, but my husband Bill is getting real worried about the situation over at the B & T. I told him not to worry, that this national Savings & Loan scandal couldn't effect our little B & T here in Alexandria even though its gotten so big, but I was wondering . . . we own a little stock you know and all this talk of Grand Juries and indictments against Mr. Henry . . . well . . . ?"

Clovis held the librarian's hand as she told how they had put all their money into B & T stock and how they could be wiped out if anything happened, even how they could lose their home since the B & T sold their note to an outfit in Arkansas that didn't know them and was threatening to foreclose.

Clovis promised to do what she could. It was a promise she had made a thousand times or more in the last month. And now that she knew what had caused all those miscarriages during the first years of her married life, and why Schuler finally took her to Europe to get her through the first months of pregnancy, it really did seem like it was time to do something.

——·63·——

Esther Anne Hendricks walked out of the J. Edgar Hoover Building onto Pennsylvania Avenue and looked across the Mall toward the Washington Monument. It had been the first thing she remembered seeing when she arrived at Union Station. And now it would be virtually the last thing she saw on he way out of town. She turned her back toward Capitol Hill and the Supreme Court and headed for Virginia. She had done what Jenkin wanted, turned state's evidence, told the FBI everything about Henry and the appraisals on the Indian Head

Slough. The agents had been delighted. They had enough now, they said, to get a warrant on Henry, if they could find him. She hadn't offered to help with that. What they did with Henry now was their own business. She was through with Washington and Alexandria, through with government and finance. She'd come here to get away from poverty and a father who confused her with his other women. She'd found money and men who had manners but weren't really much different. And there were things in West Virginia that Washington lacked, a certain decency of life, an acceptance of necessity, a passivity that she now missed and hoped to recover.

Esther Anne had already closed her office, liquidated her possessions, turned all to cash. The back seat of her car now held everything she owned. She looked at it in amazement. What all the years of whoring came down to was a few good suits and a pile of romance novels. Well, she thought, she'd saved enough to re-locate and it was high time. There were farms in the Eastern Panhandle she could buy, places that would be ideal for a single mother turned writer, and villages of trusting people who might not believe her stories about a young husband who died training for a secret CIA mission, but who wouldn't question too much, or for very long.

She headed over Memorial Bridge and turned west, up the Potomac. She felt a chill as if an icy blast had penetrated her car window from the Hill. Something was calling her back. An inner eye, if she had one, would have shown Jason Potter inflated to the size of a house trying to stop her car, chewing on the tires, plugging his fingers into her fuel injection. Esther Anne passed the chill off as nostalgia. She turned her face away and drove on.

—— ·**64**· ——

"I don't understand it," Aubrey said to Immanuel, staring at the clean patch of concrete that had been their hobo jungle for s long. "Why would the police start raiding us now? It was live and let live for so long!"

Uniformed officers wearing heavy leather gloves doused flea powder over the ragtag possessions that had accumulated on the sidewalk and threw them into a waiting trash truck. Makeshift fires were put out.

"Your question presumes a type of connection between an action and its consequences that concerns not the act's propensity to bring these consequences about, but the way in which the act is regarded as representing the valued project of which the action is a component," Immanuel said.

"You mean those new people, don't you," Aubrey said still clutching the *Toughwaugh Papyrus*.

Immanuel grunted.

"They are somewhat on the angry, violent side, I must say. The middle classes aren't really suited to this kind of bohemian existence, are they?" He eyed one interloper with particular suspicion. She was a large woman, pregnant maybe, asking for someone named Aubrey. He didn't recognize her, but he knew there was a large black spot in his recent memory, after he left the University of Virginia and before he met Granny. There was no telling what he had done.

Immanuel snorted his way through a rubbish bin and retreived the lipstick stained butt end of a menthol cigarette.

"No sense of humor in these bourgeois johnnies," Aubrey added. "No perspective of history, or cushion of philosophy. Honestly! All this crying about their precious Savings & Loans collapsing. Their deposits are all guaranteed. What are they whining about."

"The stock," a voice said from behind a massive Burford Holly. "The stock values aren't guaranteed. Those crooks wiped us out."

"Which crooks?" Aubrey asked.

"The Rock of Ages Saving and Loan in Dallas. The President's in jail, but I bet the farm on it. The stock went from $10 to $2753 in seven months and down to 0 in a week when the

truth came out. I bought on margin and I lost the farm. Lost it."
The last cry was followed by a pistol shot. Aubrey rushed forward to help, but a woman's head, still clean and well groomed though showing signs of wear, appeared. "It's only a blank," she said. "He likes to do that several times a day if he can get anyone to listen."

"Some philosophical problems remain unsolved because the mind did not evolve to deal with them," Immanuel said.

"Stock," Aubrey said, starting to worry. He ran down a sheet of newsprint caught in the wind and found the financial page. Granny's mutual fund was low, dangerously low, the Board of Directors and its lawyer, the famous Max Aceldama were under investigation, and that paper was a week old.

—— ·65· ——

The woman hesitated when the nurse asked for her name. "It's all confidential. Since you've paid cash there's no need to see any identification. Just sign your real name to the form so your consent to the operation's valid and the clinic's legally protected. I'll put it in an envelope and never look at it and then you'll need to give us a name to call you by, okay?"

The woman signed, folded the form and handed it to the nurse.

"And a name to call you by? We have to call you something."

"June," the woman said. "You can call me June."

"June . . . ?"

"Roe. June Roe."

"One of my favorite names. You'd be surprised how popular it is here at the clinic."

"How soon can you get started with the operation," the woman asked.

"Well, June, it's not that easy in your condition you know."

"I know."

"You're what . . . almost seven months along?'

"Almost." It was more like eight, but she was content to let the abortionist figure that out later.

"You'll spend two nights here. The first day the doctor will insert a little cedar peg into the cervix. The peg expands as it absorbs moisture and enlarges the opening so the instruments can be inserted."

"I know all about this."

"And then on the second day the doctor will do the porcedure."

"That's when he goes in and dismembers the fetus and takes the arms and legs and head out one by one. I know. I've seen the pictures."

"Most of our late term patients don't really want to know too much about all this, you know."

"But I know and its what I want. I even want to see the parts when they've been extracted from my body, just to make sure he gets them all out, doesn't leave anything in there left to keep on growing. I want to see them. Tell him to save them in a bottle or something."

"Well, you'll only be under an epidural. It's not normal to let the patient look, but I could check with the doctor."

"Or make him take a picture, the ones like you see on the posters."

"Well . . . maybe . . . but you know this is really unusual. Are you sure this is what you really want? Wouldn't you feel better if you had some counseling? We have some really qualified people on staff. I'm sure they could . . ."

"It's my body. It's my choice. Right?"

"Well . . . of course it's your body. Nobody . . ."

"Then I want it out. I want my baby dead. Is that clear enough for you?"

"Yes, June that's quite clear. I just hope you've thought this through.'

"I've thought it through."

" . . . so that you won't regret it later . . ."

"It's my choice."

The nurse decided then that enough was enough and said no more.

The woman called June, so transformed by sorrow and hard living that not even Karen Moelders would have recognized her as Sister Mary Scroggins, went off to a private room in the back of the building to await the abortionist's visit. It was the first time she had been in 806 Pretenders Street and she didn't think much of it. The floors creaked badly. The walls were skewed. There was a rumble and groan of earthquakes from the basement that raised serious questions about the foundation. But it didn't matter. It only had to last for a few days and she would be free. She didn't look further into the future than that.

Jason Potter, bewildered and lost since Esther Anne's departure from Washington, hovered listlessly in the back garden. He heard the boards complain as Sister Mary undressed and slipped into her hospital gown. He was used to what went on in the clinic now, the little six to eight week souls slipping so abruptly back into eternity, the teenage mothers going aimlessly on about their lives, numb to what they had done, certain that having more babies would be as easy as the first. But this was different. The woman was much too old for this. The baby was too far along, fully formed, her mind already functioning, her ears already listening to what was said about her, her spirit already tuned to her mother's heart in loving reliance. It was worse than the others.

Jason peeped into Mary's window and saw her stare remorselessly at the ceiling as she lay spreadeagled in the stirrups, the abortionist's plastic coated hand probing her vagina, the nurse preparing the sterile wooden plug for insertion. The baby girl turned and kicked. Mary winced. The doctor pretended not to notice.

Jason leapt between Mary's thighs and held himself in pugilistic readiness to defend the innocent, determined to make one last gesture for life before he was gone forever.

"This will hurt a little," the doctor said.

Jason lunged at the plug, swinging and kicking, but he missed. Mary said nothing. The pain was welcome.

Jason resumed his defensive posture. The plug hit him in the midriff. He coughed, hit back, coughed again, closed his eyes and yielded to the pressure. When he regained his senses, he was inside Mary Scroggins' womb face to face with a fully developed, beautifully formed baby girl who smiled, hugged him to her downy breast and spoke to him clearly in sighs too deep for words.

—·66·—

"I don't know where he is unless I can see him," Clovis said into a telephone that connected her to the FBI. "But I know where he will be day after tomorrow. He's got a closing scheduled for 3:30 p.m. at 806 Pretender's Street. An organization called the Wombyn League will convey 806 to one of Henry's shell corporations, which will convey it into the Indian Head Slough Property which will then be turned into a non-profit archeological trust and conveyed to the Department of the Interior for enough money to cover all the notes and put the B & T back in the black."

"But it's all a fraud."

"Not if he completes it and Congress appropriates the money. And Henry's very good at that you know. He's got something on everyone over on the Hill."

"Then we stop him first."

"Good. Do it. I'll help. I was planning to be there anyhow. 've got personal scores to settle with Henry Tuckahoe."

"Won't this ruin your bank?"

"Yup."

"But . . ."

"Henry ruined it when he made it so big and greedy. It's time closed it down and started a little home mortgage company n my own."

"It's your life Mrs. Tuckahoe."

"It is now."

—— ·**67**· ——

Aubrey stepped up on the rim of the fountain in DuPont Circle and launched into the speech that had made him famous among the homeless of the Washington area: "Homeless of the world unite," he said passionately. "You have less to lose and home to gain. You did not lose your stock investments or your Ph.D dissertations because of anything you did wrong or because of any vast economic forces over which you have no control. You did not lose your home because you were stupid or greedy. You lost your home and your job and your self-esteem because of the Devil. Now some will laugh when I talk about the devil, but I'm not talking about old Beelzebub in the Bible, or even some modern, abstract personification of evil. I'm not going to pull out any holy books and start thumping on them or tell you to believe in Jesus and everything will be alright or even tell you its God's will that you suffer like old Job. No, what I'm going to tell you is that there is a real live devil over the river in Alexandria who is personally responsible for this so called Savings and Loan crises and that if we band together we can drive him out of town. Once we do that, we can march up on the Hill and get Congress to give us our money and our homes and our jobs back so we can get on with the business of being Americans."

"Who is this devil, Aubrey?" a voice from the edge of the crowd, now numbering several hundred, asked. Usually it was Immanuel, but Aubrey's number of real disciples was growing

"This devil is named Henry Tuckahoe and let me tell you who and what this devil is. He is at least 200 years old. He lives in the sewers and along the waterfront because he isn't allowed to sleep inside a house. He eats raw fish. He'll only die if he has any grandchildren. And he's been allowed by some ancient shaman to buy and sell the lands around here as some sort of perpetual revenge for George Washington's father killing off all his tribe. He's not a red man anymore. He's turned a dusty shade of grey so that you wouldn't recognize him as an American Indian, but he can still speak his old Potowatomack language and he's plenty smart, book smart, street smart, every kind of smart.

"I'm not just making this up either, folks. I learned all this from a secret manuscript that Henry Tuckahoe's brother, Schuler, deposited in the Library of Congress. Schuler was subject to the same spell and he was turned into a devil too over a long course of time. He and Henry brought on every financial crises in the history of this country. Henry and Schuler brought on the Great Depression. They started the Mexican American War to boost real estate prices. They got us into World War I so that a torpedo factory would be put on land they owned on the Alexandria waterfront. But Schuler finally saw how evil he had become. He changed his ways, married, had a child, let her marry and have the grandbaby that meant his own life would end naturally. Then he passed away peacefully, leaving his manuscript behind to enlighten us as to the ways of his little brother so that we could put an end to all this mess."

A chant started.

Aubrey surveyed the crowd. The poor street lighting made it hard to see, and the DuPont Circle speeches always attracted a lot of gawkers from the local bars, but there were some new faces out there, people who were really interested, people who really might follow him over the bridge to Alexandria to get Henry Tuckahoe when the time was right, when he could locate Henry and expose him once and for all, bell him like a cat so that nobody would ever deal with him again.

"Get Henry. Get Henry. Get Henry Tuckahoe."

Just as he was starting to hand out summaries of his translation of the *Papyrus*, Aubrey felt a tug on his ragged sleeve. He turned to find a slender, dark headed woman in her late twenties. From her dirty face and unkempt hair, she had been on the street for a week or so, but from her clothes, she had been fairly comfortable before that.

"I'm his daughter," the woman said drawing Aubrey close to whisper in his ear. "I'm Henry Tuckahoe's daughter and I'm pregnant by the Holy Ghost with the baby that will break his spell and set him free. Isn't it wonderful."

Aubrey held the woman at arms length and looked at her face. "The book says all Tuckahoe's have a distinctive birth mark, a red carp on the inside of the left thigh."

She drew him into the shadows and lifted her skirts. Aubrey saw the mark she described. But he also saw more. The thighs and even the panties were familiar. It was her. The sleeping woman with whom he had intercourse. She was pregnant. With his child. And she thought it was by the Holy Spirit.

"I'm Talitha Cumi," she said. "You can call me Tali."

When Tali had finished telling her story and showing the letter in Granny Franny's handwriting, Aubrey realized that she really was Granny's daughter by Henry Tuckahoe. He put his arms around Tali and the *Toughwaugh Papyrus* together, unable to realize his good fortune. He told her all he knew about Granny Franny and promised to take her to the place where she was entombed. Talitha Cumi wept. She took Aubrey's hands and kissed them. Aubrey dropped to one knee, told Tali how much he loved her and begged her to marry him because he knew that they were already married in spirit, begged her to let him be Saint Joseph to her baby. She, who had become used to many strange things by now, agreed. They assembled a group of homeless witnesses around a fire of plastic refuse and exchanged vows Quaker Style as the Spirit led them. Aubrey consummated the union in the alley behind R Street.

— **68** —

Lacy Swanda read the letter again. It was simply too good to be true. It was from Aubrey's dissertation advisor congratulating him on a job well done. It was especially complimentary of the way Aubrey had worked musicological themes into the literary background, the original manner in which he had discussed the various uses of the rachet, the sackbutt and the serpent during the performance the *Menaechmi* at Guildhall in 1572. Aubrey's Professor had shown the dissertation to a colleague in the music department who was equally complimentary and praised Aubrey's synthesis of his own material with the truly original research of Dr. Lacy Swanda. Aubrey's PhD was a sure thing. Even better, he had been offered an Assistant Professorship. It was a tenure track job and would have to be confirmed by the faculty Senate, but, as everyone knew, it was really up to the English Department and he was their first choice.

Lacy moved slowly around her room at the Guest House. In the eighth month of pregnancy and with a family history of early labor, she didn't want to do anything too quickly. She took a sheet of paper, inserted it into her typewriter and wrote a letter to Charlottesville. Aubrey was delighted to accept the job and looked forward to returning to the University with his wife and family. She sealed and stamped the letter and walked it to the post office. Now there was just the problem of locating Aubrey. She had seen him from time to time out on the streets, trying to pretend he couldn't be recognized, but since leaving her room was his idea and she already had what she wanted from him, Lacy hadn't bothered him. But he was easy enough to find and this job was too good to throw away.

── ·**69**· ──

"Here's her confession, Judge, just like we told you on the 'phone." The no nonsense, all business FBI agent handed a thin file to Jenkin.

"She confessed to . . . ?"

"Conspiracy to defraud the United States Government. Title 28, *United States Code* . . ."

"I know," Jenkin said and read through the transcript. It was pretty simple really. Esther Anne confessed to signing false and misleading appraisals on the Indian Head Slough Property in accordance with a plan that the Park Service could be tricked into buying the land as an Indian burial ground. She said she assumed that evidence of the burial ground was falsified, but she didn't really know.

"It's enough to nail Henry Tuckahoe, of course," the agent said.

"Of course," Jenkin said, all too aware that police confidence was rarely warranted by conviction rates. "But what about Miss Hendricks? Did she get immunity for this?"

"Oh, yeah, full transactional immunity."

"Good."

"There's no problem with her, your honor, we just wanted to let you see this because of your being who you are and the fact that she did mention your name."

"Yes. It's accurate. I did—do—know her and she did confess all this to me and then --thank God—she did follow my advice."

"Well . . . as long as its all true. I just wanted to check, you know, because sometimes women in her condition get a little hysterical, you know, and make things up . . ."

"Her condition?"

"She told us she was pregnant and still having a little morning sickness."

"Pregnant! Esther Anne!"

Jenkin got rid of the FBI agents as quickly as he could and ran to her apartment. He found her coming down the stairs with an arm load of books.

"I was afraid you'd already left," he said.

"I had. I decided at first to leave these behind. But . . . as you see . . . I came back for them . . . all the way from West Virginia." She pointed to the signed volumes of the Complete Veronica Holloway he had given her.

"Are you . . . ?

"Am I . . . ?"

"Well . . . you know . . . I heard it from the FBI people. They said you told them about your . . . your morning sickness."

"Yes," she said picking up the books and starting down the steps, "I am, but you don't have to . . ."

Jenkin stopped her words with kisses. She dropped the books on the stairs. They fell into a pile at the bottom. But even before the racket was over, Jenkin and Esther Anne were out of the building in search of a preacher.

They found Father White of Saint Faith's Episcopal Church celebrating an evening Mass by himself.

"In the old Potowatomack tribe that lived here hundreds of years ago," he said after the wedding as he toasted their union and their offspring with a glass of communion rum, "the bride was always pregnant before the service. It made sense then to see if a girl could carry a baby through the first few months before solemnizing anything. Our Episcopal Church could learn a lot from the Amerindian spirituality, don't you think? I certainly do. Why some of the ceremonies and services, not to mention the spells and rituals, that they had would truly amaze people today. Our world has gotten entirely too rational, don't you think? There was one in particular that I recall . . ."

Jenkin and Esther Ann had slipped out of the church before Father White could finish, but unbeknownst to them, a silent spectator in a far dark corner heard all and came forward as they left.

"Have you given any thought, Father, to how those Amerindian concepts of generational continuity could be enhanced by the Vedic notions of Tantric ecstasy through the higher sex?"

"Well, yes," Father White said, nonplussed by the change in audience, "there is a movement in the Episcopal Church along those lines, something to combine the eucharistic feast with the transcendental oneness of the Vedic convergencies. I have some literature in my study if you are interested, Mr. . . . Mr . . . ?"

"Aceldama. Professor Max Aceldama."

"From the Public Television show?"

"Exactly."

"Yes, Professor Aceldama, as I was saying . . ."

"This eucharistic feast you were talking about. I don't suppose you've considered how that might tie in with my best selling *Food As Foreplay*, have you?"

"Well, as a matter of fact, we use your *Food As Foreplay* as a supplement to our Rite VII service on alternate Tuesday nights. Your insight into the oral content of religious sentiment is truly miraculous, I must say. Of course my service is not exactly orthodox. Yet. We are a church in change, you know."

"You know, Father, I think I might want you to perform a marriage for me. Maybe tomorrow. I haven't popped the question yet and the woman might find the idea a little surprising, but, assuming she says yes, do you think we could work a little *Food As Foreplay* into the service?"

"We're very open, as I said."

"This woman, my bride, she isn't the one I would have chosen, but well, there's something I can do with her that I've just never felt comfortable doing with other women."

"Oh . . ."

"All this sexual guru stuff. The truth is that I just never liked to share my spunk with anybody else. It was a selfishness thing."

"Perhaps we should move into the confessional mode, my son."

"That's a good idea. I've been needing a good confession for a long time."

"This helps I find," Father White said handing Max the bottle.

"What . . . ?"

"Confessional rum. It's a tradition of the local parish. There was an early Potowatomack convert to Anglicanism it seems who had an uncanny ability to turn common rum into . . ."

——· 70 ·——

By ten o'clock the next morning, Henry was ready with his closing documents in the conference room on the third floor of the Wombyn League. The papers were laid out so that 806 would pass directly to Henry's shell corporation and then to the Department of the Interior. The B & T would be paid off with real Government money and Henry's shady daisy chain would appear not only legal but inspired. The checks were ready. The lawyer from Interior was ready. Henry was ready. It only lacked Karen's signature on a few papers to finish it. Henry paced into Karen's office.

The young attorney who had replaced Lindsay Hayden made a call and announced that Karen was being held up downstairs. There was an important meeting with Professor Aceldama. Something about a big Supreme Court case. It shouldn't take more than a minute. Henry took a seat and tried not to look at the Government lawyer as the grumbling, scraping sounds started in the basement. The noise was worse then ever. The place was really falling down. It was the tide, of course, coming in and raising the foundation a fraction of an inch or so. Before he loosened so many of the foundation stones and cut the floor joists, the sound had barely been noticeable. Now it couldn't be avoided. A picture of Sarah Weddington moved perceptibly on the wall. Henry shifted in his chair pretending not to notice. A crack appeared in one of the windows facing Pretender's Street. The Government man gripped his chair with white knuckles and sought Henry's eyes with an expression that was rapidly turning green. Henry excused himself and went to a toilet that opened off the main hall. He sat down, put his ear to the wall and tried to pick up Karen's conversation, hoping that this Professor, whoever he was, didn't try to talk Karen out of going through with the sale. What he heard wasn't what he feared, but it was bad enough.

"Marriage! Have you lost your mind? You don't have to marry me."

"It isn't that I have to do anything, Karen. I want to. I want you to marry me. I want to be with you."

"Just because you fucked me once? Is that it? I can't have been much of a thrill after Lindsay."

"It's not just the thrill. It's because I felt with you for the first time with any woman that I could really trust you, trust you enough to . . . well to do something I've never been able to do with women . . ."

"You mean with all those other women you never let it . . ."

"No. I could never ejaculate into another woman. I know it sounds bizarre. It's something most men have no problem with at all, rather just the opposite, but somehow, subconsciously, I could never trust a woman with my sperm." Max shrugged. He was telling all, exposing himself to ridicule, giving Karen everything.

"Christ, Max," she said, "I never imagined."

"With all the women I've had, Karen, it's never been like it was with you. With you I could just . . ."

"Just do it."

"Right."

"Well, Max, you did it alright."

"Did it?"

"Knocked me up. Popped my cherry and knocked me up all at once, Max, what about that?"

"You mean?"

"I'm pregnant, Max."

"And you haven't . . ."

"Flushed it down the toilet? Not yet. I thought I'd see how it feels for a while. Just to see, you know?"

"So . . . ?"

"It feels alright, really. The whole thing felt alright. I was surprised. Watching that guy on Lindsay turned me on. And it was alright. And this thing with the baby is okay so far. I mean I don't feel stabbed or raped like I thought I would."

"So you'll marry me?"

"I didn't say that, but . . ."

"I'm the father. It makes sense."

" . . . well . . . but nobody else has asked."

"I've got the license and a priest all lined up with a really neat tantric service using some of the best lines from *Food As Foreplay*. You'll really like it."

"Well . . ."

"We can start all over. Do something new. If the Burgh &
Tuckahoe goes broke, I'm likely to get in a mess, go to jail, lose
some business. I need a new career. Something you can pick
up even if you've been in trouble, even served some time. And
I feel inspired by this priest. The Episcopal church is where we
really should be. We could both be ordained, preach abortion
and Tantric sex and new spiritualities I haven't even thought
up yet. Maybe start our own foundation. It's the best way."

"Well . . . there're going to be some conditions.'

"I'm sure."

" . . . in writing."

The conversation stopped. Henry heard a rustling of hands,
the crunch of bodies being pressed together and then a giggling
outburst. Someone, a heavy person, started running around the
room. There were heavy thumps and more giggles. The joists
on the second floor slipped out of place entirely and plaster
came down in avalanches from the ceiling. Henry came out of
the toilet in time to see the Government lawyer bolt down the
stairs. He ran to the window, dodged glass shards cracking and
flying from the twisting pressures on the building and looked
out into Pretender's Street to see something he had imagined
only in his worst nightmares. It was a crowd of people carrying placards calling for his imprisonment, his death, his treatment with tar and feathers, his deportation to French Guiana.
The only member of the crowd he recognized was Clovis who
was right in front leading. Unmarked police cars, FBI probably,
were pulling up in front of 806. The mob ignored them. A young
man with a poorly tended beard addressed the crowd through
a bullhorn. He told them that Tuckahoe was finished, that his
wife was carrying Tuckahoe's grandbaby and that meant the
end of the spell and the end of Tuckahoe. Henry searched the
crowd for the one who was supposed to be his daughter. It had
to be the darkheaded woman next to the speaker. Her hair was
almost the right color. He looked at her eyes. They were the
right color. He ducked into a closet as the mob started up the

steps. The building would never stand the weight of so many people. He had to get out, get down to the sewer where he knew he would never be followed.

Jason Potter, who had passed the night with his newfound, unborn friend, in prenatal bliss, heard the trembling of the building as what he feared the most and had prepared himself to stop. Without stopping to think, he kicked hard at the sac that surrounded him. Gradually, by focusing his mind on the sharpest implements he could imagine, he broke Sister Mary's amniotic sac and forced her into violent labor. Her cries took the staff by surprise.

"It can't be labor. Here in the clinic? We'd better call the doctor."

"He's an abortionist for Christsake, what's he know about . . ."

"He's still a doctor."

"I thought maybe he could arrest the labor and do the pro-oooo . . ."

"Cut the baby up when she's in labor? That's criminal."

"But maybe it won't live.'

"That's not up to us, is it," the nurse said taking Sister Mary's hand, helping her to breath. "There's no time for a doctor."

"Your going to have a baby, Miss Roe. Real soon. Sometime it just happens like this. Don't ask me why."

Mary screamed and cried and choked and gasped and finally, when she was told to by the nurse, she pushed out a perfect baby girl who had her chin, her high forehead, and a head covered with blond down. The nurse swaddled the little girl, tied a handkerchief around her head, and handed her to a stunned Mary only moments before another woman, a few years older than Mary, detached herself from the invading mob that had come for Henry Tuckahoe and came into the operating room.

"Can anyone help me?" she asked. "I broke my water an hour ago in this damn parade and I think I'm about to give birth."

Mary rose up as plaster fell from the ceiling and the staff nurses fled to the street. "I can help," she said. "I know all about it. Tell me your name, dear."

"Lacy," the woman said swapping places with Mary. "Lacy Swanda. And if you see a guy around here named Aubrey Wythe, would you tell him his kid is being born right now. That's the top of the head if I'm not mistaken."

"Indeed," Mary said feeling her old self again, "and here's your little boy." She handed the baby to Lacy and tucked her daughter under her arm. "I'll find your young man and send him right down." A beam fell across the door as she left, but somehow Lacy wasn't afraid or surprised when, a few minutes later, Aubrey appeared with another young woman and an enormous grey man in tow. He didn't seem to recognize her until she showed him the letter about his dissertation. The building shuddered with the rising tide. The roof collapsed. The third floor failed to hold the weight. The downstairs corridor was filled with debris and dust. It was impossible to see. The grey man took charge. He helped Lacy with the baby and led them all into a dark passage only moments before the entire house came down.

——·71·——

Mr. and Mrs. Jenkin Carroway held hands as the early flight to Boston banked sharply over the Potomac. His letter of resignation lay unopened in the mail. It would arrive at his chamber the next day. *The Post* would have the news a few minutes later. There would be a scandal and a wild effort to find him. But it would be unsuccessful. He would be in Maine again, with Esther Anne, a married man and a judge no more. He had done nothing wrong. The true story would never come out. It would all be over in a week and, by not reading the *Post*, he could pretend it wasn't happening.

Jenkin couldn't believe his good fortune or the sense of relief that came with leaving Washington. Burdens of family pride and judicial duty lifted off his shoulders as lightly as the airplane soared above the earth. He held Esther Anne's arm, squeezed her hand and kissed her ear.

"Look," she said pointing down at the river. "There's a big dugout canoe in the river. It must be fifteen feet long and looks filled with people."

"It must be a crew team from one of the local high schools," Jenkin said.

"They won't win any races in that," Esther Anne said. "Look."

Jenkin stretched over Esther Anne's thighs to see out the window. It was as she said. A solitary figure in the back paddled. There were others with him. They seemed asleep.

"It makes me think of a trapper on the Potomac about 1620 or so," Jenkin said, "a Cavalier knight cheated out of his inheritance by Cromwell and this thugs. A freak storm tips his canoe over. He's rescued by an Indian maid whose tribe have been killed in the wars with bad white men from the coast. They fall in love. They have little boys who grow up wild and free in the wilderness in harmony and favor with God and men and beasts. He makes money in the fur trade. They return to England. He recovers his lands and titles. Not easily. There will be court cases, brawls, duels. She grows lonely and ill. She does not think herself worthy of his rich patrimony and disappears so that he can marry an heiress and restore the family mansion, a great jacobean pile, back to its former grandeur. He realizes that he loves her more than his title and lands and he pursues her back to Virginia, gives up his title, and they live happily ever after."

"Their sons and daughters fight in the American Revolutionary War against the people who originally stole his estate," Esther Ann added. "But that could be a sequel."

"The first and second in a great trilogy."

"*The Sun by Day. The Moon by Night. The Sun and Moon Stand Still.* Okay as titles?"

"Great," Jenkin said. "What made you think of the sun and moon now though?"

"Because you can still see the last of the moon in the west reflected on the clouds and the sun is standing still in the east."

"Isn't that impossible?"

"I think so."

The plane banked again into the northeast flight corridor. It's silver surface reflected the sun like a gemstone, showering the river below with rays of primary color.

Jason Potter released his hold on the window as the plane headed north. It was time. He had done what he had stayed around to do. Esther Anne was doing fine after a few rough turns. The effects of his Accounting Rule 502 had been ended. Henry Tuckahoe had been humbled. And he had saved a little baby and then helped her mom escape the crumbling mess at 806 Pretenders Street. He was ready and it was time. He looked around. The blue streams seemed to have gone dry on him all of sudden. He sat in a dry course, thinking he might have to wait for a flood, but then he realized why the light hadn't been moving. It was Apollo. He had stopped. His chariot was parked over on the horizon and the guy was walking over to have a word with him, walking like a cloud would walk if clouds had to walk. And Apollo didn't even have to tell Jason what to do. Jason stood up, bounded to him, took his hand, felt the scars and the kindness of the touch and took his place in the chariot. The wheels threw off colors beyond description as it renewed its journey across the heavens.

Henry Tuckahoe felt the bands of red and blue sunlight sparkle across his face. He hadn't been on the river in the early morning since Mr. Lincoln's funeral. The pleasures of the light were a surprise and brought to mind the long dark life that was now behind him and the short time left in which to live the life he had abandoned to revenge offenses he could barely remember. He turned his face into the sunlight that seemed strangely stationary, as if it had stopped for him alone.

Turning his eyes back to the canoe, the low morning light played steadily on the strange new Tuckahoe family. His daughter, Tali, perfect he thought in her resemblance to a sister he recalled with poignant affection, slept peacefully at his feet wrapped in the arms of her new husband, Dr. Wythe. The skinny boy wouldn't have been Henry's choice for a son-in-law. There was something wrong with blond headed people. But Henry realized that this was a prejudice best forgotten, and, looking on the bright side, the boy did have a job. His first wife though, the older woman with the newborn papoose, she was another problem, but Henry didn't count bigamy a crime, and the older woman certainly did know how to take charge. She slept peacefully with her baby at her breast in the bow. She would be good for Tali, teach her the things a woman needed to know, help her keep young Wythe in line and out of trouble. And Tali would need help with her own little one coming along in a few months. Henry had accepted it all when Tali had explained it and let him read Granny Franny's letter. He remembered the student who had learned his language. He laughed when he heard the story of how she had tricked him into giving up his seed and then avoided his abortion salads and stews by disappearing.

Schuler was right, he admitted. This was the best way. The world looked fresh and beautiful as he realized he was beginning gradually to take his leave. There would be time to see the baby for a few months, time to let the last of the Tuckahoes play on his knee before he grew tired and passed on into the spirit world. And he knew something about babies. He could help. The steady motion of the river was just the thing for a little one, Henry remembered that from the talk of women around the fire. His knowledge of the old ways would come in handy. And there were lots of things Tali needed to know about her people.

Henry looked up again into the strangely stationary light, realizing that it was there for him. He blinked at its brightness and followed its falling beams back to earth, realizing that he had never quite learned to bear them. The light in the trees on the riverbank took on a new form. It became a face and then faces. It was Schuler's face and the face of Slow Possum and then the faces of all the Tuckahoe who had last gathered to feast on oysters by the river bank. They were laughing and waving. Henry laughed too and waved back.

END